CURIOSITY KILLED THE DUKE

Dukes in Danger
Book 8

Emily E K Murdoch

ARE YOU SIGNED UP FOR DRAGONBLADE'S BLOG?

You'll get the latest news and information on exclusive giveaways, exclusive excerpts, coming releases, sales, free books, cover reveals and more.

Check out our complete list of authors, too!

No spam, no junk. That's a promise!

Sign Up Here

www.dragonbladepublishing.com

Dearest Reader;

Thank you for your support of a small press. At Dragonblade Publishing, we strive to bring you the highest quality Historical Romance from some of the best authors in the business. Without your support, there is no 'us', so we sincerely hope you adore these stories and find some new favorite authors along the way.

Happy Reading!

CEO, Dragonblade Publishing

The Convenient Engagement (Book 5)

The Governess Bureau Series
A Governess of Great Talents (Book 1)
A Governess of Discretion (Book 2)
A Governess of Many Languages (Book 3)
A Governess of Prodigious Skill (Book 4)
A Governess of Unusual Experience (Book 5)
A Governess of Wise Years (Book 6)
A Governess of No Fear (Novella)

Never The Bride Series
Always the Bridesmaid (Book 1)
Always the Chaperone (Book 2)
Always the Courtesan (Book 3)
Always the Best Friend (Book 4)
Always the Wallflower (Book 5)
Always the Bluestocking (Book 6)
Always the Rival (Book 7)
Always the Matchmaker (Book 8)
Always the Widow (Book 9)
Always the Rebel (Book 10)
Always the Mistress (Book 11)
Always the Second Choice (Book 12)
Always the Mistletoe (Novella)
Always the Reverend (Novella)

The Lyon's Den Series
Always the Lyon Tamer

Pirates of Britannia Series
Always the High Seas

De Wolfe Pack: The Series
Whirlwind with a Wolfe

CHAPTER ONE

11 April 1811

S AMUEL DELLAMORE, DUKE of Chantmarle, had never seen a man dance in a skirt before.

Kilt. Kilt—he really had to remember the lingo of this place. If he was going to be courted by the very best of Scottish nobility, the least he could do was not call the blessed thing a skirt.

Samuel beamed out across the dance hall, ensuring that anyone who glanced at him saw nothing more than an idiot.

That was the best part of what he had to do, spying on behalf of the Crown. *Acting the fool.* It was starting to become so easy for him that at times—

"I said, are you listening to me, Your Grace?" huffed a woman just to his left.

Samuel started. "I beg your pardon?"

The politeness was a reflex. It was easy, being a duke, to always sound polite. Really, he should thank his lucky stars—and his childhood governess—that they had done such a superb job at preparing him for prancing about the place. Samuel tried not to grin. It was something he was perhaps a little too good at, to tell the truth.

"I am afraid I was not listening to a word you said, Lady Romeril," he said cheerfully, knowing it would rile the older woman to no end.

"I was too busy watching the dancing, you see."

He spread an aristocratic arm to their left where the dance was continuing. Skirts and kilts were flying, the dancers were whooping as they went, and the music seemed, to Samuel's ear, to be getting more and more frantic.

Really! One would never get away with dancing in such a wild manner in London!

"They call it a reel," said Lady Romeril stiffly.

Samuel examined the older woman carefully. Known, as she was, for being one of Society's most terrifying doyennes, it always amused him how swiftly he could get under her skin and ruffle the old thing.

Being a distant aunt, of course, helped. Or rather, nephew.

"Well, I think it a 'reel' shame you aren't dancing," he quipped.

Lady Romeril groaned. "Really, Chantmarle. You could not think of anything better than that?"

He perhaps could have composed a more impressive jest if Samuel had not also been scanning the crowd for the miscreants he had been sent to Scotland to search for in the first place.

Samuel's eye flickered across two young ladies seemingly bickering over a lace edged fan, two gentlemen arguing politics, and a gaggle of girls racing by who must have been permitted to attend their first dance and were showing themselves up terribly. There were sixteen people dancing, none of whom matched any description of the ruffians he had been sent to apprehend, and Lady Romeril's droning conversation did not entirely drown out the chatter around them.

"—heard the duke had rushed his marriage to a woman who—"

"—not in this Season, I don't know what my modiste was thinking—"

"—aye, ye ken the snappit of the—"

Samuel blinked. That last bit was, in truth, difficult on the ears, but he thought it meant—

"Samuel Dellamore! You are not heeding a single word I am saying, are you?"

He blinked again. The irate expression of Lady Romeril swam into view. "Sorry, old thing," he said cheerfully. "Not a syllable."

Perhaps if it were not Lady Romeril, Samuel would have paid greater attention to her words. He was able to move easily through Society on the King's orders, after all, because Samuel Dellamore, Duke of Chantmarle, was beloved and accepted in almost every drawing room in the country.

Any other woman would have been offended, and perhaps Lady Romeril was. But as it was, she merely rolled her eyes, tapped him with her fan as though he were a mischievous boy of seven who needed reprimanding, and tutted her tongue.

"When you wrote to me and requested my aid in finding you a bride," she said meaningfully, "I never presumed I would suffer such indignities!"

Samuel's smile slipped ever so slightly.

Ah. Yes. The cover story.

Well, the Duke of Chantmarle could not waltz—or reel—up to Scotland at the end of the Season without giving any explanation. Society would talk. Gossip would grow, and before he knew it, it would be impossible to hunt down the people he had been sent to find.

It was all very well being a duke, but when that distracted from one's purpose, it was smarter just to keep everyone's expectations low and the gossip predictable, to slip back into the caricature of himself he had created years ago.

Samuel, Duke of Chantmarle: idiot.

Everyone had believed it for so long, Samuel thought darkly, *there were moments when he was starting to believe it himself.*

"Well, I am grateful to you, I do declare," he said aloud for Lady Romeril's benefit. "And I do indeed need to find a bride for . . . um. Reasons."

Samuel almost rolled his own eyes. It was tiresome indeed, being treated like a complete dullard, but there it was. Everyone spoke more openly around a man they believed to be less than sharp. More secrets were whispered, more hints dropped, more statements muttered rather than murmured. It was so much easier to discover the truth of those around him.

Still. It was starting to wear, even Samuel had to admit.

At least, he would have admitted it, if he'd had anyone he could admit it to . . .

"Do not concern yourself, Your Grace, plenty of families of the very best blood find that an injection of a dowry does wonders for the name," Lady Romeril was saying in what she clearly thought was a delicate tone. "And that is why I brought you here."

Samuel forced himself to grin. "Most thoughtful of you, Lady Romeril."

And it was, in a way. He had to acknowledge that his plan to entice Lady Romeril to invite him to Edinburgh for her end of Season celebrations had been haphazard at best, ill thought through at worst. Why would anyone seek to aid a duke who had spent most of his time in Society playing the jester?

He had not accounted, clearly, for Lady Romeril's almost pathological need to be the center of attention.

The Duke of Chantmarle wishes to find a bride? Well, then Lady Romeril was going to find one for him.

"I have never been to Edinburgh before," Samuel said, saying the first truthful thing to his companion for a while. "I had never imagined it to be so . . . so . . ."

So impressive. Oh, Samuel was a London man, and other than his estates in Devon, he rarely spent time anywhere else. He was accustomed to Society and enjoyed the ability to order anything through one's butler and have it arrive that very afternoon. He liked Almack's as well as the notorious inns and gaming hells he spent time in when needing to get away from the simpering *ton*.

He had never dreamed, in truth, that there could be a city he enjoyed more. But Edinburgh was starting to surprise him.

"Precisely," Lady Romeril said, completing his sentence. "And some of the best families of the north are here."

By *here*, Samuel had to assume she meant the Edinburgh Assembly Rooms.

And they were spectacular. Not that he would ever say as much in Lady Romeril's presence, who was herself a Patroness of Almack's, but really the two were incomparable. The Assembly Rooms in Edinburgh were larger, lighter, better decorated. The food was actually palatable—quite unlike Almack's—and the music!

Samuel found, quite to his surprise, that his foot was tapping to the beat. "What do they call this?"

Lady Romeril frowned reproachfully. "Highland dancing. I have informed His Majesty that I greatly disapprove, naturally. The flinging of the hands! The whoops!"

Samuel grinned. "I rather like it."

It was easy, at times, to slip into the character he had created. Especially when his tastes matched those of a boor.

Just for a moment, a flicker of guilt seared around his heart. Was he himself perhaps rather closer in personality to that character than he would like to admit? The thought had gone before he could give it any real consideration, which was a relief. Samuel had far more important things to worry about, and Lady Romeril was only the first.

The dancing had changed, its pace increased, and the dancers were laughing and calling out to each other in the soft burr of the Scots. Samuel discovered a smile had crept across his face, and he allowed it to linger there.

Well, why not? The dancing was, in truth, impressive. Though he would never reveal a true opinion to anyone, the whole Assembly Rooms were rather fantastic. More people here than ever attended Almack's, more pleasurable music, more entertainment . . .

In a strange way, it would be difficult to return to London.

Samuel's attention sharpened. But he would, the moment he had discovered the rogues who had been passing secrets to the French.

The reminder of his true purpose in Scotland refined his concentration, even as he permitted his face to continue displaying the vague smile. He had to remember what he was here for, how he could help if he were able to track down the traitors who were sharing secrets with their greatest enemies.

"You look tired."

Samuel blinked. Lady Romeril was examining him seriously. Almost—and it made his stomach lurch to see it—with genuine care.

"It has been a long week," Samuel allowed himself to say.

Too right it had. A week of sending messages, bribing servants, receiving angry letters from London asking why he had not managed to find the blackguards yet, and a constant confusion about the language and, more importantly, the food.

The food! Why was everything boiled in its own skin up here? And why did the Scots's understanding of a cake entirely differ from his own?

Lady Romeril nodded sagely. "Ah, yes. Well, wife hunting can be a difficult business."

For just a moment, Samuel stared. *Wife hunting? He wasn't wife hunting, he was—*

"Yes," he said swiftly, hoping to goodness she had not noticed the momentary gap when he had forgotten his cover story. "Wife hunting."

He almost snorted. *Wife hunting?* Why did women have to make everything sound so ridiculous?

Besides, he could not be less in the market for a wife if he tried to be. Bring a woman into the dangerous life that he led? Risk a woman's heart, reputation, perhaps her very life? Absolutely not.

The day he allowed a woman to distract him that severely was the day, Samuel thought grimly, *he would have to pack up and retire to the countryside. Heaven forbid.*

"—outrageous, the way she has danced both the reel and the second with Mr. McDonald—"

"—never seen Miss Douglas behave in such a—"

"—has to be tonight, the letter is going to London then Dover on the mail coach—"

Samuel's ears pricked.

There was still a great deal of chatter going on around him, not including the indefatigable Lady Romeril . . .

"—consider daughters of earls to begin with, and we can then move on to—"

There was a pair of ladies behind him—he had spotted them a few minutes ago—in matching gowns of a light blue tartan. They seemed to be gossiping about a Miss Douglas—one of the dancers, Samuel had to presume. It appeared she had transgressed by crossing a very important social line, though he could hardly care less.

"—given preferential treatment! We shall have to hope Mr. McDonald will soon propose, or else—"

But it wasn't their conversation which had drawn his ear.

As Samuel continued to nod periodically at Lady Romeril—anything to ensure she did not believe he had stopped listening to her—he attempted to look lazily around, as though merely taking in the contours of the room.

His gaze narrowed. *There. Just behind him.*

Two men. One tall, the other shorter. Both stocky, both strong. One was speaking without looking at the other, and both appeared entirely unsuited to the Assembly Rooms.

Samuel looked away swiftly and nodded once more to Lady Romeril. "Yes, yes, I quite agree."

What he had agreed to, he was unsure. It did not matter. It appeared that he had, by complete chance, discovered at least two of the men who could be in this traitorous ring.

Sending an urgent letter to Dover? Why, that could only mean information sent to France. And the only people sending letters to France at this time? Spies.

It was as simple as that—but Samuel had to listen to more. Every detail would be vital, every hint that could give him insight into who else was involved would be precious.

"—never seen such ladies whooping!" Lady Romeril continued to complain in a mutter. "In my day, a lady did not whoop, not even on the occasion of the birth of her—"

"Yes, yes, I quite agree," Samuel repeated.

He allowed his attention to drift. If he was careful, he could maintain a vacant expression in his eyes and a fairly regular nod of his head to ward off any suspicion from Lady Romeril. And that would mean he could instead listen to . . .

"—recognized us?"

"I don't think so. None of these toffs have any idea. Look at them," the taller of the two men scoffed. "No clue the whole place could fall around them tomorrow."

Samuel's heart went cold as he glanced down, ostensibly to pull his pocket watch from his waistcoat pocket.

For a moment, he hardly recognized the article. Then he almost laughed. Of course, Morris had packed only tartan waistcoats. This one had a rather fetching mustard, white, and black sort of check, with a line of red running through it. The pattern was so odd, it was as though he had looked at someone else's chest.

But it was definitely his pocket watch. Opening it, Samuel glanced only momentarily at the time the watch face was displaying.

And that was because on the other side, on the back of the door of the watch, was a square inch of highly polished brass. And if he carefully positioned it like this . . .

The two men appeared in view. Though only a square inch, it was more than enough to take in their faces.

Samuel focused hard, attempting to put the faces to memory. He needed to be able to pick them out of a crowd at a moment's notice. His memory was usually strong, but the whiskey he had been given upon entry to the Assembly Rooms had rather swept to this head.

So, he needed to memorize them—find distinguishing details. One had a freckle just below his—

A movement. A sudden shock of yellow.

Samuel gasped and almost dropped his pocket watch.

"Careful, now!" Lady Romeril berated, as though that would permit Samuel to go back in time and prevent him from almost dropping the timepiece. "Honestly, gentlemen these days, they have absolutely no sense of—"

What he had no sense of, Samuel could not tell—he had stopped listening again. Attention, perhaps. His had certainly been distracted and by a shock of yellow far too bright to be allowed in such a place as the Assembly Rooms.

But there it was—a yellow gown. And it was wrapped around a woman who . . .

Samuel swallowed and discovered his amazement that his mouth was dry.

She was beautiful.

Not beautiful in the way of Society's primped and feathered monstrosities, as so many ladies at Almack's now were. Fashion and style were starting to demand more and more ridiculous ornamentation, as far as Samuel was concerned.

This woman was different. She was wearing naught but a yellow gown with what looked like black piping. The ribbon around the cuffs of her capped sleeves was a sort of gold, matched on the hem.

And that was all. No jewels. No pearls, no earbobs or bracelets or necklace. There were no diamonds in her hair, nor ribbons. There wasn't even a feather. Not a scrap of lace.

Samuel forced himself to turn back to Lady Romeril, who was still complaining in that strange way she always did.

"I told them once, if I told them a thousand times—"

Much to his chagrin, Samuel realized his heart was thumping rather powerfully. It took him a few heartbeats to understand why, then his stomach dropped.

She was talking to them.

The woman, the beautiful woman in the yellow gown. She had surprised his view in the miniscule looking glass because she had approached the two ruffians.

Samuel's brow furrowed immediately, his sense of justice and duty overpowering any good sense he had once claimed to possess.

Well, this was terrible! The poor woman had no idea what danger she was putting herself in merely by talking to them. Perhaps her companions in the Assembly Rooms were dancing and she was in need of conversation. *The poor thing had chosen the wrong people for that,* Samuel thought with a sigh.

He had to rescue her.

The thought was so strong, the sense so overpowering, Samuel had already taken a step away from Lady Romeril before he realized what he was doing.

He halted, half twisted, his mind whirling.

Where had that determination come from? He wasn't in the business of saving ladies, even from themselves. In truth, he rarely got involved in these sorts of things. Only a month ago he had given advice to a man in an inn about love, of all things. It was a small miracle the whole thing hadn't exploded in his face.

But this? This was just a woman. Just a woman at the Edinburgh Assembly Rooms. A woman he had not been introduced to, a woman who surely had a brother or father or—Samuel's stomach lurched—*husband* also at the Assembly Rooms who could care for her.

"—but your bride must be so much more than that, Chantmarle. And if you do not mind me saying so, I think it an excellent sign of character that you asked me to—"

"Yes, of course," Samuel said vaguely to Lady Romeril's monologue.

He was here, he told himself sternly, *to catch a glimpse of wrongdoing.*

To find the men who were passing secrets to the French. To bring to justice any traitors, then bring them to London. London, his home. Where he wished to return.

Getting distracted by beautiful ladies in simple muslin gowns was not one of his objectives.

Yet Samuel found himself twisting further to look properly at the woman.

His heart skipped a beat as blood rushed to his head. Oh, God. She was beautiful. And attempting to make conversation with the two men he really should be focused on.

Oh, hell, he knew what he was going to do. Becoming distracted by a pretty face was not his style, but there was always a first for everything. His curiosity growing, the need in him just to know her name propelled him forward without a second thought.

"Chantmarle? Your Grace, where do you think you're . . ."

Lady Romeril's voice faded swiftly under the music still being played for the dancers. Samuel paid her no heed; his entire focus was on the woman in yellow. He pushed past a gaggle of giggling girls, a lady who was openly weeping into the arms of her mama, and a man smoking a heavily scented cigar.

Samuel ignored them all. His gaze did not waver, not for a moment.

It was only when he reached the woman, stopping short before her and staring into her dark hazel eyes, that he realized he had prepared absolutely nothing to say to her.

The two men had halted their conversation and were staring mutinously.

"Yes?" one of them said aggressively.

Samuel ignored him. The woman had turned as though to greet him, a smile dancing on her lips.

His stomach lurched. "Would you care to dance?"

CHAPTER TWO

L ULU FINCH ATTEMPTED to take a long, deep breath.
This was what she had wanted. Why she had managed to acquire an invitation to the Assembly Rooms in the first place. And she wasn't going to miss out on her chance now, not after everything she had been through.

She was determined. It would be today that she would free herself.

"Mr. Gregory," she said, a little breathlessly as she approached.

Try as she might, Lulu found it almost impossible to ignore the glare from Mr. Gillingham standing beside him. Why were they always together? Why couldn't she ever speak to one of them at a time?

Perhaps if she could—

"You were bold, coming here," Mr. Gregory spat.

Lulu swallowed her retort, which was that they were surely far bolder to conduct their illicit business right in the center of Edinburgh Society, and tried to keep calm.

She had planned this. She had spent all day thinking about what she was going to say, how she was going to persuade them to free her. She had done everything she could, Lulu knew, and more. And it was time her efforts were recognized.

It was time the blackmail was over.

"I merely wished to speak to you, and you are astonishingly difficult to find," Lulu pointed out softly.

It was important to speak softly. She had discovered this last year, when she had attempted to speak more directly to the two men who had kept her soul in knots ever since—

Lulu pushed the thought from her mind. She wasn't going to allow herself to think about that. She had to think about the future, about how she was going to live the rest of her life happily after she made them agree to her terms.

They would agree.

"We're not difficult to find, are we, Mr. Gillingham?" Mr. Gregory sneered.

"Not in the slightest," agreed his companion.

A flicker of fear soared through Lulu. They were so much taller than she was—and stronger. She had discovered that to her peril only last week when she had asked, as politely as she could muster, for her debt to be considered paid.

Surely, by now, she had done enough.

"Well, I am glad to have the opportunity to speak with you," Lulu persisted, trying to smile. "Because—"

"You don't talk to us," Mr. Gillingham said severely. "We talk to you."

Her instincts urged her to take a step backward, but Lulu forced herself to remain where she was. She was not going to allow herself to be shouted down, even if she had seen the man break someone's arm before.

She should never have got herself entangled with—but it was too late now. Once they had the letters to blackmail her, she should have just left Edinburgh. Left Scotland.

But that had been last year. It was a belated wish now, and she had already burned the last of her bridges with anyone who could help her. That meant she had to face the fact, however unpleasant, that she had to deal with Mr. Gregory and Mr. Gillingham.

Hopefully, for the last time.

The music behind her changed as the dance came to an end and applause rang out around the Assembly Rooms.

Lulu's heart leapt. Perhaps this was the moment: her opportunity to demand—

"If you think you can convince us to wipe your debt clean," Mr. Gillingham said viciously, "you would be wrong."

And just as swiftly as it had risen, her heart sank. Despair, dark and sticky as tar, poured through her. Lulu found herself almost gasping for breath, as though her lungs had forgotten how to work.

She had gotten her hopes up, that was true, and perhaps she should not have done. Perhaps it was foolish to even consider that Mr. Gregory and Mr. Gillingham would understand her desperate need to be free of them.

But then, she thought morosely, *she was far more useful to them when in their debt.*

Despite her fear, despite the sinking feeling in her heart, Lulu forced herself to meet Mr. Gillingham's gaze.

"I thought you would say that," she said, more boldly than she felt. "That is why—"

"You don't get to make demands," Mr. Gregory said, taking a step forward.

Lulu almost stumbled over her skirts as she stepped backward, her heart skipping a beat. When would she lose her fear of these men? When would she be able to look them in the eye and not feel terror bubbling in her veins?

She should never have trusted them. She should never have believed a word they said. The moment they had made her that offer, an offer she couldn't refuse, she should have been brave enough to—

Movement, out of the corner of her eye—no, closer. A gentleman, dressed in a long coat and the most awful tartan waistcoat she had ever seen, was approaching them.

"You know him?" glared Mr. Gregory belligerently.

Lulu glanced over at the man as he wended his way through the Assembly Rooms.

"No," she said honestly.

He was tall, taller than both the men she was speaking to. He had an innocent, almost foolish look on his face, more like a youth of eighteen than the full-grown man he was.

Lulu could have groaned. What did the idiot think he was doing, approaching two men like Gregory and Gillingham? Evidently, he did not know them. No one in Edinburgh who knew them would consider speaking to them, especially not at the Assembly Rooms. So why was he making his way toward them?

"He's caught sight of a bit of skirt," sneered Mr. Gregory in an undertone, "and is coming over here to see how much you cost."

Lulu's cheeks burned.

Even if that were true, and she had no evidence to the contrary, she had never lived that life. She had been most determined never to slip into it. But if a gentleman, any gentleman, knew of her past—

"Yes?" Mr. Gillingham said aggressively as the stranger halted before them.

Well, not before them. Before her.

Lulu could hardly believe it, but there was no mistaking the gaze of interest in the stranger's eyes. He had stopped right in front her, as though they knew each other and he had merely come over to be polite.

But she had never met the man before. What on earth was he—

Her habits, however, were ingrained far deeper than she could have imagined. Though Lulu had done nothing consciously to encourage him, she found herself turning toward him, a smile lilting her lips. Anything to ingratiate herself. Anything to keep herself safe . . .

What on earth was she doing? The last thing she should be doing was encouraging this gentleman, whoever he was. No, for his own safety, he should leave Mr. Gillingham and Mr. Gregory as soon as—

"Would you care to dance?"

Lulu blinked. "What did you say?"

Astonishment was rushing through her. He could not have said what she thought he just said—could he?

Men did not ask her to dance. Oh, they asked her for a good number of other things, but she never obliged them. Lulu could not pretend her past wasn't scandalous; anyone who knew her, knew her brother, knew it was.

But this man had no idea, she saw as guilt weighed heavily on her shoulders. He did not know, whoever he was, what type of conversation he had wandered into.

Threats. Violence. Blackmail.

The man was grinning, the grin of a fool with little intelligence and even less wit.

Lulu's heart sank. For a moment, just a moment, she had thought . . . but no. This was not the sort of man who could rescue her from her situation. Only she could rescue herself.

"We'll be going, Lulu," grinned Mr. Gregory. "Don't do anything I wouldn't do."

With a dark chuckle, he and his companion moved away as heat once again scalded her cheeks.

Don't do anything I wouldn't do—honestly! The list of things Mr. Gregory would not do, Lulu thought ruefully, *was short indeed.*

"Lulu?"

Her gaze sharpened. Mr. Gillingham and Mr. Gregory may have gone—at least from her company as she did not see whether they had actually left the Assembly Rooms—but that did not mean the conversation was over, clearly.

The same idiot was standing there, vague smile and unfocused gaze.

Lulu sighed. Truly, it was most frustrating. Why couldn't she catch the eye of a man with wit and spark? Why did every man who ever wished to speak with her have nothing between his ears, no brains at all? They were entirely guided by what was between their—

"I hope those two men were not bothering you," the man said softly.

Lulu almost took a step forward to be closer before remembering herself and instantly leaning back.

How had he done that? In an instant, she had felt warmth and safety radiating from him. His soft voice had enticed her in, encouraged her to step nearer so she could hear him more clearly. If she had not had a greater hold on herself, perhaps she would have done.

Lulu tried not to take in the handsome line of the man's jaw, the way he looked at her with blatant interest.

No. Absolutely not. She was not about to allow someone else to attempt to grow close to her. She couldn't protect those close to her. Had not Malcolm proven that?

"I hope you have a pleasant evening," she murmured, gaze lowered as she curtsied.

And then she stepped away.

At least, that was what Lulu had intended. Somehow, just as her foot was about to take a step, the gentleman said something that made her halt.

"They are not the sort of men to get mixed up with."

Lulu looked into the stranger's eyes, and just for a moment, saw something completely different from the vague idiocy she had seen before.

A sharpness. A directness, a blunt intelligence that knew far more than she had revealed and probably guessed the rest. A man of intellect, of wit, of learning.

Then the moment faded and the same indefinite stupidity returned. Had she dreamt it?

"You don't say?" Lulu said dryly.

Honestly, trying to warn her off Mr. Gillingham and Mr. Gregory! It was far too late for that, though of course there was no possibility of letting this man know it.

Though that did beg the question, she thought, *why he would try to warn her off them in the first place. Now that was interesting.*

"I do not believe we have been introduced," the stranger began.

Lulu saw her chance. "Indeed, we have not. How remiss of me—well, we cannot talk here, it would be most scandalous. Good evening—"

"Oh, I am not concerned with the niceties of Society," the gentleman said cheerfully.

It was all she could do not to roll her eyes. *Well, of course he was not!* Men, especially gentlemen, never had to worry about such things. They could do what they liked, with whom they liked, and all the gossips would say is that they *probably* should not have done such a thing. The idea that they would actually be reprimanded? Heaven forbid!

"Let me introduce myself," the man was saying.

Lulu's cheeks flushed with heat. This was all going wrong—she needed to escape the man's company, not delve deeper into a connection!

"No, really, it's—"

"I am Samuel Dellamore, Duke of Chantmarle," said the man impressively, evidently expecting her to be similarly impressed.

Lulu's mouth fell open.

Oh, lord. A duke! The last thing she needed was to be connected to such a man, if he truly was nobility. That would explain the slightly gormless expression, too. Though she had little direct connection with titled men, Lulu had seen enough of those with money to know wealth was often a precursor to stupidity. Why learn anything if one could simply buy one's way out of problems?

The bitterness churning in her stomach refused to subside, so Lulu merely allowed it to fester. *Duke, indeed.*

That was probably why she spoke so directly and so openly. "Leave me alone."

The duke's eyes widened but Lulu did not linger to discover just how outraged he would declare himself to be. She pushed past, skirts flying, and attempted to make for the door.

Fresh air, that was what she needed. The coolness of the evening, a chance to stop and think, to reflect on—

Lulu gasped. *A hand—there was a hand on her arm!*

The duke examined her carefully with dark eyes. "I am not one to be ignored, Miss—Lulu, was it? Was that what they called you?"

Lulu sighed as she wrenched her arm free.

Of course he was not one to be ignored. No man wanted to be ignored—that was something she had learned long ago. Well, she would only have to suffer the man's company for a few minutes, then she could make her escape. Return to her room, start to plan the next conversation she would have with Mr. Gregory and Mr. Gillingham.

"Miss Lucy Finch, actually," she said sternly.

Her tone did not appear to work. The duke was grinning— grinning! At her!

"I believe I asked you to dance, Miss Finch," he said softly. "And I do not believe you gave me an answer."

It was all Lulu could do not to laugh in his face. "Was not my hasty retreat from your presence answer enough?"

Perhaps she had expected him to be taken aback. It was not the way dukes were supposed to be addressed, Lulu was certain. Not that she had much experience conversing with dukes. But instead of being offended, as she had presumed he would be, the duke merely tilted his head back and laughed.

"Dear me, I suppose it should have been," he said cheerfully, as though a woman had not made it abundantly clear she had no wish to speak with him. "And yet I am persistent, Miss Finch. Let me tell you, I will not leave these Assembly Rooms happy if I do not have the honor of dancing with you."

"Then I am sorry to inform you that you will be miserable," Lulu shot back, something strange rising in her chest. *Was it . . . enjoyment?* "For I have no wish to—"

"Truly? You have no wish to dance with me—none at all?"

Her answer died in her throat. The duke had stepped forward, blocking out almost the entirety of the Assembly Rooms. His gaze was sharp again, all the vacancy gone.

What sort of man was this? One who could switch his intelligence on and off as one would turn a tap?

Well, it did not appear she would escape him unless she gave into his demand. And besides, Lulu attempted to reason with herself, it was just one dance. Just a few minutes dancing a reel. How awful could it be?

"Fine," she said darkly.

Any other gentleman would have been offended at her reticence, but it appeared the Duke of Chantmarle was charmed by it.

"Marvelous," he said, offering his arm. "I intend to know all about you."

"Prepare to be disappointed," Lulu said with a brittle smile.

It was easy enough to complete the line. That was one of the things she had enjoyed the most about dancing, when she had permitted herself to do so in public. The ease with which others could participate, the sudden rush of belonging that flowed as you joined the line.

It did not rush through her now. Instead, as Lulu extended her arms so the duke could take her hands, quite a different sensation was spilling through her body.

Warmth.

It was because she was dancing, Lulu tried to tell herself. She always grew warm when she was dancing—everyone did! It was only natural!

But there was something very unnatural about what was happening to her. As Lulu caught the duke's gaze, something flickered in her heart, something she had never felt before.

They released hands as the dance moved up the line and Lulu felt a great sense of loss.

Loss? How could she feel his absence so dearly after only speaking with him for ten minutes?

But she could not deny the joy that roared through her as the duke placed his hand on her waist. The completeness that made no sense yet could not be ignored. The warmth spreading through her to the very tingles in her fingers.

"You dance well," the duke murmured.

Lulu glared, just to ensure he could not possibly guess how strange she was feeling in this moment. "I know I do."

"You don't wish to compliment me?" he quipped in return.

She almost laughed. Almost. But not quite. She was not foolish enough to lose all sense of decorum, and around a duke, too!

No. She had enough complexity in her life without bringing a duke into the bargain.

"You may think you wish to know me," Lulu began.

"You would be right. I do wish to know you," the duke said, interrupting her. "Far more than you know."

Oh, she knew. Lulu had seen hunger and desire in a man's eyes enough times to recognize it here—still, it was different. This was not pure, animalistic need in the duke's eyes. No, he was . . . well, if she did not know any better, she would have said he was curious.

Curious? About her?

Heaven forbid.

"I'm warning you," Lulu breathed as she stepped into the duke's arms—for the dance, of course. No other reason. "It's not a good idea to get too close to me."

"I wouldn't say that," the duke murmured. "In fact, I am rather enjoying it."

Her cheeks must be a brilliant red, she was sure of it. They certainly felt like they were burning. How could he say such a thing? And to her, a woman he had just met!

But perhaps all dukes were like that, Lulu tried to tell herself. Perhaps this was nothing special, just the pitter-patter of a man who was accustomed to getting what he wanted.

Well, this was one woman he was not going to get.

"Do not get involved," she said softly, but with a hint of steel beneath. "I speak the truth when I say it would go hard for you."

Lulu had intended her words to warn, to give the truth of the matter as best she could. It was therefore with a sinking heart that she saw her words had done precisely the opposite.

They had enticed.

"My word, Miss Lucy Finch," the duke said, taking her hands once more and looking deep into her eyes. "You could not have said anything that would pique my interest more."

Lulu swallowed as the dance came to an end and they stood, breathless, opposite each other in the line.

She could see that. And she would have to live with the consequences—and so would he.

"Miss Finch," the duke said, bowing his head. "Would you—"

Lulu took her chance. As the man broke eye contact with her, just for a moment, she slipped behind the vast bulk of a large gentleman who appeared to be meandering to the dining room.

"Miss Finch?"

She could hear the duke's confusion but did not dare to peek out as she rushed to the door, hidden by the crush of people who were switching places in the dance.

As she breathed in the cool air of night, half staggering through the door of the Assembly Rooms, Lulu congratulated herself.

She would never have to see that Duke of Chantmarle ever again.

CHAPTER THREE

12 April 1811

WHEN SAMUEL HEARD the gentle knock on his door, he presumed his valet was late.

"Come on in, man, for goodness' sake," he said cheerfully. "What's kept you?"

The tall door in his Edinburgh residence squeaked ever so slightly as it opened, no matter what Morris, his valet, tried to do about it. Samuel knew it bothered the man, who was methodical and careful almost to a fault.

The squeak was slower this morning, as though his valet hoped that by moving the door more carefully, the squeak would not occur.

"Kept me, Your Grace?" the valet said softly as he stepped lightly into the room. "What do you mean?"

Samuel sighed heavily as he pushed himself up on his elbows, and plumped his pillows so he could lean against them. He was hardly a man to tell off another merely for a small slip up, but really. His valet had been part of his household for near on three years. It was most unlike the man not to wake his master at eight o'clock, as he did every morning. But Samuel had been lying here in bed, eyes wide open and mind spinning, for hours past that. It must be near luncheon!

"Look, I do not mind the mistake this once," he said generously, as his valet stepped across the room and pulled back the curtains. "But please, I do like to be up for eight o'clock. Cook has my breakfast ready at that time every morning, and—"

"But Your Grace, it *is* eight o'clock," said Morris, bewildered.

Samuel hesitated. *It was?*

Surely not. He had been lying there in bed thinking of—well, someone he certainly should not have been thinking of—for what felt like an age. He had presumed he had awoken just before eight, as was his habit, then thought about Miss Lucy Finch, a woman of mysterious origin and tantalizing touch, for over two hours.

Had he really awoken at six in the morning, just because of a woman?

"Eight o'clock?" Samuel said aloud. "Truly?"

Morris pulled his pocket watch from his waistcoat, but there was no need. The servant had not closed the door to the corridor, and the chiming of the longcase clock at the end of it was still echoing.

Dear Lord. His mind had awoken more than two hours earlier than normal, Samuel thought hurriedly. Now that was a bad sign. No other woman in his acquaintance had ever—

"Well, well, so it is eight o'clock then," Samuel said quickly.

His valet was looking at him most curiously, and it would not do for anyone to realize just how rapidly the master's head had been turned.

"I'm warning you. It's not a good idea to get too close to me."

"I wouldn't say that. In fact, I am rather enjoying it."

Had that been a flirtatious comment? Samuel had thought so at the time, presumed Miss Finch had been desperate to attract his attention. But the manner in which she had slipped away from the dance . . . And he had been unable to find her after. If he hadn't known better, he would have thought he dreamt the whole encounter.

But no. His imagination was bold, but it surely wasn't that bold. He couldn't just imagine a woman that beautiful, the sense of her hands in his—

"I *said*, Your Grace," coughed his valet. "Would you like me to set out the blue waistcoat, or the—"

"Whatever you think is best, I am sure," said Samuel with a sigh as he pushed back the bedlinens. "Whatever you would recommend for a morning of visiting."

Visiting. He did his best not to roll his eyes as he walked into the dressing room that adjoined his bedchamber, where Morris had laid out a fresh shirt, his favorite slate gray breeches, and a matching cravat and waistcoat.

In tartan. Samuel groaned.

But it was what was expected for visiting, apparently. Lady Romeril had been most insistent that although Samuel had not a Scottish bone in his body, it would be expected of him that while he was in Edinburgh, he would have to attire himself to match with the customs.

And that meant tartan.

"Truly, these people could not have created a more distracting pattern," Samuel muttered as his valet carefully dressed him.

"I could not agree more, Your Grace," said Morris with a shake of his head. "Will we be staying long in Edinburgh? If so, I will send out to a tailor and order two more sets."

Samuel hesitated as he held out his hands for the shirt to be pulled over them.

Would he be here much longer? He had only intended to stay in Edinburgh a few weeks. Lady Romeril's invitation had been the perfect cover. The whole of Scottish Society seemed to be a-quiver that the Duke of Chantmarle was hunting for a bride. Even if hopes had waned in the intervening weeks, as he did nothing but attend gatherings and nod at eligible young ladies.

In truth, if last night had not occurred, Samuel would be writing to London that very morning and suggesting he return and that he could do more good in the southern capital. He had spent weeks attempting to bribe those who would know whether or not there truly was a ring of blackguards here, selling secrets to the French. All avenues had turned up naught.

But last night . . .

"Do not get involved. I speak the truth when I say it would go hard for you."

"My word, Miss Lucy Finch. You could not have said anything that would pique my interest more."

Samuel swallowed as warmth billowed across his chest. Why was he finding it so difficult to rid his mind of that woman?

She was beautiful, yes. Her face was imprinted on his eyes, his gaze unable to stop seeing her as Morris carefully tied his cravat.

But she was hardly a suitable distraction. Really, Samuel should not be permitting himself to be distracted at all. Miss Lucy Finch, as she called herself, had not accepted his pointed attentions, either, which was even more strange.

Perhaps that was why he was so curious, Samuel thought, stepping into his court shoes and wishing he could be wearing thick solid riding boots as he did so often in London. Perhaps Miss Finch's indifference to him was itself inviting his curiosity.

"Your Grace?"

Samuel blinked. Then he looked down.

Blazing hell, he was dressed. When had that happened?

"You asked me something?" he said, seeing his valet's pained expression.

"I did, Your Grace," said Morris politely, deciding not to point out his master's rudeness. "I inquired how long we would be staying in Edinburgh."

Samuel frowned. *What the devil was he asking that for? The very cheek of it!* "And what has that to do with you, pray?"

Immediately he realized his mistake. His poor valet knew no better; none of his servants knew the work their master did for the Crown. And besides, it was Samuel's own distracted nature which had caused this mix-up in the first place.

His mind flashed back to an earlier part of the conversation. *Oh, yes.* "Ah, yes, shirts and cravats and things. Well, how long I am intending to stay in Edinburgh depends on . . ."

Depends on my orders, Samuel could have said. Depends on what is required. Depends on how I can serve my country, keep England safe.

Instead, a pair of dark hazel eyes flashed across his mind. A woman who frowned rather than smiled, a woman who refused to dance with a duke instead of simpering at his attentions. A woman who was entangled, somehow, with a pair of ruffians who may just be the people he was searching for.

"A little longer, Morris," Samuel found himself saying. "We'll be in Edinburgh a little longer—order the cravats. Order whatever you like."

"Yes, Your Grace. Your Grace—?"

"I'm going out," he called over his shoulder as he made for the corridor. "Visiting!"

"At this hour?"

At this hour, Samuel thought wryly as he half walked, half ran down the broad staircase, *there were still a number of people he could call on.* It may not be a socially acceptable hour for most of the *ton*, but there were a few who understood his line of work.

If one could call it work. Dukes never worked.

The streets of Edinburgh were quiet this early—at least, quieter than they would be later. No respectable people were out, but that meant all the people not in the rigid *ton* were, and in the main they were the people whose company Samuel usually preferred.

Hawkers attempting to sell pies, meats, ale, pastries. Samuel shivered as he walked past a woman attempting to sell knitted scarves and matching mittens.

He would not have thought about it in London, of course. It was April. Spring—almost summer! But the chilly winds of the Scottish Borders were felt keenly here, and Samuel shivered as the breeze

rushed through him and the greatcoat he had grabbed from the hall
before leaving his residence. He would have to remember to ask
Morris to purchase a scarf or two.

His destination was only ten minutes up the Royal Mile. He had
recommended the location when Penshaw had written asking for a
suggestion for an Edinburgh residence, and it had three great advantages.

Firstly, it was suitable for a duke, and Penshaw was one.

Secondly, it was in the fashionable district, which was precisely
what the duchess, apparently, had requested.

And thirdly, it was only a short walk from his own residence. That
meant whenever Samuel grew tired of the pretense, tired of aping the
fool, tired of smiling at Lady Romeril as though she were *not* the most
irritating woman in the world, he could visit the Penshaws and be
himself.

"Ah, Your Grace, you are early," said the Penshaw butler politely,
opening the door.

Samuel grinned and ignored the pointed—and completely unspoken—reproof. "That I am. Is Penshaw up?"

"His Grace is in the breakfast room," said the butler sedately. "May
I—Your Grace!"

Samuel wholly ignored him. It was easy, ignoring servants. In
truth, Samuel ignored anything that did not precisely align with what
he wanted at the time. It was a hateful habit, one he had picked up
from his father and had never managed to lose.

It did come in useful, though.

"Penshaw, you old reprobate!" Samuel said with a laugh as he
opened the door to the breakfast room and took in the view. "Breakfasting before your woman makes it downstairs?"

Lawrence Madgwick, the Duke of Penshaw, chuckled as he leaned
back in his chair. "And is it always your habit to march into other
people's breakfast rooms and criticize them?"

Samuel grinned as he sat opposite his old friend. "Most definitely. May I?"

Penshaw gestured at the platters on the table, and Samuel began to help himself.

"I have never known you to respect a man's plate," his friend observed.

"Neither have you," Samuel pointed out. "I remember that time in Carlisle. Besides, we have only known each other—what, three years?"

"It feels like a lifetime," quipped the older man.

Samuel grinned as he piled two fried eggs, four tomatoes, more mushrooms than he could count, and more bacon than was surely good for him onto a plate.

That was the pleasant thing about Penshaw. They both served the Crown and, at times, had both risked their lives in the process. The man understood him; at least, understood him as well as anyone could presume to.

Even with Penshaw, though, Samuel was careful to act a little more foolish, a little more dumb than he actually was. It would never do for people to know precisely how sharp he was—even a friend.

"You look rather worse for wear, if you don't mind me saying so," Samuel said cheerfully as he pulled a knife and fork toward him. "I say, I'm not eating your wife's breakfast, am I?"

"You are not, and I am not worse for wear," said Penshaw dryly. "Much."

Samuel grinned. "You're getting extremely old."

"I'm extremely married," returned Penshaw with a laugh. "The wife kept me up last night—and don't give me that look, Chantmarle, that was not what I meant!"

It was difficult not to grin. Partly because the gormless smile was something of an instinct now, but also partly because that was precisely what Samuel had thought.

Wives. He had been surprised when Penshaw had returned from some sort of secret mission with not only the reprobate he had been sent to find, but a wife as well. The whole *ton* had been—and the fact that the new Duchess of Penshaw was untitled with no dowry . . .

Well. Samuel had been surprised, even if he had grown to admire and like her.

"Where is she, anyway?" Samuel asked, swallowing his mouthful of bacon and egg. "Too refined to break her fast with her husband?"

For some strange reason, his friend wouldn't meet his eye. "She is feeling . . . unwell this morning."

Now why was that statement in any way suspect? Samuel could not understand it, but he could see the discomfort in his friend's eye.

Well, it would have to remain a secret. There was only one mystery he wanted to uncover today, and that was not it.

"Tell me," said Samuel, in as debonair an air as he could manage. "I'm interested in knowing more about—look, there was a woman at the Assembly Rooms last night—"

Penshaw groaned. "You're meant to be here on the Crown's business, Chantmarle, not seducing—"

"I did no such thing!" Samuel protested.

Though not for lack of trying, he thought privately. Honestly, how had that woman managed to examine him with such disdain? Why had Miss Finch taken against him so?

Usually the mere mention of a title—any title—and it was easy to get under a woman's skirt. Not that Samuel did so often. It was often easier to keep his façade of being a fool if he was also terrible with the ladies.

But he had never met such resistance as with Miss Finch. Never been faced with a woman so unimpressed by him. Never wished to reveal himself, his true self, so greatly. Never been so eager to impress.

Penshaw was examining him with a knowing look. "Well. Describe her to me, and I'll tell you what I know."

Samuel was tempted to pretend the whole thing had been a jest, but he relented against his better nature. Just a few questions. Just information—how dangerous could that be?

"Her name is Miss Lucy Finch," he said quietly, playing with his fork now his plate was almost empty. "She was . . . well, remarkably aloof, to tell the truth."

His friend snorted. "You mean she was not willing to be seduced in the Edinburgh Assembly Rooms?"

Samuel forced down his retort that no man should be jesting about Miss Finch.

It was odd, this possessiveness, this determination to protect her. He could not tell five facts about the woman, knew almost nothing about her . . . yet she drew something from him he had never experienced before.

It was maddening.

"Miss Finch . . . I have not heard the name, though I am sure there are sufficiently numerous ladies in Edinburgh's *ton* that I have not encountered them all," Penshaw was saying.

Samuel grinned. "That's because you never accept any invitations anymore. Being married has—"

"Being married has been the greatest joy of my life, I tell you," Penshaw said, trotting out the same line most men entrapped in matrimony repeated. "You should try it some time. I hear that's the gossip around why you're here."

His friend affixed him with a knowing look.

Samuel shrugged. No more needed to be said. Penshaw had served the Crown, he knew the lies which sometimes had to be told to keep the scandalmongers away.

"One day you will get married," Penshaw said quietly, an irritatingly knowing look on his face. "And more than that, you'll like it."

Samuel rolled his eyes. "Perhaps I will. Perhaps I'll find a woman I don't mind being tied down to, an anvil around my neck, when I'm no longer able to serve my country."

"You can serve your country still, if you find the right woman," Penshaw countered.

Now that was curious. Samuel had met the duchess a few times, and she had appeared perfectly pleasant—but not the sort who would permit her husband to put himself in danger. Perhaps there was more to this duchess than met the eye.

And where was she, anyway? A little sickness in the morning, what did that—

"Oh, dear God, you're going to be a father," Samuel breathed.

Penshaw did not confirm his conjecture, not in words, but he did not need to. The flush that scalded his cheeks and his immediate bluster was enough.

"We haven't—that is, it's not certain that—we lost a child early so we didn't want to announce—"

Samuel's heart sank.

Poor sod, losing a child. He couldn't think of anything worse. *And now, that was that.* His friend was truly lost to him. If husbandhood hadn't completely stolen him, fatherhood would.

"I must be going," Samuel said quickly, rising to his feet.

Penshaw looked wretched as he mirrored him. "I was going to tell you, old chap, it's just—well, she didn't want anyone to know until—"

"It's quite all right," said Samuel, hardly knowing what he was saying. "I'll see myself out."

The bracing Edinburgh air was a shock to his lungs as the Penshaws's butler closed the door behind him. Still, despite the sharpness in his lungs, Samuel breathed in deeply.

Well. There was going to be an heir to the Penshaw line. Or a daughter, he supposed—a prospect for alliances. He should be happy—he knew he should be delighted for his friend, glad the man's life was evolving and growing.

But he couldn't push out of his mind the certain knowledge that all the adventure, danger, laughter would be gone from Penshaw's life.

That part of his time was over. Now it would be . . . oh, Samuel didn't know, as he started to walk down the Royal Mile once more. Baby names, and governesses, and—

"Have a care, sir!"

Samuel started. So lost had he been in his thoughts, he had accidently walked into someone!

A lady someone. A woman with dark hazel eyes and a mortified expression.

"You," breathed Miss Finch.

Something astonishing stirred in Samuel's stomach. What were the chances—it was a miracle! In the whole of Edinburgh, who had he bumped into but Miss Lucy Finch?

Her cheeks darkened. "Good day."

She had bobbed a curtsey before Samuel could collect himself, and he had to race after her down the street.

"Wait—Miss Finch!"

"I have nothing to say to you," she said firmly.

Samuel's heart was thrumming, his lungs tight, every breath a challenge. His curiosity unsated, he had to know—had to know everything. Anything.

"How long will you be in Edinburgh?" he asked, keeping pace with Miss Finch's long strides easily.

The question was brushed aside as though it was nothing. She did not even look at him. "I said good day."

"And I said how long will you be in Edinburgh?" Samuel persisted. "You are not a Scot, I can tell by your acc—"

"Do you always ask ladies impertinent questions?" shot back Miss Finch.

Samuel almost stumbled as she swiftly turned a corner, pushing past a gentleman on the pavement and ignoring his shouts of irritation. "Only when those ladies don't answer any of them. I always get the information I need."

"Well then, prepare to be disappointed," said Miss Finch, her cheeks pinking. Falling back into trite sentences, then? Hadn't she said that the last time he—"For I have no intention of—"

"Are you being courted by anyone, Miss Finch?" Samuel asked, much to his surprise.

That caught her attention. Miss Finch halted, her cheeks now a blazing red, and she glared with unconcealed anger. "Why would you ask—who do you think you are?"

"I am the Duke of Chantmarle," said Samuel, stepping to her, closing the gap between them. "And I want to know you, Miss Finch. I want to know . . . everything."

What possessed him to say it, he had no idea. He was intoxicated by her, entirely lost to the tantalizing Miss Finch who appeared truly shocked at his words.

As well she might. What he was saying was ludicrous, disgraceful . . . and precisely what was on his heart.

His mind, Samuel corrected hastily. This woman was merely a puzzle, that was all. He wished to understand her. That was no surprise—he was a curious soul. It was what made him so advantageous to the Crown.

The Crown. He really should be hunting down those two men he had seen . . .

Seen talking with Miss Finch.

"Who were the two men you were speaking to last night?" Samuel said softly, not shifting his gaze. "At the Assembly Rooms?"

He was not mistaken. There was a definite look of guilt on Miss Finch's face.

"No one."

"No one is no one," Samuel said, irritation prickling around his heart. "Who—"

"I am no one, and you should leave me alone," Miss Finch said, her voice breaking as she turned away. "Before it's too late."

Samuel watched her go, unable to collect his senses swiftly enough to follow her. This woman! She was absolutely the most irritating, confusing, and strange woman he had ever met.

The smart thing, he knew, would be to focus on his mission. On discovering whether the two men she had been speaking with were anything to do with the traitors sharing secrets with the French.

So why did he have the distinct need to find Miss Lucy Finch again, and seduce her into spilling all her secrets?

CHAPTER FOUR

13 April 1811

L ULU LOOKED AT the coins spread out across the table, and wondered whether counting them for a third time would make any difference.

It wouldn't. She knew that. It was foolish of her to even consider—

Breathing out slowly, Lulu scraped the coins off the table and into her sweaty palms and started counting them onto the table again.

"One penny, a penny and a half, fourpence . . ."

Her stomach tied itself into an even tighter knot as soft spring light shone through the partially open window. The sounds of the street below rose, packed full of horses' hooves and the shouts of men arguing over a trifle.

She might have smiled if the situation weren't so dire.

" . . . one pound and six shillings," Lulu finished, looking at the pile of silver and coppers on the table.

Table. It wasn't exactly a table. The lodgings she had taken two years ago had become more and more sparse as her financial woes had increased, which was saying something. She had only taken the two rooms. She now had nothing more than a bed in the bedchamber along with a single candlestick and a trunk for her clothes. In the other room there was a fire, a pot for cooking and a teapot, a chair, and what had once been a crate. Lulu had begged it from a sailor who smiled at her on the Thames docks, and it made a perfectly serviceable table.

Even if it had smelled of fish for the first few months.

Lulu bit her lip as she leaned back in the old wing backed armchair she had salvaged from a hotel which had been about to chop it for firewood. The springs creaked ominously, but it remained intact.

"One pound and six shillings," she repeated, her words the only sound in the room. "But is it enough?"

Enough. At times, she wondered whether money could ever be enough. If there would ever be an amount of money that would satisfy Mr. Gregory and Mr. Gillingham. It was as though her debt, once small, was now completely insurmountable.

And true, they had not given a particular price for her freedom. Perhaps freedom was the wrong word, but she could think of no other.

"Freedom," Lulu whispered, rolling the word around her mouth. It felt as though that was the closest she was going to get to it. "Freedom."

Freedom from fear. From terror. From looking around each corner and wondering whether there would be someone behind it who would hurt her. Freedom from worrying that at any moment the truth could be released, scattered to the winds, ruining reputations.

Lulu shook her head as though that could dislodge the fear. But how could it? She had lived in fear so long, she was starting to wonder if she would ever learn to live without it.

One pound and six shillings.

It was a vast sum of money, but even without finding old Gillingham and Gregory, wherever they were hiding at the moment, Lulu was certain it would not be enough. She would have to find more.

The window rattled as a harsh wind suddenly blew. Lulu rose from her seat and stepped over to the small diamond-paned window, the source of the only natural light that flowed into what she sometimes called her "drawing room." Her only room, other than the bedchamber.

The whole world appeared at her feet. Well, that was, down below on the street. Men and women, old and young, rich and poor. Lulu amused herself for a few minutes by trying to imagine where all the people beneath her were going. What their worries were. What their joys could be. It sufficed to distract her from her own situation for about five minutes, before the heavy, leaden weight of the burden she carried crushed her heart again.

"You may," Lulu whispered to herself, "have to consider another route to riches."

Her heart rebelled at the implied notion, even unspoken. Stomach still churning, she tried desperately to convince herself that a few weeks working as a—would not be the end of the world.

Probably.

It was the last thing she wished, but she could no longer live with this hanging over her. This blackmail, it was going to be the death of her!

And the realization that unless she did something drastic, she would die under these circumstances, appeared to be the instigation Lulu needed. As though acting on the orders of another she closed the window, drew the curtains—well, curtain—and hunted for her thickest, warmest shawl. Who knew what time that evening she would be back?

The wind felt even brisker on the landing. Lulu had rushed down the stairs of the building where her rooms were lodged as swiftly as she could manage, before she had time to change her mind.

Every time she felt desperate, she promised herself she would never do it. The nauseous feeling of regret which always settled in her heart wasn't worth it.

She was not a bad person, Lulu told herself firmly as she started to walk along the busy pavement. *She was not a bad person—she was just—*

"My God—Miss Finch!"

Lulu suddenly halted. There, blocking her path on the pavement, staring with wide eyes was—

She groaned. "Your Grace."

"I cannot believe it!" grinned His Grace, the Duke of Chantmarle. "Just think, only yesterday you—"

"—attempted to get away from you," Lulu snapped. "Unsuccessfully."

This could not be happening. The whole of Edinburgh, and she had to be the woman who suffered this idiot's presence three days in a row!

Lulu glared at the man who was still talking happily, seemingly unaware she was not listening. What was wrong with him? Why did every gentleman assume their words were the only ones worth hearing?

Of course, he wasn't just a gentleman. He was a duke.

Lulu's heart skipped a beat.

Ridiculous, she told herself sternly. A duke, indeed. He was just a man! An impressive title was only impressive if you allowed yourself to be impressed.

And this Duke of Chantmarle, or whatever he called himself, was hardly impressive. There was a stupidity about him, in truth—

"Who were the two men you were speaking to last night? At the Assembly Rooms?"

"No one."

"No one is no one."

Lulu's stomach lurched. But he wasn't completely foolish, was he? There'd been a moment, the day they had first met at the Assembly Rooms. A moment when he had seemed almost clever. A sharpness in his eye she had not expected.

"You're staring at me, Miss Finch."

Lulu started. There was a knowing smile on the man's face that she dearly wished to remove. If she had been a man, she would have undoubtedly done it with her fist. As it was . . .

"I am," she said boldly, ignoring all instincts to walk away from this imprudent man. "And there is no crime in that."

"None indeed," quipped the duke swiftly. "In fact, I take it as a compliment. You strike me as a woman who does not suffer fools and spends even less time with them."

Lulu opened her mouth, hesitated, then closed it again as heat blossomed.

See, that was where the man was so infuriating! An unintelligent man would not have been able to reply so swiftly, so cleverly. So was he witty? Or was he merely lucky?

"Here, take a good look," said the duke, spreading out his arms and getting in the way of everyone walking around them. "Ensure that you examine me fully, Miss Finch. I would rather have an accurate opinion from you than a good one."

"Rather have a—" Lulu could hardly breathe. *Was every duke this arrogant?*

It was impossible to know, as this irritation was the only one she had met.

Still, it was not like her to back down from a challenge, and so she pointed her chin in the air most determinedly as she beheld him.

It was unfortunate indeed that as she did so, her heart skipped another beat.

Well, she would have to be blind not to notice just how handsome he was. Dark hair, longer than was fashionable, but it suited him. Curls gently dusted the tops of his ears, just visible above his collar points and cravat, which was tied in a most fashionable manner.

In fact, now she came to think of it, all his clothes were fashionable. He had been well dressed at the Assembly Rooms, save for the tartan, and he was well dressed now.

But there was more to it than that. Lulu had seen her fair share of gentlemen who were well dressed, but no amount of tailoring could create the breadth of his chest, the muscles that tightened in his sleeves. There was strength there, real strength. And poise. And—

"I don't have time to look at you," blustered Lulu, tearing her gaze away almost too late.

Goodness. She had almost got lost in the moment there.

"No time?" asked the duke, twisting to follow her as Lulu stepped around him. "But we have all the time in the world!"

Lulu rolled her eyes as she strode away. *All the time in the world, indeed!* There went a man who had never had to work a day in his life. Even worse, he had no comprehension of what it was to work at all.

All the time in the world!

At least she was free of him. She could continue on her way, find Mr. Gregory, and—

"You know, if I were an easily hurt man, I may start to think you were avoiding me," said a conversational voice.

Lulu did not permit herself to glance to the left. She did not need to. Somehow she could sense the duke's presence alongside her.

How had he managed to catch her?

"Longer legs," supplied the duke, as though he could read her mind.

She recoiled, almost as though he had physically injured her. Perhaps he had. Lulu could not understand the heat soaring through her, or how she was so uncomfortably aware of the duke's presence beside her.

The pavement was rushing along faster and faster as Lulu attempted to out-stride him, but the Duke of Chantmarle was correct. He had much longer legs, and before long she had to admit a silent defeat and slow down.

The duke grinned beside her, his smile so dazzling she could not help but see it. "You could just talk to me, you know."

"I have no wish to talk to you," Lulu snapped.

What a fool the man was! Anyone could surely see Mr. Gregory and Mr. Gillingham were dangerous men. Men that one would not wish to get involved with. She certainly regretted every moment she had ever spent in their company. The moment this duke had seen her with them, shouldn't he surely have stayed away? Ignored her, refused to get mixed up in anything untoward?

Perhaps he truly was a buffoon.

"Where are you going?"

"Right," snapped Lulu, suddenly halting and turning on the duke.

The man was grinning inanely. "Hello."

Lulu sighed and tried to collect her wits. This was ridiculous—but it was also a mixed blessing. The man was clearly a few spoons short of a drawer, and though he may think her pretty, or whatever reason it was that he was following her around Edinburgh, that could be easily solved.

"Are you following me?" Lulu said, pointing a finger.

The duke looked at the finger she had held up. Though she managed to hold it for almost a full silent minute, she eventually lowered it.

Not silent, exactly. They were now standing on the pavement of Grassmarket. The market sounds around them were growing in volume with every passing moment, and Lulu could feel the gazes of a hundred eyes.

Perhaps not a hundred. Perhaps no one had noticed that she was being followed, for she could think of no other word for it, by a duke.

Lulu's lungs tightened. She was just a woman, a woman alone in a city. No protection, no brothers or fathers. No occupation, no independent wealth. Why would anyone care about a woman like her?

"Following you?" the duke repeated. "I mean, I have been, just now."

Lulu fought her instinct to roll her eyes. If the man truly was dim—

"But I know what you're asking, and no. It has been chance, luck, fate, whatever you want to call it," the duke said suddenly, his gaze focusing and his voice lowering as he stepped closer. "No matter where I go in this city, there you are. I cannot escape you, Lucy Finch, and I am starting to think you cannot escape me."

Lulu swallowed. There it was again: that sharp wit, that focus and determination which utterly belied the gormless conversation they had otherwise shared.

What kind of a man was this? Who was the true Samuel Dellamore, Duke of Chantmarle?

"You . . . you aren't following me?" she said, uncertainly.

It was impossible not to be disarmed by the way he so rapidly changed. What sort of a man could elevate his intellect to such heights, only to permit it to fall to such depths?

A slow, lopsided grin spread across the duke's face. "How would I follow you? Edinburgh is a large place," he pointed out.

"And you are a duke," Lulu pointed out in return. "You could— oh, I don't know. Have a servant follow me, pay people to find out where I lived."

For a moment, she thought she had gone too far. A strange flicker of something danced across the tall man's face, but when she blinked, Lulu saw she must have been mistaken.

The duke was still smiling. "Now, why would I do that?"

"Because—" Lulu began instinctively, then halted.

It was an excellent question. *Why would he?*

He was a duke, a man clearly with more money than sense. But certainly with money. There were a thousand and one entertainments he could be enjoying in Edinburgh. He could be in London, in Bath, in Brighton. He could go to his manor. Every duke had a manor, didn't he? He could visit friends, relations, enemies.

So why would he be in the streets of Edinburgh, paying people to find her?

Unless, a small dark voice in the back of Lulu's mind whispered. *Unless . . .*

Lulu shook her head as though to rid herself of that thought. *No. That was impossible.*

"Because," she said firmly, as though that answered his question.

The duke raised an eyebrow. "You think I am tracking you, stalking you."

A cold gusty wind blew past them. That had to be why Lulu shivered at that precise moment.

Stalking her. Like a fox stalking prey. Like a hunter stalking a deer.

Yes, there was something of the hunter in the way the Duke of Chantmarle looked at her. Lulu was no fool. She knew what a man and a woman could share. She knew of the desire a man felt, the need that erupted within him.

And if she were not mistaken . . .

"Well, I think you are taking advantage of the fact I cannot outrun you," she said hastily, pushing aside the thought and taking a step forward. She was unable to take a second step because the duke blocked her path.

"And you would be right," he said softly, his dark gaze meeting hers. "I am banking on the fact you cannot outrun me."

Lulu opened her mouth in outrage. *The cheek! The audacity to admit—*

"I am curious about you, Miss Lucy Finch," the duke continued, his voice low. "And I have asked a number of people after you—people from all walks of life, from all classes of Society. And few know anything about you. Isn't that strange?"

Lulu swallowed. Not nearly as strange as the fact that a duke was asking after her! Now that was strange indeed.

Still, a prickle of pride in her heart reminded her that she had, at least, been discreet. A duke would have significant resources, wouldn't he? Yet he had been unable to find out much about her. That boded well for the future. When she needed to slip away into the night.

"I am a private person," she said aloud.

For some reason, her voice was soft. Lulu could not understand it. She could also not understand why her fingers were tingling, why the hairs on the back of her neck were standing up.

The duke stepped closer. There were only a few inches between them now. *Why,* Lulu thought wildly, *if someone were observing them, they may even think—*

"Who were you talking to?" he said quietly.

All the warmth drained from her body as Lulu stared at him. For a moment there, just a moment, she had allowed herself to believe. It was a darling fantasy, wasn't it? The idea a duke could genuinely be interested in her. That her beauty, what little of it she had, was sufficient to draw in a man of such pedigree.

She had been a fool to permit herself, even for a moment. Now he had revealed his true colors.

It was not *her* the Duke of Chantmarle was interested in.

"Talking to?" Lulu said as lightly as she could manage. "I truly don't know what you mean—excuse me, I am late for an appointment with—"

"With the men you were speaking to at the Assembly Rooms?" cut in the duke swiftly.

Lulu had intended to walk away, but somehow the man's gaze kept her pinned onto the pavement.

"You should be careful, Lucy," said the duke softly. "They are dangerous men, I am sure."

Lulu hardly knew what to chastise first: the arrogance of telling her who she should associate with, the audacity of calling her by her first name, or the assumption that he could speak to her so intimately! Even if she did rather enjoy two of the three, he was not to know that.

Lulu pulled her shawl around herself more tightly and attempted to focus. The last thing she needed was for the Duke of Chantmarle— for anyone—to know she was in any way mixed up with Mr. Gregory and Mr. Gillingham.

And that meant there was only one thing for it. Lie.

"I am sure I do not know what you mean," she said airily. "I was off to the flower market. You may accompany me, if you wish."

The duke held her gaze. It was the same mixture of intellect and inanity. The same disconcerting confusion swelled in her heart as she observed him.

Was she really bold enough to allow a duke to accompany her all afternoon?

"What an excellent suggestion," said the duke with a smile, stepping out of her way. "Lead on, Macduff."

Lulu rolled her eyes as she set off slowly along the pavement. "It's 'lay on, Macduff,' you idiot."

Well, there was nothing for it now. She would have to attempt to be as dull as possible. This curiosity of a duke could simply not be permitted to continue.

CHAPTER FIVE

16 April 1811

S AMUEL GLARED AT his informant. "And is that all?"

The man squirmed.

He was being too harsh, Samuel knew, but there was no other way of getting information out of people these days.

Money? Oh, he longed for the days when money was sufficient to gain all the details one required. Money would pour from his lap, and back into his lap would pour delicious information.

Information that had, in the past, saved lives.

But now? Now honor, respect, and duty were far more important.

Samuel almost scoffed as he leaned back on the hard bench he had been seated on for nearly an hour. It had been all very well when he had been the only one with honor. That had been easy to take into account. He was a duke. He was supposed to be honorable.

But honor amongst thieves? Wasn't the whole point that there wasn't any?

Blakely, his current informant of choice, was still squirming on the other side of the table in the inn where they had met.

"I know I should have more information, I know," he said wretchedly. "But it's so hard to get stuff from people nowadays."

Samuel managed not to roll his eyes. The irony was not lost on him, even if it was on Blakely.

"I am well aware of that," he said quietly. "But I am certain there is something else you have to tell me. No, not more direct information, I know you've given me that. Something else. Something you've noticed, or overheard that you thought nothing of at the time . . ."

Allowing his voice to trail away, Samuel hoped to goodness it would jog the man's memory. He was a coalman, after all. Blakely went all over Edinburgh, was allowed to walk happily into every kitchen, every servants' hall. He overheard much, Samuel was certain.

It was why he had brought the man into his employ in the first place.

Samuel waited patiently as Blakely sat quietly trying to think. That was the important thing. *Give them enough time to think.* Some of the other men who served the Crown were all for rushing in, guns blazing. Samuel did not see the point.

Good things come, as he had proven over and over again, to those who wait.

Samuel allowed his gaze to drift around the inn. It had been Blakely's suggestion. In London, that would have caused alarm bells to ring. He much preferred talking to his informants in a place of his own choosing.

But in Edinburgh? He hardly knew the place. Any recommendation from a man like Blakely was naturally suspicious, of course, but he couldn't allow the man to see he might be concerned. To the *ton*, he may be Samuel Dellamore, Duke of Chantmarle: idiot. But to his informants, he was Mr. Samuel, the harsh man who would get what he wanted. How long could he be both? Could he ever be more?

The place was packed. It was late in the afternoon, too early for the evening rush, but even so there was a mixture of downtrodden gentlemen and uppish tradesmen meeting here.

Samuel almost smiled. *No dukes, of course. Other than himself.*

"There was something . . ."

His attention snapped back to Blakely. "Yes?"

Blakely smiled nervously. "Just something I overheard, you understand—I wouldn't call it information, more—"

"You would be surprised how often information was never information when it was shared," Samuel said dryly, trying to keep his voice level.

Something within him told him this was important. There was that flutter in his stomach, that expectation he was about to hear something crucial. He may not understand how it all fitted in now, but he would later, when he had a few more pieces of the puzzle.

"It was a woman."

Samuel blinked. "A woman?"

Now that, he was not expecting.

Blakely was nodding. "Yes, I was almost certain I heard a woman's voice when I went to visit—but I couldn't have, could I? What woman would associate with Gillingham? What woman would actually *go* to his lodgings?"

Samuel frowned as he leaned on his elbows on the table between them.

It was an excellent question. Most interestingly, it led him back to Miss Lucy Finch. She could know this mysterious woman who was bold enough to visit a man's lodgings after dark. The whole thing would not be so mysterious, of course, if the man in question were not Mr. Gillingham.

The very man she had been speaking to at the Assembly Rooms.

His heart skipped a beat. Well, it was an excellent excuse to see her again. The meander they had shared together at the flower market a few days ago had been highly unsatisfactory. She had been so monosyllabic in her replies to his prompts for conversation that he'd been bored nearly to tears.

"No."

"Yes."

49

"Perhaps."

"No."

Yet Samuel could not pretend he was not intrigued. And as well as she seemed to know Gillingham, Miss Lucy Finch must also know this woman who had visited him. Perhaps she would be willing to give up the identity of this woman . . . for coin.

His stomach lurched at the thought. *Money would sully what they had.*

No, that was ridiculous. What they had? Had Miss Finch not made it perfectly clear that she had no appreciation for his company and no interest in ever seeing him again?

"I hope you have satisfied your curiosity," she had said with a wide smile as Samuel had finally admitted he was late for a dinner invitation. "The flower market is so fascinating."

And he had glared, hating that he had been outwitted.

And by a woman, too!

But this information from Blakely—it was just what he needed to see her again. Lucy.

"Sir?"

Samuel started. For perhaps the first time in his career—if one could call it that—in service to the Crown, he had not pretended to be gormless. He truly had drifted off.

Dear Lord, that wasn't a good sign.

"Yes, yes, here's your half a crown," he said quickly. "Be off with you."

Blakely snatched at the coin eagerly and scarpered, disappearing far quicker than Samuel had thought possible. That was a talent. One he needed to bear in mind for the future.

The future?

Samuel groaned as he sagged onto his arms on the table. *The future?* He couldn't put up with Edinburgh much longer. The Season was reaching its peak in London and then all his friends and acquaintances would be disappearing off to their country residences. Summer balls, long weeks of visiting, the opportunity to make new connections . . . he was missing it all. Before he knew it, the hunting season would be back, and autumn would be here.

He couldn't still be in Edinburgh then. Heaven forbid.

No, he had worked too hard, Samuel thought as he rose from the bench and threw down a shilling to cover the cost of the drinks he and Blakely had consumed. He was not about to abandon Edinburgh merely because he was frustrated.

He would find out who was sharing secrets with the French if it was the last thing he did. And now he had the perfect excuse . . .

It did not take him long to return to his lodgings. That was one of the more pleasant things about Edinburgh compared to London, Samuel thought begrudgingly. It was far smaller. You were never that far from your front door.

"Dressing for dinner, Your Grace?" asked his valet smoothly on entering the bedchamber.

Samuel suppressed a grin. "Yes. Would you mind having a note sent to the Royal Arms Hotel asking for a table for two, around eight o'clock. And another note to a Miss Lucy Finch, Stewart Buildings, to inform her that her presence is required. Same time. Same place."

If his servant was surprised his master—a duke!—would demean himself by dining out in public, he did not show it. He did not even inquire as to who this Miss Lucy Finch was, or why it was so crucial that his master dine with her. A commoner!

Instead, Morris merely bowed. "Of course, Your Grace. I will return momentarily and aid you into your formal dining attire."

The door closed with a snap behind him, and Samuel permitted himself a moment of exhaustion as he dropped onto the sofa at the end of the resplendent bed.

Was he playing with fire here? Allowing his curiosity to overwhelm him?

There were other lines of enquiry he could pursue, after all. There was that note someone had spotted being passed on a ship bound for France. That could have been something. Or the strange conversation overheard by his butler, of all people, when the fishmonger had delivered the weekly supply to the kitchens.

But somehow, of all the different opportunities he had to discover the traitors, he thought this was the most important one.

No surprises there, Samuel thought wryly.

He had never permitted a woman to distract him the way she did. Well, that ended here, he decided. He would have dinner with Miss Lucy Finch, entirely rid his system of her, and never spend a waking moment on her ever again.

It would be that simple.

It did not feel that simple, however, a few hours later. Samuel had arrived at the Royal Arms Hotel out of sorts and ten minutes late— another irritating practice he had not managed to avoid inheriting from his father.

"Your table awaits you," said the maître d'hôtel, nerves showing in the sweat beading on his brow. "I must say, we have never before received such a request from—"

"—a duke, yes, I thought so," said Samuel smoothly, wishing desperately to put the man out of his misery. "A bottle of your finest red wine."

"Yes, yes, of course, I—"

"And when my guest arrives," Samuel added as he started toward the dining area. "Ensure she—"

"Miss Finch has already arrived."

Samuel stopped dead in his tracks and stared at the maître d'hôtel, who flushed. "I beg your pardon?"

"She . . . your guest, she—well, she arrived just before eight o'clock," said the man miserably. "Was that wrong? I do apologize, Your Grace, I—I showed her to your table. I presumed—"

Samuel swore under his breath, cutting the man off.

Well, damn. He should have guessed there was a chance she was already here. He had hoped to have more time to collect himself. What woman arrived on time for dinner? It was outrageous!

Still. Drawing himself up, Samuel reminded himself that at least he now had less time to wait until he saw the pretty woman again. There was always a silver lining.

"—had known it would disagree with Your Grace, I would never have—"

"Yes, yes, very well," Samuel said with a vague wave of his hand. There was nothing to be done, after all. "My table?"

"I-It's near the back, far from a window, I thought the most private—"

"Fine," said Samuel, stepping away from the poor man and putting him out of his misery. "The wine."

The stammering of the maître d'hôtel disappeared swiftly as Samuel stepped into the dining area.

It truly was most impressive. The string quartet in the corner was playing Mozart, and there was some sort of fountain tinkling on the other side of the room. The chandeliers glittered with candlelight, and the other patrons were talking in low, genteel voices.

Samuel's shoulders relaxed, tension melting away, as he stepped through the fern-bedecked dining hall. Where was she? Half the tables were hidden behind fronds. Perhaps this had not been such a poor idea after all. Perhaps this could—

"And what," came Miss Finch's icy tones, "was the idea of inviting me here?"

His stomach lurched as he beheld her.

She was magnificent.

She was always rather striking. Miss Lucy Finch had caught his eye at the Assembly Rooms precisely because she outshone everyone else who was there, even without the adornments typical of her sex.

Here in the opulence of the Royal Arms Hotel, he had expected her to be diminished.

Nothing could be further from the truth. Lucy was seated at a table right at the back, half hidden by a screen and two large ferns in oversized pots. She was leaning back with an air of absolute contentment, wearing a blue gown of muslin that shimmered in the candlelight. On closer inspection, it had seen better days—like all of her gowns, now he came to think about it. Once again, she wore no jewels, no ribbons, no feathers. A lady who had fallen on hard times?

Samuel swallowed. The most beautiful lady he had ever seen.

"Why good evening, Miss Finch," he said breezily as he stepped over to her table.

A footman pulled out his chair and he sat slowly, ensuring that he got a good view of his dining companion before he settled.

Dear God, she was magnificent. Did she have any idea how she caught the eye?

"I asked you a question, Your Grace," Lucy said sharply.

Samuel caught the eye of the footman. "One of everything."

"One of—"

"That was what I said," Samuel said, adding just a little flint to his tone. "Is that a problem?"

The footman's mouth fell open. In his hands were what Samuel presumed were menus. But he had no need for menus. No wish for them.

"O-One of everything, Yer Grace," stammered the footman, bowing low and retreating without turning his back.

Samuel tried not to smile. The maître d'hôtel had obviously been attempting to impress upon his staff the importance of a duke dining with them. That boded well.

"Do you always do that?"

His attention snapped to the woman seated opposite. For some reason, she was glaring.

"That?" Samuel said, allowing his standard idiotic smile to slip onto his lips. "I don't under—"

"Yes, I think you do," said Lucy slowly, her eyes narrowing. "I think you are far more intelligent than you let on, Your Grace. I think you do it because you enjoy making other people feel stupid, inferior. I think it's all a game to you."

Samuel's smile disappeared.

Now that was something he had never heard before. Was that truly the impression he gave? Was he in fact not as clever as he thought himself, pretending to be a fool? Was he in fact turning aside potential informants—nay, potential friends?

It was a harrowing thought.

"You know, I thought I would come here just to see how much of a charlatan you truly are," Lucy said, standing in a rush of skirts. "But I have no interest in becoming the fool in your little charade. Good evening, Your Grace."

It was all going wrong. Samuel could not bear it, the thought of her leaving, but Lucy had already taken a few steps away from the table.

He needed to do something. Fast.

"I am sorry."

The words had slipped out before he could consider them, but apparently they were far more powerful than he gave them credit for.

Lucy halted in her tracks. She turned slowly, then returned to her seat. "You just apologized."

Samuel was just as shocked as she appeared to be. When was the last time he had apologized? In truth, he could barely remember ever doing so in his life.

What was coming over him?

"You . . . you were right."

Samuel clenched his jaw shut but it was impossible to take back the words. What, was he now admitting to the only trick he had in his book?

55

Lucy raised an eyebrow. "You—"

But she was interrupted by the footman, who was followed by—

"Just how much is on this menu that you ordered one of everything from?" Lucy asked slowly.

Samuel groaned. "I didn't check."

Perhaps he should have done. What appeared to be over twenty servants, mostly footmen but a few maids, were trailing out of the door to the kitchen, each holding a platter. Evidently "one of everything" was a far greater number of dishes than he could have imagined.

Well, his steward would not like the expense, but it would make for a marvelous story.

"We're going to need bigger stomachs," Samuel said, grinning at Lucy.

She treated him to a rare smile. "We're going to need a bigger table."

After a frantic five minutes in which the maître d'hôtel apologized for the size of the tables, the size of the room, the dearth of footmen, and seemingly everything Samuel did not immediately approve of, they were settled. Two additional tables had been pushed either side of the one Samuel and Lucy were seated at, and every square inch was covered.

"I never had you down as a glutton," Lucy observed, looking at the plethora of dishes. "Now, what have we here? Chestnut soup, mackerel with fennel, roast potatoes, roasted pheasant . . . such a shame so much will go to waste."

"Do not pretend you are not hungry," Samuel said softly. "I know you have known hunger. If I were a betting man, I would say you know it now."

Yes, there was the soft flush in Lucy's cheeks. "Of course I am hungry, it is dinner time."

"You know what I meant," he cut across her gently.

It had not been difficult to spot. It was part of his responsibility to notice things. And Lucy Finch looked hungry. As though she had not seen a hot meal recently. As though the memory of a hot meal was fading.

Lucy met his eye with a determined air. "You were busy apologizing, I think, not prying into my private—"

"Ah, yes," said Samuel with a heavy sigh. She was not going to let it go, he could see that. "Well, I am sorry. There it is."

She watched him as he plated a good deal of grouse and more than a few potatoes onto his plate. Even when not examining her, he could feel her examination of him.

What was this sensation? Of being too aware of a woman? What was it called?

"And what precisely are you apologizing for?"

Samuel swallowed. This would not be easy. Perhaps it was not wise. But he would never forgive himself if he was not honest in this moment.

In truth, he had never been so tempted to be honest before in his life.

He sighed. "I play the fool. It is not a clever trick—it is certainly not as clever as you. You saw through me within days."

"Play the fool?" Lucy repeated, playing with her wine glass. The wine itself she had not touched. "What does that mean?"

Samuel squirmed in his seat. Now he knew how Blakely had felt. "It's just . . . I am a duke."

"I am well aware of that."

"What you might not be aware of is that many people treat me as someone to use for their own gain, rather than someone to get to know," Samuel said heavily.

Strange, how deeply he felt this. How he had never been able to explain it before.

Lucy raised an eyebrow. "Am I supposed to feel sorry for you?"

"It wouldn't do my ego any harm," Samuel said honestly with a dry laugh. "But seriously—imagine knowing that everyone you meet, everyone who looks at you, is only admiring you for your title, for your wealth, for your grandeur—not yourself. And they think you a fool. You haven't earned any of it, they think. And so I . . . give them what they expect."

The look on Lucy's face was somehow softer. The way she looked at him made Samuel's heart patter painfully.

"What they expect?" she repeated slowly, with no malice or teasing in her tones.

Samuel nodded. "They expect a fool, so I give them one. I play up my ignorance, I offer a stupid smile. Pretending to be dim has rescued me from countless situations in which I would have been encouraged into something dangerous"—well, that was not completely untrue—"and I believe that most of the time, it prevents anyone expecting too much of me."

There. It was said.

Strangely, some of the weight always resting on Samuel's shoulders appeared to be . . . gone. Now how had that happened?

"And do you feel happy?" Lucy asked quietly. "Never having much expected of you?"

It was such an odd question, Samuel hardly knew where to begin. "I think—"

"I don't want to know what you think, I want to know what you feel," interrupted Lucy softly. "How you feel about being underestimated. How you feel about people immediately believing the lie, that you are a fool. How you feel about being ignored by those who think they cannot gain anything from you."

Heat was twisting in Samuel as she spoke, but he did not know how to interrupt her. Her questions were so strange, so unexpected. But now he came to think about it . . .

"Hurt," Samuel said awkwardly. "Lonely."

Lonely? What was wrong with him? Gentlemen like him weren't lonely! He was a duke!

Lucy held his gaze, just for a moment. The moment seemed to last forever.

Samuel found he was holding his breath, and it was therefore a great relief when she smiled and he could release the tension in his lungs.

"There," she said softly. "I think for the first time, I have seen the real Samuel Dellamore, Duke of Chantmarle."

Samuel smiled inelegantly. That she had, and it had made him feel most vulnerable. Not a sensation he would have believed he could enjoy, and yet . . . yet it was rather pleasant. How odd.

"Now," Lucy said, helping herself to a portion of the chicken. "Now we can dine together."

Samuel's heart skipped a beat. "We can?"

Why did it matter so much? Why did every moment in her presence lead to something entirely unexpected?

Her smile was shy, but it did not disappear. "At least for tonight. I make no promises for tomorrow."

CHAPTER SIX

19 April 1811

L ULU EXAMINED HERSELF critically in the looking glass. That was, the small amount of looking glass that she still had.

"Breaking a looking glass," she murmured under her breath as she attempted to pin the last curl in place. "What did you expect, Lulu?"

She had never been one for superstitions. She never had to be. Everything had been wonderful and easy, and then—

Well. She could no longer recall what had come first, the disaster and the blackmail, or the breaking of the looking glass. But she had to admit, even if only to herself, that it was a hell of a coincidence that the two events had occurred in the same summer.

Lulu sighed. The portion of looking glass she had rescued was only a few inches square, which made it difficult to pin her hair back. But from what she could see, the overall appearance wasn't too bad.

"If you only had some jewels, or even a ribbon," she said to her reflection. "But that all had to go, didn't it?"

Had to go. The euphemism for "being sold" did not lessen the pain in her chest. But this evening was not about feeling sorry for herself. Lulu drew herself up. No, tonight was the night she was going to tell Mr. Gregory and Mr. Gillingham, for the final time, that she was done playing their game. No more blackmail, no more secrets, no more doing what she knew was wrong just to save her own skin.

She was not going to be that woman anymore.

"Ah, going out m'dear?" said Mrs. Abernathy as Lulu stepped out onto the hall.

Lulu forced a smile. It was not the older woman's fault that she was so nosy. Perhaps she would have been too, if she was too unwell to go out into Society anymore.

"Yes, to the Assembly Rooms," she said as she stepped past her neighbor and toward the staircase.

Mrs. Abernathy nodded. "Aye, I ken as much. Ye keep yersel safe, y'hear?"

Lulu smiled warmly. "I always do, Mrs. Abernathy. I always do."

In truth, she had never felt more in danger. The Assembly Rooms were packed when she arrived, and it was difficult at first to push through to the table where punch was being served. Lucy had to physically elbow a gentleman out of her way to get a glass.

"Oh, sorry," sneered the man, not sounding sorry in the slightest. "I was watching the Duke of Gilroyd. Did you see, he—"

"I just wish for a glass of punch," Lulu snapped, not bothering with any social niceties. "Get out of my way!"

The man, whoever he was, looked affronted, but that was none of her concern. Her gaze was scanning across the room, seeking desperately the faces of the two men who held her future in their hands.

Lulu's stomach lurched as she sipped her punch. Most of her days since their . . . agreement, she had studiously avoided seeing either Mr. Gregory or Mr. Gillingham. Anything, rather than be subjected to their satisfied smiles.

But this was the end of their arrangement, Lulu promised herself as she watched the Assembly Rooms quieten after the Duke of Whatever disappeared into the night. She would never again have to fear seeing either Gillingham or Gregory. Never have to rush down an alley to escape them. Never have to slip out of a inn because they were there. Never need to—

"Ah, Lucy," came the sneering voice of Mr. Gregory. "I thought you'd be here."

Lulu's heart contracted painfully. She had not noticed the man approach her. Her gaze had been focused on the door, watching for when they arrived.

But they were already here.

"I didn't," said Mr. Gillingham darkly. "I thought she'd be cleverer than that, turning up to the Assembly Rooms when she knew we'd be here."

Lulu swallowed. Her mouth was dry, her heart pattering, but she had to go ahead with her plan. "May . . . may I have a word?"

She cursed the weakness in her voice. She was about to negotiate for her freedom. She would have to be more direct than that! Perhaps her self-frustration showed on her face. Though she had said no more, Lulu could see Mr. Gregory smirking at his companion.

"She wants a word," said Mr. Gillingham with a snort. "She thinks we've got all the time in the world."

Lulu managed to bite down the retort that they did. They were extorting from so many people, they barely had to work.

Instead, she said demurely, "I only wish for a few minutes of your time."

She watched, heart racing, as the two men exchanged a glance. The Assembly Rooms had been the right place to accost them. The place was too public for them to do anything too—

"Over here, then," Mr. Gregory said, the unspoken conversation with Mr. Gillingham coming to a natural end. "Come on."

Lulu gasped. Gillingham had grabbed her arm, pulling her away from the main hall and across to a small alcove, partly hidden by a large fern.

Far more private than she had intended.

"Now," Mr. Gregory said as Mr. Gillingham roughly released her arm. "What d'you want?"

Trying desperately to gather her thoughts, Lulu began, "I wish to renegotiate—"

"We don't change our minds," said Mr. Gregory sternly. "You should know that by now, Lucy."

"Unless of course, you've got something else to offer," Mr. Gillingham said with a leer. "I would never say no to a kiss, Lucy. You know that."

Lulu swallowed the bile that rose at the very thought. The idea that she would permit Mr. Gillingham—

"Consider it," Mr. Gillingham breathed, stepping close and pinning her against the wall. His breath smelled terrible, his hands were on her waist." I would be minded to consider a renegotiation if—"

"Get your hands off me," Lucy croaked, panic flooding her lungs.

No one could see her. The music was loud, the cheering at the reel being danced overpowering all other speech. No one would hear her. She would be forced to—

"Release Miss Finch or suffer the consequences," said a dark voice.

Lulu was suddenly released. The abrupt absence of Mr. Gillingham's disgusting breath and clammy hands felt like being reborn. Air was rushing into her lungs, her head was pounding, and there stood—

She could not believe it.

"And who the hell are you?" snapped Mr. Gillingham to the tall gentleman standing by the fern. "Interrupting a man's private business, that's—"

"Miss Finch, there you are," said Duke of Chantmarle pleasantly, reaching out a hand. "I was looking for you."

Lulu did not hesitate. Determined as she had been, clearly there was no reasoning with these people—and now she wanted to be as far away from them as possible. Any caution she may have felt toward the strange duke had been diminished by their dinner a few nights before.

Though she would never admit it, she had spent more than a little time since that evening thinking back on their conversation. The laughter they had shared. The secret the duke had spilled about why he acted the fool in company.

He was not acting the fool now.

"Chantmarle," she said grateful, reaching out and taking his hand, rushing swiftly away from Mr. Gregory and Mr. Gillingham. "I-I thought—"

"Let's go," said the duke meaningfully, glaring at the two men standing mulishly by the wall. "I see no men of honor here with whom to converse."

Lulu clung to his arm as the duke turned and marched out of the Assembly Rooms. Her mind was spinning so rapidly, she could barely perceive where they were going. All she could take in was Chantmarle. The strength of his arm, the comfort of his hand. The intoxicating scent of his musk, the power of his presence.

Despite the hustle and bustle of the Assembly Rooms, the crowd parted. Whispers started, whispers Lulu was vaguely aware of.

"—the Duke of Chantmarle—"

"Who is that with him?"

"Lucky woman . . ."

Lucky. Yes, Lulu supposed she was lucky. If the duke had not happened to see her—

"What," the duke said heavily as they stepped down the Assembly Rooms steps to the pavement. "What in God's name were you doing back with them? You told me yourself, they are dangerous!"

Lulu swallowed and released the man's arm. She had to. She was being swiftly overpowered by his mere presence.

How did he do it? Was it simply part of being a duke? Was that how Chantmarle was able to affix her with such a stern and yet compassionate eye?

"I . . ." Lulu hesitated. *How on earth was she supposed to explain this?*

She certainly could not tell him the truth. No, the truth would be the death of her. Though she had never sought the man's attention, she had to admit that being addressed so intimately by a duke was rather pleasant.

Particularly when it was this duke.

And all that regard he had for her, whatever it was, from wherever it had come . . . it would all disappear if he learned what she had done.

"I'll walk you home, Lucy," said the duke sternly, offering his arm. "But I want you to promise me you won't go near those men again."

Lulu was so distracted by his dominant orders, she found herself saying, "Lulu."

His arm was solid. Dependable. Warm. She took it and fell into step beside him before she really knew what she was doing.

"Lulu?"

She blinked. "I beg your pardon?"

The duke was grinning. "I think you just asked me to call you Lulu. Is that a family name?"

Oh, bother. She should never have breathed in so deeply as he rescued her. She should have known her senses would betray her. He was deeply intoxicating at the best of times.

No. No! She was not going to allow herself to think like that!

"My family called me Lulu, yes," Lulu said, grasping onto the only fact she knew she could share without disgracing herself. "I-I suppose you can, too."

Their footsteps were taking them down a street she did not know. It was far more impressive than any place she had ever lived, but she permitted the duke to guide her. Time with him, somehow, was never wasted.

"In that case, I suppose you should call me Samuel."

Lulu looked up, horrified. "I can't do that!"

"Why not?" the duke countered. "It's my name."

"But . . . but . . ."

How could she explain to a duke that it was impossible for her to speak so intimately like that with a man? With any man it would be scandalous. With a gentleman it would be outrageous. But a duke? Disgraceful!

"I cannot call you Samuel," she said firmly.

She felt as well as heard him chuckle.

"I suppose that would be particularly familiar," he owned with a shrug. "But still. I don't like the idea of you calling me "Your Grace" all the time. Not after . . . well, not at all."

This was a mistake, she knew. With her past, the last person in the world she should be associating with was a man who had a reputation to lose. All she needed was to lose her nerve and actually agree to call him Samuel! And yet . . .

"What about Chantmarle?" she suggested shyly.

Where had all this shyness come from? She was not the sort of woman to cower in a man's presence!

But the Duke of Chantmarle was no ordinary man. He did not make her cringe, nor hide away any of herself. In truth, she had been more open in her temper with him than with most people in her acquaintance.

She had not thought it would matter. And now it did . . .

"Chantmarle? I suppose that is a fair compromise," the duke said with a chuckle as he turned left at a crossroads. "I suppose I shall have to be content with that. For now."

Heat blossomed within and she was grateful for the darkness of night. Hopefully Chantmarle would not notice.

This was beginning to get out of hand. She couldn't be meandering the streets of Edinburgh in the dark of night with a duke! No, she needed to thank the man, direct him to her rooms, then firmly say goodbye, Lulu told herself. And that would be an end to it. An end to an acquaintance she should never have had, and one such as she would never have again.

She swallowed, and the knot in her throat momentarily disappeared. Then it returned.

Well, it was not as though she had any other choice.

"Thank you," Lulu said awkwardly.

Chantmarle raised an eyebrow. "For . . ."

He was doing it on purpose, she thought irritably. Purposely misunderstanding her!

"For rescuing me. From Gregory and Gillingham."

"Oh, that's quite all right," said Chantmarle cheerfully. "I would have done it for any lady in distress. Any gentleman would."

Lulu's shoulders slumped as she steered them down the next left. For any lady? Was she truly as insignificant as all that?

That was the trouble, she thought fiercely, of allowing one's thoughts to run away with one! There was absolutely nothing in his demeanor, his manners, or his conversation that should have allowed her to think that the Duke of Chantmarle saw her any differently to the maid who lit his fires.

Would have done it for any lady, indeed!

Well, I hope that teaches you a lesson, Lulu Finch, she told herself. There is no point feeling deflated. Chantmarle never promised you any—

"But I am glad," came Chantmarle's quiet voice, "that I could do it for you."

Joy rushed into her heart to replace the despondency. Lulu caught his eye, a slow smile spreading across her face as she did so.

"Truly?"

"Truly," Chantmarle said softly. "It was an honor. A privilege."

Warmth was spreading to the very ends of Lulu's toes. *A privilege!* Perhaps there was some reason to hope, after all.

Only as she nodded at the third right did Lulu realize what she had almost allowed herself to do. She had almost permitted herself to think of the Duke of Chantmarle as . . . well, as a prospect!

"So tell me," Chantmarle said easily as he allowed her to direct them. "Why is it that I keep finding you in their company anyway?"

Lulu blinked. She had been too busy looking at the way his side-burns crept into the curls of his hair to pay attention. "Whose company?"

"Gregory and Gillingham, of course," he said softly. "Lulu, you know they are dangerous. You warned me about them. Why do you seek them out?"

Looking at the pavement appeared to be the only way to keep her attention on her words. Even then, it was difficult. Chantmarle's warm and sturdy arm under her hand was doing strange things to her concentration. Lulu was not entirely sure they were even walking in the right direction.

What was this man doing to her?

"I mean, there must be countless gentlemen, real gentlemen, in this city who would be eager for an acquaintance with you," Chantmarle continued.

Lulu gave him a teasing smile. "Was that a note of envy in your voice?"

"Absolutely," said Chantmarle, returning her grin. "What, you think I don't have a vested interest in these questions?"

Heat flooded her cheeks. He was such a—

"Do you not have a brother or father who can tell you these things?" Chantmarle asked, his curiosity getting the better of him. "No . . . no gentleman courting you?"

Though her cheeks were assuredly pink, Lulu forced herself to meet his eye as they turned onto her street.

"You are very curious, aren't you?" she pointed out. "A very curious duke."

Chantmarle shrugged. "I am curious about you."

Despite herself, Lulu was unable to hold his gaze any longer. How did he do it? The moment she believed she had a hold of the conversation, that she had turned the focus back on him, he immediately twisted it so that she was once again under the microscope.

A curious duke indeed, but that did not quell her own curiosity. What was an English duke doing here in Edinburgh? Did he not have friends, family? Was he so truly experiencing such a dearth of good conversation that he would befriend a strange woman?

Lulu almost laughed. *The poor man had no idea what he was getting entangled in.*

The thought had been a passing one, but as it settled into her heart, she knew she had to say something. She would warn anyone off Mr. Gregory and Mr. Gillingham. She had already done so with Chantmarle, but he had not heeded her, and Lulu could not live with herself if she did not warn him again. These were dangerous men. She had entangled herself too deeply, she would never truly recover from her connections to either of them. But that did not mean Chantmarle had to suffer the same fate.

Lulu's jaw tightened. She would not permit anyone, let alone a duke, to ruin their reputation because she had not sufficiently forewarned them. Particularly not Chantmarle. He was starting to become . . . special to her. Even if she could never admit it.

"Chantmarle," Lulu began softly. "Oh. Here we are."

They had arrived at her rooms.

"This is where you live?" asked Chantmarle. "I shall have to remember that."

"You already had my address, you reprobate," she pointed out with a frown. "When you invited me to that dinner."

The man's grin was outrageous. "What a coincidence. Well, it's nice to see it in the flesh, for when I return."

She glared. "And what precisely makes you think that you will ever be here again?"

Chantmarle's lazy smile was not supposed to make her stomach flip like that. "Why, to see you, of course."

Lulu took a deep breath. This was going to hurt her more than it would hurt him. Even if he would never know that. "Look—"

"If you are attempting to warn me off, please don't," said Chantmarle quietly, dropping her hand but not stepping away. "I am accustomed to danger."

Lulu laughed dryly. "Not like this."

"I can look after myself," Chantmarle said, lifting a hand to cup her cheek. "It's you I'm worried about."

She had intended to say something, anything, to convince him to keep his distance from her. She was dangerous, rotten goods, spoiled. Treacherous. But the sensation of his fingers on her cheek—it burned into her skin as nothing else ever had.

"I warn you," Lulu breathed, unable to break the connection, gazing deep into his dark eyes. "You shouldn't get involved with me. With any of this."

Chantmarle chuckled as he smiled ruefully. "You say that, Lulu, like I can stay away."

CHAPTER SEVEN

22 April 1811

"WHY DID NO one tell me I was—"

"Well, you never dine out so early," his butler said in a rush as they both careered down the stairs. "It's only six o'clock, Your Grace, and—"

Samuel groaned loudly as he tried to pull on his greatcoat inside out when he reached the bottom of the stairs. "I needed to be there at six o'clock, not leaving at—"

"I am so sorry, Your Grace!" Fitzhugh was wringing his hands now, as if that could somehow change the time. "Next time, please inform me—"

"I did—never mind," Samuel snapped.

There was no point in attempting to explain it. In truth, he had not given the servant a huge amount of detail, precisely because of the nature of the rendezvous. Other gentlemen, Samuel knew, would plan secret meetings with lovers. He, on the other hand . . .

"Hat, hat, hat! Oh, blow it, I'll go without," he said with a weary sigh, wrenching open the door. "What is it?"

He had halted, just for a moment, as his butler thrust something into his hands. It felt like paper.

"A letter? From whom?"

The butler shrugged helplessly. "I know not, Your Grace, it came with the afternoon post, and I thought—"

"Fine, fine, I'll take it with me," said Samuel, chest heaving. He could not be late. If he missed it—Blakely had been very clear on when the meeting was to take place, and if he was going to have any hope in eavesdropping . . .

"Shall I keep dinner warm for you, Your Grace, or—"

"Eat the blessed thing yourself!" Samuel retorted with a laugh. "Oh, Fitzhugh, I am not truly angry—but I am late. Enjoy the dinner!"

He did not wait for his servant to respond. Instead he slammed the door behind him and started to half walk, half run along the street.

It was too bad. The information Blakely had sent that morning had been perfectly clear. There was going to be a meeting of some of Edinburgh's most notorious ruffians that very evening, at six o'clock, at Deacon Brodies Tavern. All Samuel had to do was be there ahead of time, place himself somewhere in the vicinity, and he could eavesdrop on the entire thing.

Except, of course, his butler had not informed him of the time when he had requested. Five o'clock had gone, completely ignored as Samuel had lost himself in thoughts of a certain young woman . . .

"I warn you. You shouldn't get involved with me. With any of this."

"You say that, Lulu, like I can stay away."

Samuel's jaw tightened as he hurried along the street, taking a right turn. Lucy Finch was fast becoming a liability, one he could ill afford. There were still secrets about English supplies being fed to French troops. If they could not plug the leak, there was going to be increasing danger for the British in France.

And the war, he had been told, was not going well.

He had to get there quickly. Though he was late, perhaps there would still be somewhere he could hide.

The streets of Edinburgh were crowded, but the people thinned as Samuel continued into the less reputable district. It was fortunate indeed that he had once met one of his informants at this tavern—he knew right where he was headed.

The letter was still clutched in his hand. Samuel shoved it in a pocket. If it were truly important, he could read it when he arrived. First, he had to choose his spot.

The place was absolutely packed. Evidently it had been payday for some of those in the city, for beer and ale were flowing. That was all to the good. The crowded noise and merriment was an excellent cover. So too was the coat he had chosen, one of his underfootman's. No one would give him a second glance.

"Two ales," Samuel said, dropping the genteel tones his voice typically carried. "I'm waiting for a friend."

The landlord leered. "A lady friend?"

Samuel carefully ignored him. He picked up the two tankards and pushed his way through the riotous crowd to a small table near the back, far from the five candlesticks that were dotted about the place.

That was it. Nice and dark, where he could see but not be seen. It was with great relief that he half sat, half fell onto a chair by the table. It could not be more than ten minutes past the hour. And they were not here.

Samuel sagged. Perhaps, if he continued to be watchful of the door so he did not miss the entrance of any new persons, he could also read whatever this damned letter was. When he pulled it from his pocket, however, he groaned.

It was not important. Well, it was from an important person. Most of the *ton* would be delighted to receive a letter from the Duke of Ashcott. But as it was, Samuel knew precisely what it would contain.

Taking a long sip of the disgusting ale he broke the seal, unfolded the letter, and prepared himself for paragraphs and paragraphs of pining.

Dear Chantmarle,

Your last letter was most remiss in sympathy, I must say. Even though I am helplessly in love, never able to be with the woman I care about, forbidden from her presence, never gifted with sight of her again, you think somehow I should be upbeat?

You have never been in love.

If you had ever cared about anyone, you would understand. You would know the torture I feel. You would sympathize with the agonies my waking moments are filled with. You would comprehend the nightmares I suffer.

Lady Margaret is as lost to me now as she was when her brother ordered me from their house. And yet she has not married another.

Is it possible? Could she be thinking of me?

I dread to think what the future brings, and I know that any possibility of reconciling with her is long gone. She is Lady Margaret Everleigh! The only woman I have ever loved.

Dear God, what is wrong with me?

My friends say I am pining. You, you dolt, say I should just forget her. Forget her? Have you ever forgotten the most beautiful woman you have ever seen?

Perhaps I shall go abroad. Perhaps escaping this godforsaken isle is the only way I can ever rid my heart of the beautiful, the lovely, the peerless Lady Margaret.

Oh hell, I've wasted another sheet of paper.

Come back to London and knock some sense into your faithful friend—

Ashcott

Samuel rolled his eyes as he folded the letter and placed it back in his pocket.

It was always the same. Ashcott—the Duke of Ashcott, to most of Society—had been whining about this woman for months now. No, wait. Perhaps even a year. And every time Samuel presumed the man must finally have given her up, he received a foolish letter like that. It was pitiable!

The moment he was ever . . . ever trapped in such miserable affection like that, he would have to hope one of his friends would give him a good kicking. It was shameful, the way Ashcott was carrying on. As though Lady Margaret Everleigh were the only woman in all of London!

Have you ever forgotten the most beautiful woman you have ever seen?

The line echoed in his mind, making his stomach lurch.

Well. When Ashcott put it like that, no. He hadn't ever forgotten the most beautiful woman he had ever seen. But then it was rather difficult to do so when Lucy Finch appeared to be filling his days, one after another.

A slow, lazy smile drifted across Samuel's face. She truly was remarkable. Every time he thought he had entirely understood Lulu . . . He must remember to call her Lucy, it would never do to be on such intimate terms. Or at least, to make their intimate terms so obvious.

His most recent memory of Lucy surfaced in his mind, and his heart skipped a beat. He had wished to kiss her then, standing as she was outside her rooms. Perhaps, if he had managed to kiss her, really shown her the pleasure he could give her with just one kiss . . . perhaps she would have invited him up.

Samuel shook his head and took another sip of the repulsive ale.

He was getting ahead of himself. That was, he was going along the wrong path entirely! He had no plans to seduce Lucy Finch. No plans whatsoever.

Even if his loins stirred for her as they did for no other.

And—

Samuel blinked. It was a trick of the light. It was because he had been thinking about her, reminiscing on the way she smiled, the sound of her laugh.

Lucy couldn't actually be here. Not in this tavern. Not at this time.

But she was. He had not imbibed sufficient ale to be completely stupid, and Samuel would have known her anywhere. The contours of her face were becoming as dear to him as—

Shaking his head as though forcing the thought from his mind, he watched Lucy pick her way through the crowd. She ignored the leering shouts of the men, holding her head high as only Lucy could, her presence noticed due to her irrepressible beauty, not the maid's gown she was currently wearing.

What the devil was she doing here?

Panic started to rise. Himself, he could protect. It wouldn't be the first time he'd used his fists to escape a dangerous situation. He didn't like it, but if push came to shove, he was ready.

But Lucy? Was he strong enough to protect her, protect both of them? And why was this infuriating woman always managing to find herself in the most hazardous of situations?

Samuel watched, heart thumping painfully, as Lucy approached a table on the other side of the room. Thanks to the smoke of a few pipes, it was impossible to see precisely who was seated there. At least three men, two of them dressed better than the third.

One of them rose to welcome Lucy to the table. Samuel hissed with a swift intake of breath.

Gillingham. The very man that he had rescued her from but days ago!

"Thank you."

"For . . ."

"For rescuing me. From Gregory and Gillingham."

What the blazing hell—

It was a long twenty minutes. Samuel knew it was precisely that long that Lucy spent with the three men because he could not stop himself continuously looking at his pocket watch.

Twenty minutes. Twenty minutes during which he expected shouts and cries of pain at any moment. That she would be manhandled, and he would rush forth and rescue her, be the man she needed.

Samuel's head ached as, eventually, the three men rose and without even bowing to Lucy, left the tavern. Only then could he loosen the tension in his shoulders.

Right now, in this moment, there was nothing for it but to demand answers.

The fact he had not been close enough to overhear any of the conversation flickered in Samuel's mind, but he pushed it aside. There would be other chances to eavesdrop on the men he was half-certain were tangled up in the French plot he'd been sent here for in the first place.

For now, he had to do what was most important, and that was keep Lucy safe. With tact, of course. He was a tactful man.

"Do you have a death wish?" Samuel demanded, standing behind Lucy at her table.

She whirled around, fear in her eyes—fear that swiftly mellowed. "Chantmarle."

He ignored the soft warm feeling that settled in his stomach as he heard her speak his name. He mustn't allow himself to get distracted. He had to make Lucy understand just what dangers she was meandering into, once and for all.

"I said, do you have a death wish?" Samuel said flatly, dropping into the chair beside her so recently vacated by Mr. Gregory. "What do I have to do to keep you safe, Lulu?"

A gentle flush tinged her cheeks at the sound of her nickname. He tried, unsuccessfully, not to notice.

This would be so much easier if the woman weren't so damn charming!

"You're following me again, I see," Lulu said quietly.

If he wasn't mistaken, there was a brittleness in her voice. Samuel did not understand it. What woman would associate with such men at the best of times—but especially after Mr. Gillingham had attempted to force a kiss?

"I'm not following you," he said thoughtlessly.

Lulu raised an eyebrow. "My, my. Then what is a duke like you, Chantmarle, doing in a place like this?"

Samuel cursed his own arrogance. Once again, Lulu appeared to prove that perhaps he *was* the dimwitted fool he pretended to be.

Because that was the obvious question, wasn't it? Why would a man like him be in an inn like this, when there were plenty of places a gentleman should be: the Assembly Rooms, a drawing room, a card party.

Not a dirty tavern with regulars who smelled like they needed a good wash.

"You're learning my habits."

Samuel's head jerked up. "I am certainly learning something about you."

He had not intended to sound so combative, but he could not help it. What danger this woman allowed herself to get into! Did she even comprehend, for a moment—

"I wouldn't learn my habits, if I were you," Lulu said with a wry smile. "They're not good habits to accumulate."

Samuel leaned forward, unable to help himself. He had to be closer to her. Something in Lulu Finch drew him in like nothing ever had before.

"I . . . I want to know everything about you," he murmured.

As expected, Lulu's cheeks flushed. "No, you don't."

"Don't tell me what I—"

"No, really, you don't," she repeated, emphasizing the last two words. "You are the one who keeps spotting me with dangerous men. Has it ever occurred to you that I am a dangerous woman?"

Samuel stared. *A dangerous woman?*

He was a duke often in danger, and most of the time, the danger was calculated. It was a means to an end, a way for him to secure a greater achievement. There was risk, yes, but he could see it and so could avoid it.

There was no avoiding Lulu Finch.

"You're not dangerous," he said, wishing to goodness he had the bravery to reach out and take her hand.

What was stopping him? It was not as though they were in polite Society. There were no rules nor restrictions preventing them from touching.

Just as Samuel reached out for Lulu's hand, she removed it from the table and placed it in her lap.

"You don't know if I am dangerous or not," she said softly, meeting his gaze. "You don't know anything about me."

That was true. Samuel may not like it, but he could not help but admit it. "Yes, perhaps. All the more reason for you to tell me about yourself."

She scoffed. "Chantmarle—"

"Samuel," he said desperately.

Anything, anything to feel closer to this woman who made him feel more alive, more on the edge of something spectacular than anyone ever had.

Lulu's severe gaze raked across his face. "You truly want to be on first name terms with a woman who associates with brigands, a woman you know nothing about?"

Samuel swallowed.

She was right. There was not a single syllable she had uttered he could disagree with. And yet everything within him fought against it. "I want to know you."

Lulu's dry chuckle was almost lost in the noise of the room. "Don't you ever worry your curiosity will lead you somewhere dangerous?"

Samuel shrugged, ignoring the rushing sensation of tingling anticipation up his spine. "No."

"You're lying," said Lulu with a look of mischief. "Don't lie to me, Samuel."

He was clay in her hands. If she had asked him to drop to the ground and allow her to walk all over him, Samuel would have done it.

He had never felt this way before: this rebellious, this vulnerable, this lost. This at one with someone he hardly knew, yet so confused that nothing seemed to make sense.

"Tell me about yourself," he persisted.

Samuel waited with bated breath as Lulu examined him.

Then she sighed. "There's not much to tell. I was born, I had a family that I lost, and now I live here."

After waiting for more, Samuel blinked. "Is . . . is that it?"

Lulu shrugged. "What else is there to know about me?"

Everything, he wanted to say. I want to know the soap you use, why you smile at me so darkly when you think I'm not looking. Where "Lulu" came from. Did you ever have a dog? Where were you born? How did you lose your family? Why do you wear no jewels?

Not that he could ask a single question, of course.

He was dancing with fire here. Samuel knew that the closer he got to Lulu, the more distracted he was becoming. The harder it was to care that this woman was derailing everything he had worked for in Edinburgh.

And so, although questions whirled in his mind, making it impossible to think clearly, he did not ask a single one.

Instead, Samuel was forced to smile. "You really don't wish me to know much about you, do you?"

"Get to know the me you see now," Lulu said softly, just a hint of hesitancy in her voice. "Anything more could be dangerous."

Samuel leaned forward. There were but a few inches between them. The tavern was growing noisier as more people entered, calling out to friends as they did so. Yet somehow, at this table, it was just the two of them. As though he and Lulu were in their own private world.

"I rather like your flavor of dangerous," Samuel breathed, working hard not to lean forward and capture her lips with his own. "What's a little danger?"

Lulu smiled as though she could sense his thoughts. "You could be killed."

He nodded. "And yet you're the one killing me."

Her eyes widened in shock. "I'm—"

"You're killing me every second that I don't kiss you," Samuel confessed, manhood stirring desperately against his breeches. "Damn, I want to kiss you, Lulu."

Lulu's flush told him everything he wanted to know. She wanted it too, wanted his kiss more than almost anything.

Almost.

"Well, I am afraid you are going to have to accustom yourself to being slowly killed," Lulu said with a wry smile. "Because I . . . I am not going to kiss you, Samuel."

Samuel groaned.

"At least die a little more quietly," she teased. "And order me another drink, and you can ask me all the questions you want."

He perked up at that. "I can?"

"Of course," said Lulu with another mischievous grin, "I didn't say I would give you any answers."

CHAPTER EIGHT

23 April 1811

T HE MCBARLAND GAMING hell was riotous—as Lulu would expect of a Tuesday evening past ten o'clock.

Candles were lit throughout, though a few had already guttered. Cigar and pipe smoke wafted through the air, making it impossible to see more than ten yards along the wide, long room where almost twenty gaming tables had been set up. Music was being played by a trio of musicians in one corner and serving maids wandered around the tables, offering refreshments and top ups of wine.

And Lulu smiled. *There were certainly worse places to spend an evening.*

She had almost, though not quite, been tempted to seek out Mr. Gillingham and attempt to buy back the letter directly. She had almost two whole pounds in her reticule now, though what she was going to eat next week . . .

As it was, Mr. Gillingham was not where she had presumed he would be. As Lulu knew her two rooms would be freezing without a fire in the grate, she had come here, to McBarland's gaming hell.

Her meeting with the French agent had gone well. At least, she had managed to recall her message almost precisely, and she had not caught a single eye while she had done so. Shame burned within her, but she had no other choice. It was that or starve.

She had breathed a sigh of relief when the man had slipped out. Never again, she promised herself for the third time that year.

The usual crowd was here. Lulu could not quite remember precisely how she had managed to descend to such depths of Edinburgh Society, but she was now on first name terms with the McBarlands, and that offered a sense of protection.

Typically, this would suffice for an evening. If a certain gentleman had not walked through the door.

"Samuel!" Lulu breathed.

"What's tha', darlin'?" snapped the man opposite, holding six cards close to his chest.

Lulu swallowed. She had not intended to say Samuel—the duke's name. It had been an unconscious reflex the moment she spotted his handsome face enter the gaming hell.

She knew this was not a man she could predict, but even so. *A duke, here?*

A man was more likely to be robbed of what little coin he had managed to win in this place than walk out of here safely!

"I can't believe it," said a woman at her table.

Lulu's attention jerked. "What?"

It was impossible, surely, that she was not the only woman Samuel had been speaking to?

"You're killing me every second that I don't kiss you. Damn, I want to kiss you, Lulu."

"Well, I am afraid you are going to have to accustom yourself to being slowly killed. Because I . . . I am not going to kiss you, Samuel."

Her skin went cold. If she discovered she was merely one of a dozen women Samuel was paying attention to—

"Three aces!" crowed the woman, placing them on the table. "Look at that, I—"

"Now how, madam, have you achieved such a thing, when I hold two aces?" the man opposite Lulu snapped, laying down his hand.

Lulu acted instinctively. There was only one way a conversation like that could end at the McBarland gaming hell, and she had absolutely no intention of being a part of it.

The argument rose in both volume and heat as she strode away, weaving between the tables and almost upsetting an empty chair. Her gaze at no point left the tall gentleman who was slowly meandering around the edge of the room.

She was being foolish. Lulu knew it, knew her fascination with this man was only going to lead to trouble. Hadn't she, only a few nights ago, warned him off her?

Lulu swallowed. Yet she could not deny she had been pleased her warning had not been heeded. The selfish part of her—the part that struggled and never got what it wanted, not for years—was relieved, and more than a tad astonished, to discover Samuel saw no need to retreat from her.

Still, this was going too far. Was she not permitted to have a single evening in Edinburgh without him? It was not as though he was . . . was her husband, or anything!

Heat seared her cheeks just at the moment Lulu accosted him. "You."

If she had expected shame, embarrassment, or repentance, she was to be sorely disappointed.

Samuel's face broke out into a smile. "Why, Lulu! I had not expected—"

"Look," Lulu said, keeping her voice low. The last thing she needed was for the entirety of the McBarland gaming hell to realize Samuel was an easy target. *Why, the man could hardly protect himself!* "You may not realize this, but McBarland—"

"Yes, it's rather a favorite of mine," said Samuel smoothly. "I come here every time I am in Edinburgh, in fact."

Lulu, conscious of how she had publicly approached a gentleman and was already receiving a few curious gazes, rocked slightly on her heels. What on earth did he mean, every time? She had never seen him here. None of the McBarland regulars had ever mentioned a duke coming by! That was something she—and they—would remember.

Only when Lulu caught the mischievous glint in Samuel's eye did she sigh weakly. "You come here every time you are in Edinburgh . . . of course. This is your first time in Edinburgh, isn't it?"

Samuel's eyes twinkled. "It's still technically true."

If it had been anyone else, Lulu would have rolled her eyes, informed one of the doormen there was an undesirable looking at people's cards, and that would have been the end of it. Samuel would have been removed. Forcibly.

But something halted her. Perhaps it was the honesty with which he had spoken to her about his false stupidity. Perhaps it was how he made her feel so . . . so safe.

Lulu was almost certain—almost—it was nothing to do with his handsome expression.

She sighed. "You have got to stop following me."

Her words were weary, even if she was delighted. As a serving maid pushed past them and Samuel hoisted a tankard of ale from her tray, Lulu could not help but admit to herself that it was rather flattering.

Well. What woman did not like to be pursued, particularly if it was by a gentleman? A handsome gentleman? Good. A handsome, wealthy gentleman? Even better. A duke?

Lulu could never have imagined such a thing.

But still—Samuel had not actually requested to court her, she reminded herself. And he never would! Dukes did not marry down-on-their-luck women entangled in a mess of their own making.

Which made it even more peculiar that Samuel was once again following her.

"Following you?" Samuel repeated, taking her arm and pulling her over to the wall. "I have no idea what you—ah, Penshaw!"

Lulu rolled her eyes as a man, almost certainly another gentleman, entered the McBarland gaming hell and raised a hand in welcome.

Now, this was getting out of hand. Half the attraction of the McBarland was that there were no gentlemen. This class of people, Lulu well knew, operated on a slightly different moral code. One which included far more fisticuffs, for a start.

She couldn't have Samuel bringing half his gentlemen friends into a place like this!

"Samuel," she hissed, trying to attract his attention. "You can't—"

"Have you met Penshaw?" Samuel said brightly as the man approached. "Penshaw, this is—"

"A woman you have no interest in meeting, I am sure," Lulu shot back, glaring at Samuel as directly as she could.

For some reason, the duke managed to avoid her gaze. "Lulu, this is—"

"Penshaw, yes, good evening Mr. Penshaw," said Lulu hastily.

Oh, this was becoming a nightmare! How did Samuel manage to cause chaos and confusion everywhere he went? It would be most irritating if he weren't so charming.

Lulu swallowed. She was not going to be charmed. Even if Samuel was receiving admiring looks from half the women in the place, and jealous ones from the men.

"You have got to stop this," she said softly.

Samuel stepped closer, leaning nonchalantly against the wall. "This?"

Warmth flickered in her cheeks. "This! Always being where I am. I don't know how you are managing it, but—"

"You are quite mistaken this time," the duke said softly. "This is just a coincidence. I promise."

Lulu smiled ruefully. "You think I believe that?"

There was growing chatter in the place, a growing sense there was something happening to disturb the peace. Eyes were flickering over, and she was getting that horrible prickling on the back of her neck.

This conversation had to end—and he had to go. Even if it would be the ruin of her evening.

"This is no accidental meeting, both you and I know that," Lulu hissed, wishing to goodness the man weren't so alluring. "Look, whatever this, *this* between us—"

"There's a *this?*" Samuel interrupted with a beaming smile.

Lulu hesitated, longing heartily for the capacity to think. *How did he do it?* Samuel was a charming man, yes, and a handsome man. But he was not the most handsome or most charming she had ever seen.

And yet . . . something about him, the combination of all his faculties, features, and faults created a man she was drawn to beyond all others. A man she could hardly tolerate and yet desperately needed. It was exasperating!

"You have to stop following me," Lulu repeated, returning to that certainty. "I haven't the faintest idea how you knew I would be here tonight—"

"He didn't."

Lulu blinked. The Mr. Penshaw, or whoever he was, was smiling blithely. Now there was a tall man. An arrogant man—he spoke as though anything he said was to be immediately believed!

"Well, thank you, Mr. Penshaw, for that contribution," she said, as kindly as she could manage. "But—"

"It's Your Grace, actually."

Lulu's eyes widened as Samuel's friend spoke with a depreciative air that was in no way deceptive.

Your Grace? Your—of course he was.

"You brought another duke to the McBarland?" Lulu hissed, dropping her voice as low as she could manage as panic rushed through her. "Are you mad?"

"Actually, I was the one who suggested this place—I used to come here when I lived in Edinburgh," said the Duke of Penshaw serenely. "The place is worse for wear since I last visited, but I see Mrs.

McBarland is still in fine spirits."

Lulu did not need to look over her shoulder to hear Mrs. McBarland, the owner of the gaming hell, singing with gusto along to the current favorite song.

"You . . . *you* were the one who suggested this place?" she breathed.

Despite her better judgment, she allowed her gaze to drift over to Samuel.

He was beaming. "Told you."

"I don't think that's helpful, old thing," said the Duke of Penshaw happily.

It certainly wasn't. Embarrassment was burning through Lulu like she had been branded. It was not Samuel's curiosity which had brought him here, then . . . it had been his friend. Her accusations of him following her, again, had been incorrect.

"I think I'll go deal myself in at a whist table," said the Duke of Penshaw awkwardly, evidently sensing the tension. "Don't leave without me, Chantmarle."

"Wouldn't dare," said Samuel happily. As his friend stepped away, his gaze lingered on Lulu. "You are angry with me."

Lulu hesitated. She was angry, it was true, but not with him. But it was far easier to be angry at oneself, she had discovered a long time ago, than apologize.

She took a deep breath. "I am sorry."

Samuel jerked his head, as though ridding his ears of water. "I do apologize, I think my hearing just went then. Did you say—"

Lulu shoved him, none too gently. "You heard what I said!"

"I did indeed," he replied with a grin, the noise of the gaming hell rising as Penshaw joined in with Mrs. McBarland's duet. "And I can see it took a great deal to say it."

The flush turning her cheeks crimson was only increasing, much to Lulu's annoyance.

How dare he—how dare he be so right! It was galling. Men were not supposed to be right, they were supposed to be amazed! Her whole body was tingling with annoyance—at least, she was half certain it was annoyance.

Lulu pushed aside all thoughts of what else the sensation could be. *She was not going to lose her head.* She was in too deep with Mr. Gregory and Mr. Gillingham. She had to free herself from their grip, long before she thought of walking into the clutches of someone else.

"You know," came Samuel's quiet voice. "It is rather pleasant to see you ruffled. For once."

Lulu's attention snapped back. "And what do you mean by that?"

"Only that it is rather intimidating to be around a woman with such poise," came his gentle reply. "You are always so proud, Lulu. So determined, so sure of yourself—"

She had heard this all before and was disappointed to hear it from him. "And those are not attractive traits in a woman, am I right?"

Having half a mind to turn away and leave, it was only when Lulu caught the look of admiration—*admiration?*—in his eyes that she halted.

"Not attractive?" repeated Samuel in wonder. "Dear God. It's a miracle I am ever able to step away from you, Lulu Finch."

Partly to distract herself, as well as him, from the outrageous things he was saying—even if she did rather appreciate them—Lulu gestured around the McBarland gaming hell.

"Well. Welcome to your first visit to Mrs. McBarland's," she said as airily as possible. "I don't suppose many gentlemen like you—"

"We'll have less of the 'gentlemen,' if you don't mind."

Lulu almost snorted. The discomforting shame at her apology was melting away, replaced by a mirth that settled happily in her stomach.

"You think you can hide your breeding, the facts of your birth?" she laughed.

To his credit, Samuel looked sheepish. "Is it that obvious?"

Lulu shook her head as she started to walk toward a card table that was almost empty. Only Mr. McBarland seated there. "The clothes, the way you walk, the accent—"

"The accent?"

"You can't hear it?" she asked, half amazed. "It's the way you speak, the way you breathe. You know yourself to be superior. It's an interesting trait of gentlemen, I find."

She was speaking nonsense, Lulu knew, but it was clever nonsense—and it had managed, just for a moment, to distract her long enough to sit at the table without falling over.

Well, that was some victory.

"Does that mean you cannot hide the fact that you are a lady?" asked Samuel, raising an eyebrow as he sat opposite her.

A strange flickering excitement was playing havoc with her ability to concentrate. Typically, a woman like Lulu would have to be careful in a place like the McBarland gaming hell, even with a friendship with the owners. But somehow, though Lulu could not explain it, she knew she was in no danger. Samuel would protect her.

At least, he would protect her from anything else that could hurt her. But could he protect her from himself?

"Cards," Lulu said.

Samuel blinked. "I beg your pardon?"

Cursing herself silently for losing all ability, it appeared, to speak rationally, Lulu reached out and picked up the deck of cards laying on the table.

"Cards," she repeated airily, as though she had always intended to make such a bold statement. "I suppose you would consider it beneath you to play with a woman."

Try as she might, Lulu could not keep the teasing air from her voice. Oh, it had been so long since she had flirted. The danger she had put herself in with this letter—Mr. Gregory and Mr. Gillingham had taken all her focus for months.

But it was pleasant, was it not, to flirt a little with a gentleman? No one would begrudge her that.

It was not a flirtation in which she acted alone. Samuel leaned back, eyes never wavering from her face. "I'll win."

"I doubt it," said Lulu lightly, dealing out the simplest form of poker. Well, she didn't want to confuse him. For all she knew, the man had never played in an actual gaming—

"Aces high, joker in the pack, and double eights leave you out?" Samuel said carelessly, picking up his hand.

It was all Lulu could do to prevent her jaw from dropping. *How did he*—

Samuel was grinning. "I said this was my first time here, at the McBarland gaming hell, not that I had never picked up a hand of cards before. I'm a duke, Lulu, as you keep reminding me. I know my way around a deck."

That flicker of excitement was pooling in her and though Lulu attempted to hide it, she was almost certain he could see on her face just how much she was enjoying this.

The noise and rush of the gaming hell continued on around them, but it faded into the background, a noise she could hardly hear. All she could take in was the man opposite her, shifting his cards in his hand.

"You think you can beat me?"

Lulu smiled, a dart of joy warming her heart. How was it possible to feel so free with this man—and yet at the same time, so in danger?

"I always win," she said softly, glancing at her cards.

Two queens, a king, and an ace. Well, she hadn't been the one to shuffle the pack, old Mr. McBarland had done that. She couldn't be blamed for—

"And what happens if I win?" Samuel asked softly.

Lulu swallowed. They had shifted into dangerous ground—how, she was uncertain. But there was a possessive look in Samuel's eyes she had not seen before.

A hungry look.

"You will never know," Lulu said softly, belying the dread in her heart. "Here."

She laid down her cards.

Samuel gazed at them with goggled eyes. "How the—"

"By hook or by crook, I always win," she said, greatly enjoying his astonishment.

"But—but I thought you had nothing!"

"I have had nothing," Lulu countered, brittleness seeping into her voice. "But I have always known what to do with the little I had."

Samuel met her gaze. For a moment, just a moment, it was as though he was looking into her very soul. As though everything she was, all the worst parts of her, were visible to him. And he did not care.

The moment ended as soon as it had begun.

"Well, damn," Samuel said ruefully. "And here I was, hoping to win a kiss."

A kiss . . .

Lulu's heart skipped a beat. No. She absolutely was not about to allow this man, this good man, this noble man, to tangle himself any further in her nonsense. She had risked too much already.

And so she smiled as best she could. "You'll have to play a lot better than that. Another hand?"

CHAPTER NINE

24 April 1811

S AMUEL SMILED AT the soft silk in his hands.

Well, it was not as though he had purposely orchestrated this. Not entirely.

He would have to hope Lulu would see it that way as well. His footsteps echoed on the Edinburgh pavements as early evening revelers started to leave their homes and enter their carriages. Calls to remember greatcoats, that children should be put to bed, and that the milk cart would be delivering tomorrow and would require sixpence rang out in the air.

None of them distracted Samuel from his intended destination.

Lulu's rooms.

He had memorized the route to where she had said she lived but Samuel had no excuse to visit until today. Until last night.

"I have had nothing. But I have always known what to do with the little I had."

"Well, damn. And here I was, hoping to win a kiss."

His wry smile deepened as he turned a corner and recalled the conversation he had shared with the most bewitching woman in the whole of Edinburgh. Perhaps the whole of Scotland. A woman who seemed determined to surprise him at every turn and doing a remarkably good job of it.

But though she had accused him, not once but several times, of following her, this was the first time Samuel was purposefully going out of his way to see her.

The shawl in his hand rustled against his skin, teasingly reminding him of what he had not been able to touch yesterday.

It wasn't as though he had intervened. Lulu's shawl had slipped from her shoulders onto her chair as the evening at McBarland's gaming hell had continued. He saw no reason to point it out as their conversation deepened, their laughter grew. When the shawl had slipped to the floor, Samuel had again been silent.

It was therefore probably his fault in part, he thought with a chuckle as he turned onto Lulu's street. He could have pointed it out. He could have helped her put it on, taken the chance to brush his fingertips across her shoulders—

But no. This was a far better plan.

Besides, Samuel's curiosity about Lulu had only increased after their evening at the gaming hell. Who was this woman who knew how to play cards like a sharp, but smiled so prettily through dark lashes? Why did she continuously attempt to dissuade him from getting close to her, then look at him like . . . like . . .

Samuel swallowed as he stopped outside the building where he had once escorted Lulu back. There were lights in most of the windows. She was surely home. Eagerness bubbled in his chest, sparking hope through his heart. He would be seeing her in just a few moments.

The door to the building was unlocked, but after that point Samuel was forced to halt.

Now where?

There appeared to be three apartments here on the ground floor, but there was also a narrow, sweeping staircase that appeared to go up at least two additional floors. *That meant nine apartments, at least,*

Samuel thought with a groan. And he had no way of knowing—

"Ah, that'll be Miss Finch's shawl," came a voice from above.

Samuel's head jerked. "I beg your pardon?"

"I said, that'll be Miss Finch's shawl," repeated the voice.

He placed a foot on the first step, craning his neck to see who had spoken. An elderly woman's face appeared over the banisters, looking a mite distrustful but curious.

Samuel tried not to smile. There was always someone in every building who could be guaranteed to spill secrets with gentle flattery. Even coin, sometimes, was unnecessary. And older women . . .

When, he wondered, *would the world realize the power of older women?* Given half a chance, they would probably be running the world.

They would probably do a better job than the present incumbents.

"Yes, I believe it is Miss Finch's shawl," Samuel said aloud, taking a few more steps up the staircase and tilting his head to look at the woman. "I hoped to return it, but I admit—"

"You don't know where her rooms are," said the woman with a grin. "You dinnae have to be coy wi' me, sir. I seen enough people tramp up and down here to ken precisely what Miss Finch does to get by."

Samuel's smile faded.

Ah. Well, perhaps he should have expected that. It was rare, after all, that a woman was able to support herself. Lulu had never struck him as a woman of independent means, and she said she had no family . . .

The disappointment rushing through him, however, was not expected. He did not own her—Lulu owed him nothing, not even the full truth, not if she had no wish to give it to him. Still, Samuel could not help but feel morose to discover the woman he was starting to care for was *that* sort of woman.

"I see," he said listlessly. "Well, in that case—"

"Up here, second door along," said the woman brightly. "She's not home now, but the door is never locked."

Samuel frowned. *Never locked?* Why on earth would Lulu make herself so vulnerable? Did she not have any care of her safety?

He looked at the shawl in his hands. Well, he had come this far. He was delivering a lost possession, there could be no arguing with that. All he had to do was place it inside her room and leave, and she could thank him another time.

And, Samuel thought with a rush of intrigue, *he would have a chance to see inside Lulu's rooms.* There was something so personal about one's living quarters. Surely he could gauge a great deal about the mysterious Lulu Finch by seeing them.

Somewhere in the back of his mind, Samuel knew this was taking a step too far. He certainly did not think Lulu would appreciate knowing he had peeked into her private quarters.

His nosiness stirred. But she was not here. Would she be returning soon?

Samuel cleared his throat. "Second door, you say?"

"The middle one," nodded the woman. "You let Miss Finch know I let you know."

"Yes, but—"

The woman was gone before Samuel could discover her name.

Well, there was nothing else for it. He had already determined his course of action in his mind, and there was no going back. The temptation had been faced, and he had given in.

The doorhandle to Lulu's rooms creaked under his touch. Samuel found he was holding his breath, which made no sense whatsoever. There was of course the faint possibility that the older woman had been mistaken, and Lulu was inside . . .

"Lulu?" breathed Samuel as the door opened just a few inches. "Are you there?"

He waited, heart frantically beating as though he were breaking and entering.

Which he had done before, though this could probably only be considered trespassing. Naturally, a duke should require one of his informants to do such a thing, but sometimes there simply wasn't the time.

This was difficult. This was not a person betraying the Crown, breaking the law, or getting involved in anything more dangerous than associating with cads like Gillingham and Gregory.

No, this was simply trespassing in a woman's rooms, a woman who held a fascination for him that he could not explain.

Before he knew it, he had stepped into the room and closed the door. Eyes adjusting to the darkness, Samuel groped about for a candle. He pulled out his tinderbox, lit a short stub of wax, and peered about.

It was . . . not what he had expected.

And in an odd way, he didn't know why. Every time he had seen Lulu she had been unadorned, unjewelled, and unpretentious. Fraying at the edges. She had not worn silk gowns or fashionable pelisses. There had been nothing in her attire to suggest she was a woman of means.

But Samuel had not quite realized just how without means she was.

The room was almost bare. He stepped forward, his footstep echoing horribly thanks to the emptiness of the room. The fire had not been lit in the grate for some time. The single chair was worn, far more worn than he would have expected, and there was not much else in the room. He would not have permitted his lowest maid to have such a thing in her bedchamber, let alone someone like Lulu.

He took another step forward. There was a door on the other side of the room, and Samuel half hoped that this was some sort of servant's quarters, that the rest of the lodgings, Lulu's real home, would be through the door.

Opening it only revealed the large, almost empty bedchamber.

He closed the door and walked to the window, looking out

through the worn curtain. The room was freezing, and there was a horrible dampness to the air that made his nose itch.

Samuel swallowed. Somehow, seeing a woman's poverty felt different to seeing a woman's luxury. He should not be here. He should never have come.

Leaving the shawl would only reveal to Lulu he had intruded. Tightening his grip on the fabric, Samuel turned.

He almost dropped the candle.

"Well," said Lulu dryly, closing the door to the corridor and leaning against it, eyebrows raised. "This, I did not expect."

Panic rushed through him so violently Samuel was unsure if he could breathe.

This was the very worst situation he could have found himself in—the very worst. How could he ever explain it? All his justifications, all the reasons with which he had placated himself the moment he had put a hand on Lulu's doorhandle, rushed from his mind. *What had he been thinking?*

The silk of the shawl shifted in his fingertips.

Without another thought, Samuel thrust it forward. "I-I brought your shawl."

It did nothing to pacify the irate glare in Lulu's eyes. "And do you often steal women's possessions and use that as an excuse to barge into their homes?"

Had he ever felt this wretched? Oh, Samuel wished he could go back five minutes and leave Lulu's shawl with the woman who had pointed him in this direction. Why hadn't he realized that was the right thing to do? When had he so completely lost sight of his own morals?

What was it about Lulu that did this to him?

"It wasn't like that," he said hastily. "I saw you had left your shawl at McBarland—"

"You mean, you took it," Lulu snapped, her glare showing no sign of receding.

Discomfort sparked along Samuel's shoulder blades. "No, I—"

"And then you thought oh, this will give me the perfect excuse to ignore Lulu's privacy, march into her home, and have a good poke about her possessions?" said Lulu, pain evident in her voice.

Samuel swallowed the defensive retort that it wouldn't have taken long, as she did not appear to have many possessions.

What had happened to put Lulu in such a situation? Had her father never thought to provide for her? Was there no one she could go to for protection?

"You don't have to be coy with me, sir. I've seen enough people tramp up and down here to know precisely what Miss Finch does to get by."

A bitter, almost nauseous sensation rose in his stomach as the words of the woman on the stairs echoed in his mind. If she *had* sought the protection of others, it had not borne fruit.

Guilt was not a sensation Samuel was accustomed to. He was an agent of the Crown. He was one of the few men in London who had known where Penshaw had been last year. He had been informed of Sedley's desperate attempt to catch the Glasshand Gang. He had known where Caelfall was while hiding from Society. He'd even received a begrudging invitation from Wincham after he'd lost his leg, though he'd been too busy to accept it.

He was a good man.

He did not feel particularly good in this moment.

"I am sorry," Samuel said softly. "I—"

"We seem to be doing a great deal of apologizing to each other. I cannot help but think we are simply unsuitable to be acquaintances," Lulu said, eyes blazing. "How—how dare you!"

It would rather have inflamed the situation, Samuel knew, to point out just how marvelous she looked when she was angry. He had attempted that once with Lady Romeril and it had been a mistake. One he would not make again.

Still, he could not pretend he did not think it was true. Seeing Lulu riled was like seeing the glories of the heavens unfolding. There was something majestic about her, as though nature herself were thundering in Lulu's every syllable.

"I—I wanted an excuse to see you," Samuel admitted, deciding on the truth. *How much trouble could that get him in?* "Besides, I am not sure it was an accident you left it there."

Lulu halted in her advance, which came as both relief and disappointment to Samuel. He had half hoped she was going to kiss him, though her hands had clenched into fists which did not bode well.

She glared. "Not an accident?"

"I think," Samuel said, rushing forward before he lost his nerve. "I think you wanted to see me again."

The thought had been flickering right at the edges of his mind since he had pocketed the shawl last night. Lulu wanted more, he was sure. She looked at him sometimes like he was the most fascinating man in the world, and Samuel was absolutely certain he was not.

Why couldn't she just admit it?

Perhaps she needed to hear of his growing interest and affections first. Yes, that would be it. What woman wanted to be the first to be vulnerable?

"Lulu," Samuel began. "I—"

"What precisely are you doing in Edinburgh, Your Grace?"

Samuel froze.

Not because Lulu's tone had been combative, though it certainly was. Not because he had just noticed a leaf entangled most becomingly in her hair, which he had. And not because she had called him "Your Grace," which jarred. But because the question itself was one he should have asked himself a week ago.

What was he doing in Edinburgh?

He was supposed to be hunting those who were traitors to the Crown. He had been sent, after all, to find those who were sharing secrets with the French. Their mortal enemies!

And at first, that was precisely what he had done. Samuel had sent out messengers, built a network of informants, and started to follow up on the tastiest morsels of gossip. So why had he, for the last few weeks—ever since he had first encountered Miss Lucy Finch—become so distracted?

Guilt of a different flavor rushed through him. Samuel placed the shawl on the armchair and tried desperately to think of a response which would not shame him, but there wasn't one.

"I just want to know you," Samuel said helplessly.

The words had spilled out before he could stop them. They were filled with such longing, such desire, Samuel could tangibly feel the room warming with his embarrassment.

A scarlet flush tinged Lulu's cheeks. "You—"

"I want to know everything about you," he said quietly, stepping toward her. "I know you've fought your inclinations for me, Lulu—"

"You don't know anything about me," she whispered, still flushing.

Samuel gritted his teeth. "That's what I have been saying! Damn it, woman, I didn't think I would have to debase myself to such a level just to—"

"You think because you are a duke, you do not have to ask politely?" Lulu shot back, almost vibrating with anger. "You think because you are wealthy and I am—am not, you can merely demand things of me?"

Samuel bit back his response that it had always worked in the past. *This was not helping!* Every time he seemed to take a step nearer to understanding Lulu, to gaining her trust, he put his foot in it.

He met her gaze. Lulu's eyes were shimmering with passion or with unspilled tears, he could not tell which. There was a defiance in her air he had only seen in her presence, and it warmed him as nothing else ever had.

"Fine," she said curtly. "Fine. You want to know about me? Here is what you can know about me."

There was such brittle pain in her words, Samuel immediately changed his mind. *Why did this happen so often in her presence?* "No, I—"

"I am a woman of no means, no support, and no options," Lulu said, gaze unwavering. "I am down on my luck, as those in the McBarland gaming hell would say. I have done . . . I have done things in the past to survive, things I—I am not proud of."

Samuel cleared his throat as the older woman's words rang once again in his ears. He knew precisely what the woman had meant, and now Lulu had confirmed it. She had been a courtesan, a lady of the night, a street walker: whatever you called it, it all amounted to the same thing.

"I had to do what I knew to be wrong to get by," said Lulu, her voice breaking. "And I may just have to do that again. Are you happy, now you have wormed your way into my secrets? That is why I do not tell people about myself, that is why I hide myself away, that is why I—what are you doing?"

Her gaze had finally left Samuel's face to look at the hand which had taken hers.

His hand.

Samuel's heart was pattering painfully, but he had never been more certain that what he was doing, right now, in this moment, was the right thing.

Her fingers were cold. She must have been freezing outside.

"I am sorry I am once again apologizing," Samuel breathed, and he smiled as Lulu snorted. "I am sorry I pushed you to reveal more than you were comfortable with."

"Oh, what are secrets revealed when you have marched into my home?" Lulu snapped.

Samuel winced. "I am sorry for coming into your home uninvited. It was wrong."

Strange. After going so long in his life without so much as a single apology, he was starting to make a habit of it.

Lulu's wry look warmed, her smile deepening. She stepped closer, her breasts grazing his chest as she looked up at him. "You are forgiven. Mostly."

"Mostly?" murmured Samuel, fighting the instinct to pull her into his arms and show her precisely what an apology from the Duke of Chantmarle should look like. He would make a great deal of apologies if the results were like this.

Lulu's eyes glittered. "Mostly. I suppose I shall have to keep you around to see if I can be persuaded to forgive you entirely."

Samuel lowered his head ever so slightly, and his heart skipped a beat when Lulu tilted her chin. She wanted him to kiss her, that much was obvious. And there was no reason to stop now, no excuse. He would kiss her.

Almost moaning at the anticipation, Samuel lowered his head, his lips a mere inch from Lulu's, and—

"Miss Finch! Miss Finch, I told a man—oh."

Lulu whirled around, dropping Samuel's hand. "Mrs. Abernathy! I—"

"Never mind," said the woman, cheeks flushed. "I dinnae intend to—never mind."

The door closed with a snap.

Samuel cursed darkly under his breath.

Lulu was smiling as she turned back to him. "I think you should go."

Samuel groaned. "You cannot mean to almost kiss me then—"

"You will just have to wonder," said Lulu with a laugh. "Curiosity becomes you, doesn't it? This will just have to be one more thing that you are curious about."

Chapter Ten

27 April 1811

"WE SHOULDN'T BE doing this," Lulu murmured, trying to strengthen her voice but not managing it.

Samuel's chuckle made her stomach lurch and her face flush. "I know."

"Well then—"

"If you want me to leave, order me to leave," he said softly. "I am completely in your power, you know that."

Lulu swallowed.

He was right. She did know that. Ever since she had discovered the rascal of a duke in her rooms last week, a change had occurred between them. It was a shift she could not put into words but could feel through every inch of her body.

A difference in the balance of power between them.

Oh, Samuel was still a duke. He was still terribly handsome, and his mere presence was enough to make Lulu sometimes forget what she was about to say. He was still infuriating at least once an hour and made Lulu glare as she had never glared before.

But the partly spoken, partly unspoken desire between them had almost come to a point with the kiss that had not been. That altered things. They were no longer simply two people in Edinburgh who were acquaintances. They were something more.

Precisely what, Lulu did not know. But she knew for certain what they were doing was absolutely outrageous and should not be countenanced.

That had not stopped them.

"We shouldn't," Lulu said, far more firmly than she felt.

Samuel grinned from the chair he had arrived with that evening outside her lodgings. "And yet we are."

She smiled as she shifted in her old wing backed armchair.

It had been Samuel's idea. Why, he had put to her, should they suffer through the indignity of having to pretend in public that they were anything less than . . . friends?

Friends. Lulu had repeated the word back to him and reveled in the way his cheeks pinked at the mere hint of heat in her words.

Friends, he had said. Far better, Samuel had argued, that they arrange to meet in her lodgings. Her rooms would provide more than enough privacy for them to converse without being concerned about the world's incorrect assumptions.

"Incorrect?" Lulu had said, raising an eyebrow as Samuel had arrived outside her building that evening. "I am not certain what would be incorrect."

They had moved into uncharted territory, and though she was curious to see precisely where it could lead, Lulu knew she was stepping onto dangerous ground. After all, most ladies in Edinburgh did not have dukes turn up at their homes with an armchair, a basket full of food undoubtedly prepared by his cook, and another full of coals.

The fire blazed merrily in the grate. *The first fire*, Lulu thought sadly, *she had enjoyed in many a week.*

"I still think the news will get out," said Lulu, taking another sweet pastry from the basket between them.

Samuel snorted as he sipped from the bottle of wine he had

brought. Lulu had been forced to admit, a little shamefaced, that she had no wine glasses. Since then they had merely taken it in turns to sip from the bottle, which she had tried not to think too much about. It was so . . . intimate.

Samuel offered her the bottle. "What, you have a reputation to lose?"

Lulu took the bottle, made a great show of wiping the neck as though that would make any difference to the intimacy they were now sharing, and took a sip. The wine was heady, far more impressive than anything she had tasted before.

But that was the benefit, wasn't it, of being a duke? The man probably had a cellar older than her building.

Pushing aside the thought of just how wealthy the man opposite her might be, Lulu tried to smile. "It may shock you, Samuel, but I do actually have a reputation. One I would be remiss to abandon just because a certain duke decided to knock on my door."

Samuel grinned. "A reputation lost can always be found, I say."

Lulu did not bother to disagree with him. What would be the point? The man—and Samuel being a man did make a difference here—was unlikely to understand.

A reputation lost could always be found? Evidently he had never paid much attention to the gossip columns, either in London or here in Edinburgh. Lulu could think of three ladies, just those she had read about recently, who had lost their reputations and been unable to remain in good Society.

In fact, one of them was prodding her memory. Had not Lady Margaret Everleigh—

"Reputations are overrated," Samuel was saying with a grin as he pulled what appeared to be a pork pie from the cavernous basket. "I always thought . . ."

Lulu tried not to smile. There was a youthfulness about Samuel that belied his actual age, which she would estimate to be about thirty.

Reputations overrated. Only a duke, a man unlikely to ever lose who he was, could think that way. Why, even a gentleman was at more risk than losing his good name than a duke.

The church clock at the end of the street chimed. Nine times.

Lulu's smile faltered. *She was going to miss it.*

"—as I said to Ashcott myself!" Samuel was saying. "If the woman truly did not care about her reputation, or for her brother's, then she would surely—"

It had taken almost two weeks to force Mr. Gregory to agree to meet her, Lulu thought wretchedly, and now she was going to miss it. Perhaps her best chance to cease the disgusting work she had been forced to carry out and make the man relinquish any hold over her.

Her chance of freedom.

So why did she find it so difficult to leave Samuel Dellamore, Duke of Chantmarle's presence? Why was it somehow more important to stay here with him, a man she did not even know a month ago?

Lulu sighed. She had a job to do, one she had agreed to. And she was not doing it. This Samuel, he was far too much of a distraction.

"You're not listening to me, you know."

Her gaze sharpened. "Yes, I am."

Samuel had a knowing smile about him that had at first irritated, but over time she'd discovered he only looked that way when he knew what he was talking about. Worse luck.

"Really?" he said, his charming smile broadening. "Then what was I saying?"

Lulu grasped about for a sufficiently vague answer that would suit. "You were talking about—about reputations?"

"Anything more specific than that?" Samuel said, starting to chuckle.

Lulu allowed herself to laugh with him. "No!"

"There, I told you, you weren't listening," he said with a shake of his head. "Which is all to the good, I suppose. I shouldn't really be talking about Ashcott's private business."

Her ears pricked up. Private business—Ashcott? If any of her previous encounters with Samuel were anything to go by, the man would be a duke.

Well, there was no harm in asking. "Not . . . not the Duke of Ashcott?"

Samuel groaned. "Blast it all to hell! How much wine have I drunk?"

"Not nearly enough to blame it on the vintage," Lulu said with a giggle, handing him back the bottle. Their mingled laughter filled her almost bare room and made her believe, just for a moment, that this could be her new life.

Well, why not? This was a man she was coming to adore, whose conversation made her smile or rail against him in a most invigorating way. He had money. Few gentlemen could turn up outside a building with a leather chair finer than any she had ever seen.

And that was the problem, wasn't it, a voice whispered at the back of her mind. She was all too distracted by him. Whenever she seemed to be getting somewhere with Gregory and Gillingham, Samuel was there to divert her.

"Did you have an invitation to attend this evening?"

Lulu focused once more on the man opposite her. "An invitation?"

Samuel shrugged. "I should not have presumed, I know, but—"

"You think I would be sat here talking to you if I had anywhere else I could be?" Lulu lied with what she hoped was a convincing smile.

In truth, she should feel more disappointed she had not made her rendezvous with Mr. Gregory. She would regret it in the morning, she was certain, but right now . . .

Right now, the only place that she wanted to be was here.

Samuel's smile made her heart skip a beat. "I should think so. After all, we've been talking for hours, yet I have barely noticed time pass.

Isn't that strange?"

Not nearly as strange, Lulu could not help but think, *as the fact that I just gave up an opportunity to be free, just to sit and drink wine with you.*

"Not so strange," Lulu said softly.

Samuel's gaze was too penetrating. "You don't come from here, do you?"

It was a most startling change of direction, but she was starting to become accustomed to that. The duke's mind jumped into so many different topics, their conversation had already included the weather in East Africa, just whether or not the Americas deserved to be independent, Plato, and the price of a pork pie. With anyone else, Lulu would have guessed they were being pretentious. Attempting to demonstrate their knowledge.

With Samuel . . . it was hard to tell.

"I'm a Londoner by birth," Lulu found herself revealing, regretting it the moment the words were out of her mouth.

Samuel's interest narrowed his gaze. "Now that is interesting."

"Not really," she said hastily. "I came here to be with my brother and . . . and he died."

She would not say his name. She would not draw near to the pain—

"And you have never thought of going somewhere else?" asked Samuel quietly. "Somewhere different? Leaving behind the painful memories that so obviously cling to you?"

Lulu drew a hasty breath, unsure why she had been holding it in the first place.

How did he do it? Read her so clearly, as though she were an open book. There was no need to be curious, it appeared, if Samuel could look straight through her and into her heart.

She shrugged as nonchalantly as she could manage, pulling apart the remains of the pastry. "Where would I go? I have no family, no friends, nowhere that has a particular tie."

"Not . . . France?"

Lulu stiffened.

It was a coincidence, she told herself firmly. France was a common topic, after all. The war had been going on for some time, and the Revolution before that, though she could barely remember it. It was a natural topic for a nobleman, certainly.

So why were tendrils of panic starting to curl around her heart?

"Of course not," she said, more sharply than necessary. "Why would I go to France?"

She met Samuel's eye as boldly as she could manage, but perhaps it was not enough. There was a directness in his gaze, one she had only seen a few times. The first evening they had met, in the Assembly Rooms. He had looked at her and she had wondered just how dimwitted the man actually was.

Lulu knew now, without a shadow of a doubt, not very.

So why this sudden interest in France—or was it merely a meandering thought that would not last?

Lulu swallowed. "I do not know anyone there. There would be no reason for me to go there. And besides, it is far too dangerous."

She needed to stop talking, she knew that, but she could not. Panic was rushing her mouth, tumbling her tongue in all sorts of directions.

Get a grip on yourself, Lulu!

"I don't suppose you have ever been?" she asked as airily as possible.

Samuel had not taken his gaze from her for one moment. "I think you aren't telling me the whole truth, Lulu."

Lulu fought the instinct to immediately argue. She needed to think, not react. Her inclination to barrel into a conversation and escape out of it later had already led her into significant harm. The last thing she needed was to do it again!

Besides, there was no possibility Samuel actually knew what he was asking about. Oh, his conversation had meandered close to the truth—a truth he definitely did not need to know.

But that was all chance. He didn't actually *know*.

Samuel sighed and Lulu immediately flinched. There was a look of decision on his face, chilling her to the very bone.

Well, this was it. It had been pleasant while it had lasted, but she should have known her past would come back and bite her. It hadn't even been her mistake in the first place! If her brother, Malcolm, had just—

"Listen, Lulu," Samuel said softly. "I know."

Lulu's heart skipped a beat. "You . . . you do?"

How? She had been so careful, so desperate to keep the shame of the blackmail she suffered to herself. She had not even confessed to Mrs. Abernathy, who had been so kind and understanding to rent her the two adjoining rooms.

Surely no one could know. No one in Edinburgh expect . . .

Lulu went cold. *Except for Mr. Gregory and Mr. Gillingham.*

"I mean, it's obvious you are the victim here," Samuel was saying. "And I admit, I feel sorry for you. This isn't the life you would have chosen for yourself."

Lulu swallowed. *It certainly wasn't.* "I—I never thought I would—"

Guilt washed over her as she saw kindness in Samuel's eyes. "I don't suppose you did. I suppose you thought you would never lower yourself to that."

All of a sudden, Lulu was blinking back tears. No, she had not. The idea of doing such a thing, just to survive—she would never have thought that of herself. She was not that sort of woman. Except she was, now.

Samuel was still speaking. "And would I prefer it if you did not have to offer your services to men—well, of course. But that doesn't mean I think any worse of you, Lulu. If anything, I have more respect for you."

Lulu blinked. Something wasn't quite adding up here. "I beg your pardon?"

Samuel sighed. "You don't have to hide it from me, Lulu. You're a courtesan! Plenty of women have chosen that life in order to survive. You are no different. No worse."

Her ears rang with his words. *Courtesan . . . courtesan . . .*

Lulu's shoulders sagged with relief. *Of course, he assumed she was a courtesan!*

Well, it made sense. There were plenty of women, Lulu knew, who had to resort to that to keep their families off the streets. It had never been something she had been forced to do, thank goodness, but perhaps in a way she had chosen a worse path.

She would never know. And she also, Lulu realized with a sinking feeling, would not reveal the truth to Samuel. He was smiling with such acceptance, such . . . well, she would not call it love, but it was not far off.

Lulu could not bear it if she lost that support, that affection. Though he was most understanding about the lengths a woman may go to protect and support herself, she was almost certain Samuel would think very differently about what she had *actually* been doing.

That was a secret she would take to her grave.

"I just wish . . . well." Samuel shrugged with an awkward smile. "I wish I could take you away from all this."

It was all Lulu could do not to laugh. "This?"

"This!" Samuel gestured around the room. "You cannot truly tell me you are satisfied with living like this?"

"I have never been offered much choice," Lulu said. "Though if you are offering . . ."

Her voice trailed away. *What was she even asking?*

Samuel appeared to notice her discomfort, and it was mirrored by his own. He silently offered her the wine bottle, appeared to think better of it, and placed it on the floor by his chair.

"I don't know what I am saying," he said ruefully.

Lulu tried to smile. All she had to do was make light of the situation. *That was all!* "You could offer to make me your mistress."

Immediately she saw she had gone too far. Though the fire had not been stirred by either of them, the room immediately blossomed with heat. Or was that her own scalding shame rushing through her?

What would he think of her?

Samuel bit his lip, his gaze drifting to the fire.

Oh, if only she had kept her mouth shut! All she had to do was be silent, and it would have been a kind, considerate moment. Instead she had to go and—

"I do not think you would enjoy being my mistress," Samuel said quietly. "I . . . my life takes me all over the place. I'm never in one place for long."

Lulu's heart constricted painfully. Was he attempting to tell her he would be leaving Edinburgh soon?

She had no ties here. Nothing, save Mr. Gregory's and Mr. Gillingham's blackmail to bind her. If she could just be free of that—

Being Samuel Dellamore, Duke of Chantmarle's mistress had to be better than the life she was leading now.

"Perhaps I would not enjoy it," Lulu said softly, giving him an opportunity to take it back.

But Samuel did not take it. Settling deeper into his leather armchair, he cracked a smile. "I suppose I should not speak so lightly of taking a mistress."

"Better that than speak lightly of taking a wife," Lulu shot back before she could stop.

What was wrong with her?

It appeared Samuel was not stunned by her words. He raised an eyebrow. "Oh?"

"Though it would take a great deal to make me marry you," said Lulu hastily, hoping to goodness she could blame the warmth of her cheeks on the heat of the fire. "I mean, you are exhausting to be around at the best of times."

"Oh, I am, am I?" rejoined Samuel with a laugh.

"And your arrogance!" she continued with a laugh, relieved to find the tension of the room dissipating. "Oh, you are unbearable!"

"And far too charming, I suppose," he quipped.

Lulu giggled. "Far too charming. No, I am sorry, Your Grace, but I must absolutely refuse to marry you."

Samuel held her gaze for just a breath too long.

She swallowed. It was all a game, wasn't it? Just a bit of mischief. They were not actually speaking the truth, were they?

"So what would it take?"

Lulu blinked. "I beg your pardon?"

"What would it take?" Samuel asked, his voice sounding serious. But he could not be serious. It was still a jest, wasn't it? "To make you marry me?"

Perhaps she had drunk more wine than she had intended. Lulu's head was certainly spinning.

"A scandal," Lulu said slowly, lips curling into a smile. "I would only marry you, Samuel, if absolutely necessary."

CHAPTER ELEVEN

30 April 1811

"THIS IS A mistake."

"You've got to stop saying that," hissed Samuel under his breath, though he couldn't stop himself grinning in the dark of the carriage. "Someone might hear you. Someone might actually believe you."

Even in the gloom, he could make out the glare Lulu shot him from the opposite side of the carriage.

His grin widened.

Because she was right. In a very real way, this was a mistake. This was a dangerous decision, one that could not only get him into a heap of trouble—not something he enjoyed at the best of times—but worse . . .

He could attract the ire of Lady Romeril.

Samuel shuddered in his greatcoat as his carriage rattled along the Edinburgh streets.

And yet, here he was. Doing the thing Lulu had told him, resolutely, she would not consider. She thought it far too foolish. Which was why, when he had pulled up outside her building not ten minutes ago, he had been half certain she would not come down.

He needn't have worried. Lulu had already been standing on the pavement, waiting for him. That gold and black piped gown suited her even better in the darkness of the evening. It had been all Samuel could do not to pull her into his arms and—

"There's still time to change your mind," came Lulu's soft words, breaking through his thoughts.

"Absolutely not."

"You are perhaps the most radical man in the whole of Edinburgh, you do know that?" Lulu said conversationally, as the carriage started to slow. "I mean, you must be the only person who would consider this acceptable!"

"I haven't the faintest idea what you mean," Samuel said loftily, though he could not help but continue to smile. "I have received an invitation. I am expected."

"*You* are expected," Lulu pointed out, pulling her shawl closer around her shoulders. "Yes, the Duke of Chantmarle is very expected. I am sure Lady Romeril will be delighted to have you attend her ball. But a woman of low repute—"

Samuel winced.

He hated it when Lulu spoke of herself like that. So, she had fallen on hard times. She had found it difficult to survive and had made decisions many would consider unsavory.

Did he particularly like the fact that she had acted as a courtesan? No. But that wasn't who Lulu was. It was something she had done, not an intrinsic part of her. And it was Lulu, all of her, that he wanted to accompany him tonight.

"Who is going to stop the Duke of Chantmarle attending Lady Romeril's ball with his guest?" Samuel said aloud.

Even in the dark, he could almost hear the eye roll. He certainly heard the scoff.

"You are being purposely obtuse!"

"That I am," Samuel said happily as the carriage drew to a stop just outside Lady Romeril's Edinburgh residence. "Ready?"

Outstretching his hand, he saw Lulu was still not completely convinced of his plan.

And why should she be? Samuel had spent little to no time on it, after all. The moment Lady Romeril had declared—not invited, declared—that he would be opening the dancing at her frustratingly dull May Day Ball, he had known precisely what he would do.

Take Lulu with him, of course. Who was to stop him?

"There is still time," Lulu said softly.

Samuel allowed his hand to fall into his lap. "Time for what?"

"For you to go in, and for your carriage to take me back home," she said awkwardly. Though the darkness obscured her face, it was clear how discomfited she was. "Samuel, I barely belong in the Assembly Rooms as it is! Attending a private ball—"

"If I say you are my guest, no one will question it," Samuel said, far more fiercely than he had intended. "No one will question you!"

There was a wry chuckle opposite him as the noise of footsteps outside the carriage grew louder. "No one will question you, you mean. Samuel, I really think—"

"Your Grace," said a voice smoothly as they were suddenly bathed with light.

Samuel squinted in the direction of the carriage door. Someone had opened it, allowing light from the mansion ahead of them to cascade blindingly into the carriage.

"Please, allow me," said the voice.

Only then did Samuel recognize Lady Romeril's butler. They had sent out the finest servant to their finest guest. All he had to do was convince Lulu to come with him.

Samuel did not look around as he stepped out of the carriage. He had to act as nonchalant as possible—as though everything were perfectly natural.

"And how is our ladyship tonight?" he asked smoothly as the servant held out a hand for his companion.

"Miss?" said the butler softly.

Samuel's throat constricted. If Lulu refused to come out, she would leave him little choice but to send the carriage back. It would not be the end of the world. But it would be the end of his evening.

"Miss?"

If only the thought of an evening without her was not caustic to his heart. Perhaps then, Samuel would not have spent the last six evenings in her rooms. *Perhaps he would have spent it doing what he was supposed to do,* he thought feverishly, *hunting these traitors.* Perhaps it was for the best if Lulu did not get out of the carriage. Perhaps—

"My, what an elegant house," said Lulu genteelly as she stood beside Samuel on the pavement. "Your arm, Your Grace."

Samuel beamed as he offered his arm. "How could I say no?"

His stomach twisted as she met his eye: a mixture of stern reproof and delighted charm.

"How indeed," she said dryly.

There was nothing quite like the feeling of stepping into Lady Romeril's ball with Lulu on his arm. Staying away from her—Lulu, not Lady Romeril—was an impossibility. Like the sunflower that twisted its head to stare at the sun, unable to look away, Samuel found himself staring as a footman stepped forward to take her shawl.

"Allow me!" said Samuel before he realized what he was doing.

All eyes in the hallway were on him, he was certain. Lady Romeril's butler, two footmen, a couple of gentlemen who had just arrived, and a trio of ladies were staring avidly.

Samuel swallowed. He had not intended an audience, and Lulu seemed highly conscious of the attention. But that did not stop him gently slipping his fingers under the hem of her shawl, brushing his fingertips along her skin, slowly allowing it to fall into his hands.

He was breathless, his chest tight. The shawl was warm in his hands. Lulu was not looking away.

A cough. "Shall I take that, Your Grace?"

Samuel blinked. The butler had approached respectfully, the pair of gentlemen were tutting, and the trio of girls were giggling.

Ah. He had already managed to make a complete fool of himself. *Excellent.*

"Yes, thank you," Samuel said, as coldly as he could. "We'll just go on in and—"

"There you are! After all this time, too, I was starting to think you had forgotten!"

He did not need to turn around to know whose voice that was. Lady Romeril's tones were far more foreboding than anything he had ever heard.

Lulu stepped closer to him, and Samuel felt courage rise as though he were about to fight a lion.

Really, it wasn't far off.

"How," said Lady Romeril as she stepped out of the ballroom and into the entrance hallway, "am I supposed to arrange you a marriage if you insist on being late to my ball?"

Samuel's heart went cold. Lulu stepped away.

Oh, hell. How had he managed to completely forget the pretext on which he had come to Edinburgh in the first place? How had he managed to fail to recall he had told Lady Romeril, quite erroneously, that his only purpose in coming to Edinburgh was to find . . .

"An arranged marriage?" repeated Lulu under her breath. "Samuel, what—"

But there was no possibility of holding that conversation, not here, not now. Before Samuel could open his mouth, Lady Romeril had pulled his hand onto her arm and started marching him into the ballroom.

"So many lovely and eligible ladies, it truly is too bad of you not to review them as they entered. But there it is, you will simply have to dance with as many of them as possible. Now, Miss Fitzroy, the eldest of course . . ."

Samuel jerked his head over his shoulder in desperate search of Lulu.

There she was—just a few feet behind him, following with a demure expression and eyes downcast. It was most unlike her, now he came to think about it. The Lulu he knew—

Lulu lifted her gaze, shot daggers at Samuel with such accuracy he could almost feel the blades slipping between his ribs, then returned her gaze to the floor.

Samuel swallowed. *Ah. Oh dear.*

"Now, you promised me you would open the dancing," said Lady Romeril severely as she brought him to a halt. "You still intend to carry out that promise, don't you Chantmarle?"

Try as he might, Samuel was unable to catch Lulu's eye again. This was what his mother had called a pickle and his father had called a bloody nuisance. How was he supposed to extricate himself from Lady Romeril's grip? How could he explain—

"Yes, the first dance," he said slowly, seeing light at the end of the tunnel.

Well, he would be obeying Lady Romeril, wouldn't he? He would be doing precisely what she wished. There was no restriction on *who* he had the first dance with.

"Miss Finch," he said aloud.

Lady Romeril frowned. "I have never heard of such a person, and I doubt such an insignificant would dare—"

"Yes, Your Grace?" Lulu said sweetly, stepping up to himself and Lady Romeril.

Samuel tried not to smile as Lady Romeril bristled.

"Who the devil are you?" she said sternly. "I certainly did not invite—"

"Miss Finch is my special guest," Samuel said smoothly, stepping between the two women. He wasn't sure how far Lady Romeril could be pushed, but he wouldn't discount a fistfight. "And she is my partner to open the ball."

As he said the words, Samuel hoped beyond hope Lulu would accept his hand. It would be embarrassing if, after all this, he were forced to find another woman to dance with.

Not that it would be impossible. As he glanced about the room, it was to see to his merriment that Lady Romeril had apparently invited half of Edinburgh to her ball.

Well. The female half.

"Open the ball?" Lady Romeril repeated blankly. Then a knowing smile quirked her lips. "Ah, I see. Invite an unknown woman to dance the first to spark curiosity and envy in the others! Well done, Chantmarle."

Samuel's heart sank. "No, no, that's not what I—"

"No better time to start than the present," said Lady Romeril sternly. "Hie, you there! Tell the musicians to start playing, His Grace wishes to dance!"

Groaning under his breath in the hope his hostess would not hear him, Samuel wished to goodness he had thought more about this. Of course Lady Romeril had only agreed to host a ball in his honor because she thought she was here to find him a bride! How had he managed to be so stupid as to forget?

With every day that passed, he thought grimly, there was more and more evidence that he was, in fact, the dullard he purported to only pretend to be.

"Well," said Lulu faintly. "I suppose I must make the most of this opportunity to make every woman in Edinburgh jealous for your hand."

Samuel did not know what made him reach out for her fingers. Frustration, perhaps. Quelled passion. Fury at himself for forgetting the cover story which had seemed such a clever idea at the time. Irritation with Lady Romeril for being . . . well, Lady Romeril.

Whatever it was, Lulu gasped. "Samuel!"

Scandalized looks followed them as he led her by the hand into the middle of the ballroom as the musicians struck up.

"Did you hear that—"

"—called His Grace by his first name!"

"Never before have I heard such impertinence . . ."

Samuel grinned as he released Lulu's hand and moved to stand opposite her, creating the beginning of a line. "Well, I think we've firmly become gossip."

Lulu's eyes were sharp. "You never told me that you were here hunting for a bride. All those evenings—"

"I'm not—"

Genteel applause rang out around the ballroom, deafening his words. Lady Romeril had stepped graciously toward the line with a partner and others were pouring toward it, desperate to take part in the opening set.

When Samuel managed to meet Lulu's eye again, she was still glaring.

"It's nothing to me whether you are seeking a rich bride or not," she murmured as the line of ladies curtseyed. "Nothing to me at all."

"I want it to be something to you," Samuel shot back in an undertone as he and the other gentlemen bowed.

Dear God, how he wanted it to be. Every inch of his body was tingling with the anticipation of dancing with Lulu again. Every moment, he wanted to be close to her. Every second that passed, he railed against the fact he could not speak openly to her.

But perhaps in this dance, he could show her.

"—after all, you have made no promises to—Samuel!" hissed Lulu, eyes wide.

Hers were not the only ones. Murmurs echoed around the ballroom as the gentlemen stepped forward to take their partners' hands. Which would have been entirely normal.

Except for what Samuel had just done.

"You—You've removed your gloves!" she breathed.

Samuel grinned. "That I have."

Outraged murmurs were rustling around the room now, like wind through trees.

"You'll never live this down," murmured Lulu as she stepped to the side and accepted his hand once again.

Samuel resisted the urge to pull off her glove as well. Oh, to feel the softness of her skin against his own . . .

"I suppose I never will," he said aloud, just quietly enough so Lulu was the only one to hear him. "But as I never actually intended to find a wife when I came to Edinburgh, it's of little consequence to me."

The expression on Lulu's face as she met his gaze told Samuel more than enough about her feelings on the matter. His heart skipped a beat. *She had been hurt.* She had cared—really cared—that he had perhaps been seeking a wife elsewhere.

And it brought him such happiness, Samuel hardly knew what to do with himself.

"You . . . you aren't here to seek a wife?"

"Definitely not," Samuel said firmly, as she slipped her hands in his and they paraded down the set. "I may have inadvertently misled Lady Romeril on that matter, of course . . ."

More than misled. *That conversation could be had another time,* he told himself firmly. It was certainly not a conversation he wished to have now. Not when he was conscious of Lulu's body so close to him. The shortness of her breath as his hand moved gently to her waist. The rise and fall of her breasts—

"And have you inadvertently misled me?"

Samuel almost stumbled on the next step of the dance but managed to right himself. "I beg your—"

"You heard me," Lulu said with a mischievous smile, leaning ever so slightly into him as they turned and started to promenade back up the set. "Are you misleading me, Samuel? What is it that you want?

What is it that you need, that you crave? Is it a wife?"

He swallowed, his manhood lurching at the highly suggestive questions.

Samuel knew what the answer should be. He should want to find the blackguard who was endangering the lives of English soldiers. He should be hunting down that miscreant, the cad who thought nothing of their own safety if it meant jeopardizing another.

But that wasn't what he craved. Dear God, no.

Tingles of pleasure rushed through him as he looked into Lulu's eyes and saw desire matched in her looks.

"I want you," Samuel whispered as they returned to their place in the set, heart pounding. "You, Lulu."

The moment elongated, stretching painfully until—

"Ah, what a wonderful dance!" Lady Romeril boomed as elegant applause at the end of the dance rang out. "Your Grace, you comported yourself . . . relatively well."

Samuel paid her no heed. There was a wicked glint in Lulu's eye he must investigate. Now.

"I'll be right back, Lady Romeril," he said firmly, reaching out and taking Lulu's hand before the entire ball. "Miss Finch and I have something important to discuss."

"Chantmarle!"

He ignored his hostess, ignored the shocked murmurs of those around them, ignored the scalding heat rushing from Lulu's fingers to his own.

"Your Grace!"

"Where is the man going?"

"And who is that?"

Samuel ignored them all. He had only one thing on his mind—had done, in truth, for almost a week now—and he could wait no longer.

Thankfully, he had been to Lady Romeril's Edinburgh home before. The ballroom had a great number of doors leading off it, but only one led from the ballroom to this vestibule with columns spaced around it like a Greek temple.

Samuel almost slammed the door behind him.

"Now what," Lulu said coolly, slipping her hand from his and meandering to look at a column, "do you mean by this?"

Samuel stepped forward, his pulse thundering. *This was it.* "I have something very important to say to you."

She turned, her back against the column, her eyes wide. "You— you do? What is it?"

"This," Samuel growled before crushing his lips on hers.

Oh, God, it was worth the wait. The sweetness, the fire, the passion in Lulu's kiss as she clutched him tight. Her fingers wound in his hair, the way she arched into him—

Samuel could not help it. His desire for her had been constricted for so long, it was pouring out of him in a tangled mess. His eagerness forced Lulu to take a step back and she was pressed up against the column, pinned between solid marble and the strength of his chest.

"Samuel," she moaned.

It was enough to push him off the precipice. Samuel's hand scrabbled to her gown, lifting up the skirt so that he could pull her leg up around his hip—and she obliged eagerly, parting her lips to invite him in.

And he was kissing her, kissing her with such passion he hardly knew where he ended and she began. Lulu was everything, everything he wanted, everything that was distracting and glorious and sweet and tender and—

"Your Grace!"

Samuel broke the kiss but did not release the woman in his arms. Her gaze had shifted to over his shoulder, and he watched as Lulu's cheeks burned.

"Samuel Dellamore, Duke of Chantmarle," came Lady Romeril's voice behind him. "Put that woman down!"

CHAPTER TWELVE

"Y OUR GRACE!"

Lulu felt the kiss end and moaned at the lack of contact. She didn't want less of Samuel, she wanted more of him. She wanted everything. She may never have kissed a man like that before in her life, but that did not mean she wished to stop finding out what it was to be held in the arms of a man.

"Samuel Dellamore, Duke of Chantmarle," came a stern woman's voice. "Put that woman down!"

Lulu's gaze drifted from the slightly panting gentleman who still had a hold of her leg to a point over his shoulder. There stood—

Her cheeks burned. Lady Romeril. She was looking at them so severely, Lulu was uncertain whether she would ever be able to walk down an Edinburgh street again.

Even worse, the door behind Lady Romeril was open. The door to the ballroom.

Gasps and even some screams were pouring through it.

"Dear God, that's the—"

"Scandal! How he could consider—"

"—have to marry now—"

Lulu would have retreated if she could, but where could she go? Her breasts were pushed up against Samuel's chest, his breathing ragged. Her back was against the column. Oh, it had felt so wonderful to be pinned there, between his passion and the cold harshness of the marble—but now she had nowhere to run.

Even if she could, she thought feverishly, *she could never outrun this scandal.* The gossip would be spreading across Edinburgh this very moment. It would be everywhere.

Worse, Mr. Gregory and Mr. Gillingham would hear about it. They may decide she was no longer useful, that she could no longer pay off her debt in the way they'd agreed. And that would mean—

"What is the meaning of this?" Lady Romeril stepped toward them.

Samuel slowly lowered Lulu's leg to the ground. She tried not to catch Lady Romeril's gaze as he did so, her heart beating frantically.

She had made a terrible mistake. Not just the kissing, though that was certainly part of it. Perhaps her mistake had been dancing with Samuel beforehand. Guilt tinged the memory of all her actions as Lulu attempted to calculate when she had stepped onto this terrible road that would lead to such humiliation. Was it agreeing to come with him to Lady Romeril's ball in the first place?

Or was it earlier than that? Was it permitting his curiosity, something which should have made her run from him rather than allow him to grow closer?

Lulu's mind was whirling with so many thoughts, it was difficult to separate them. And through it all, through the murmurs from the ballroom, Lady Romeril's rambling critique, through her scattered breathing and the wild sense this was happening to another—

There stood Samuel. Right before her, her breasts still pushed against him. He had not moved, said nothing, and . . . and had not met her eye.

Lulu swallowed. "I—"

"I don't want to hear a single word from you, Miss Finch," Lady Romeril snapped. "The very idea of losing all sense of decorum to such an extent you would permit a duke to kiss you!"

Lulu flushed. The duke had assumed she was a courtesan, and she had certainly done nothing to dissuade him from that misunderstanding. In truth, she would have permitted Samuel to do far more than kiss her.

Little did he know that he had given her something truly precious: her first kiss.

"What do you have to say for yourself, you rogue?" Lady Romeril demanded.

Lulu glanced at Samuel, but he still would not meet her eye. His gaze was drifting, almost as though the column were not there and he was seeing something else entirely. His face was pale, his left hand still on her waist though no longer clinging to it as though she were the only thing he wanted in the world.

Dread started to pour through her. "Samuel?"

"—never seen such an outrageous display—"

"Move the ladies along, there, they can't see such an immoral—"

Slam!

Lulu started as Lady Romeril slammed the door behind her, blocking out the appalled mutterings.

"That's enough of that," their hostess said forcefully. "They have more than enough fodder for their scandal sheets now."

Lulu closed her eyes, just for a moment, and tried not to think about what she had done to Samuel's reputation. She had warned him, hadn't she?

"It's not a good idea to get too close to me."

"I wouldn't say that. In fact, I am rather enjoying it."

True, she had not expected the danger to come from this particular direction. She had been certain his continued fraternizing with her would bring him to the attention of the ruffians she was forced to associate with—Gillingham and Gregory. She had never dreamed it would be his reputation that would be killed.

"Samuel," Lulu whispered, desperate to hear him speak. "Samuel?"

Yet the duke did not meet her gaze. He did not step away, true, but neither did he look at her.

A sinking, desperate feeling was hollowing out her chest. *Regret.* That was the expression on the man's face. She did not need him to say it to—

"I regret this," Samuel said stiffly, removing his hand finally and stepping back.

It was fortunate indeed that Lulu had the column to lean against. Without it, she was almost certain she would fall, her legs no longer able to support her.

Their moment of passion, of connection, their moment that had meant more to her than anything—*of course he regretted it.*

She just hadn't expected it to hurt so much.

Lulu stared in horror as Samuel hung his head. If only Lady Romeril weren't here, she would directly ask the man what in God's name he thought he was doing! But the presence of the doyenne of Society gave her pause. She couldn't demand an explanation from a duke!

Oh, how she wished Lady Romeril would disappear. Then Samuel could explain—he could tell her what the kiss meant, why he would lie to Lady Romeril and say he regretted—

"Well," Lady Romeril said with a heavy sigh.

Samuel nodded.

Lulu could not understand why. She reached out a hand instinctively to take his own, but he shifted ever so slightly on his feet, leaning away.

Ashamed, Lulu allowed her hand to fall to her side. *She should have expected this.* She should have known any connection with a duke was bound to lead to trouble—but it was not her reputation that was sullied now.

"You know what you have to do," said Lady Romeril severely.

Lulu swallowed. Yes, she knew. She would have to leave Edinburgh; she had no choice. The Duke of Chantmarle could not be expected to live down a scandal of this nature. If his reputation was ever to be recovered, she would have to go.

Where, she did not know. She had no family, no friends. No relations upon whom she could lean. London, perhaps. Returning there had never felt right while her brother was alive, but now Malcolm was dead . . .

It would be a difficult road, but Lulu knew she had to take it. For Samuel's sake.

Oh, if only her curiosity, her desperate need to know what it was like to kiss a duke, had not killed the duke's reputation!

"I will pack immediately," Lulu croaked. She swallowed, her throat dry. "I—"

"Not you, you little—" Lady Romeril took a deep breath as she glared at Lulu, then turned back to Samuel. "You know what is expected of you."

Lulu glanced at the man who was standing simultaneously three feet away and a mile distant.

What was expected of him? Of Samuel?

It did not make sense. He was a duke: his reputation, such as it was, would remain intact. It was never gentlemen who paid the price for such indelicacies. It was always—

Samuel nodded. "I know, and I will meet those expectations."

Lulu had never heard him speak so dully. When he had pretended to have little intellect and no wit, he had been cheerful. Almost radiant.

But this? Samuel's face was still pale, his expression drawn. He appeared to be staring at the door behind Lady Romeril, and there was no warmth in his gaze, no interest in his look.

Lulu could not understand it. *What were they talking about?*

Lady Romeril sighed, shaking her head ruefully. "And under my roof, too! To think, another scandal!"

Now that was a statement which could not be ignored. "Another scandal? What—"

"I do not think I gave you permission to speak to me, Miss Finch," said Lady Romeril, cutting across her with a sharp look. "You have already done enough damage, I think. Perhaps it would be best if you just remained sile—"

"Perhaps it would be best," said Samuel quietly in that same quiet, dull voice, "if you returned to your guests."

Lulu watched, bemused, as a strange look passed between the older woman and the man who had, but ten minutes ago, been kissing her as though his life depended on it. It was a look she had never seen before. Resolute understanding in his eyes, and dark sympathy in hers.

"I suppose you are right," Lady Romeril said with a sigh. "And you will need to speak with Miss Finch."

Lulu's gaze darted to the older woman. "Why—"

"Yes, I think that would be appropriate," Samuel said in a low voice.

If the situation had not been so bizarre, Lulu would have laughed. Appropriate! Nothing in their connection had been appropriate, and it felt ridiculous to start attempting it now, after they had just been caught kissing at Lady Romeril's ball!

Lady Romeril curtseyed low to Samuel, then gave her a cursory glance. "I will expect to hear all about it tomorrow. Good evening, Your Grace."

"Lady Romeril," he murmured, inclining his head.

Lulu watched with bemusement as the woman left the vestibule through a different door. Only when the sound of Lady Romeril's footsteps disappeared did she turn to Samuel.

Finally, they were alone. Finally, he could explain precisely what was meant by—

"Well, damn," Samuel breathed heavily.

Lulu laughed awkwardly, hoping it would dissipate the tension. "My word! I have no idea what Lady Romeril was speaking about, but—"

"She meant there was only one thing I can do to fix this," he said quietly.

Taking a step forward, Lulu was hurt to see the man she cared for so deeply take a step back. Had he lost interest in her that swiftly? Was one kiss enough? Was one moment of passion enough to rid his system of her? Lulu's heart constricted. Was that it? Did the man she had thought could be something wonderful already find her dull?

"I . . . I don't understand," she said helplessly.

It appeared Samuel did, though the knowledge clearly injured him as well. Lulu had never seen him look so utterly bereft of joy. As though all hopes for the future, all plans, were lost.

What was going on?

Samuel's deep breath echoed around the room. "I am a gentleman. That affords me one option, and one only. It was my own curiosity that did it, of course. I had to find out—"

"Samuel, you're not speaking any sense," Lulu said softly, this time stepping forward so swiftly that the man could not retreat from her.

His hands were clammy, even through her gloves.

And finally, for the first time since Lady Romeril had so shockingly interrupted them, Samuel met her gaze.

Lulu almost dropped his hands in surprise. There was such a medley of odd emotions in his gaze, she hardly knew what to do with herself.

Not disappointment. Not quite—but something similar. Something that made it almost impossible to look at her. Yet he did. And she could see how it pained him.

Oh, the thought that merely looking at her was injurious!

"I don't understand," said Lulu helplessly. Perhaps she should try to inject merriment into the moment. Distract him. "I mean, it's not as though I am a lady of the *ton*, not really. If I were, I suppose you would have to marry me!"

Her laughter sounded false in the large echoing room.

Samuel did not smile. But he did not drop his gaze.

Lulu's laughter faltered, trapped in her lungs as her smile faded.

No. No, it was not possible. That happened to lords and ladies! It occurred rarely, to be sure, though every now and again she was almost certain a marriage announced in the newspapers had been a little too rushed, even for an arranged marriage.

But this—a marriage of convenience? One intended only to avoid scandal?

"No," she breathed.

Samuel nodded curtly. "A marriage of convenience is the only way to—"

"Absolutely not," Lulu said, staring as though he were mad. "Samuel, no!"

"You have been brought to Lady Romeril's Scottish May Day Ball," Samuel said steadily, his voice firm. "You were introduced, as though you were a member of Society—"

"B-But I'm not!" Lulu stammered, hardly able to get her words out as her mind whirled. "I'm not!"

"It will take a great deal of convincing to persuade the hundred or so people who just watched us dance and kiss that you are not," quipped Samuel dryly, turning away to pace.

Lulu could not have followed him if she had tried.

A marriage of convenience? Her and Samuel?

She could not deny, in the privacy of her own heart, that it had leapt for joy at the mere thought. But, though she had teased him about becoming his mistress, marrying Samuel had never been something she had truly considered.

"What would it take? To make you marry me?"

"A scandal. I would only marry you, Samuel, if absolutely necessary."

Lulu's cheeks flushed. But she was not that sort of woman. She was not one to entrap a man into matrimony merely because it suited her!

"No," she said, her voice surprisingly hoarse as she watched Samuel pace. "No, this is ridiculous!"

"This is what Society is," Samuel said as he paced. "Rules, restrictions, regulations—we may not like them, Lulu, but without them, what would Society be?"

"Far more enjoyable, I suppose—"

"You are being deliberately facetious," he snapped.

Anger rose. "And you are being deliberately dense!" she shot back. "Have you, even for a moment, thought this through? Considered that by marrying me, you will be removing for yourself any chance of finding a woman to whom you are better suited?"

"I do not think I have ever found a woman better suited to my character," Samuel said with a dry smile as he halted his pacing and shook his head ruefully.

Lulu swallowed. It was a compliment, given at the strangest of times. And here she was, arguing with a duke at a ball hosted by Lady Romeril, because he wanted to marry her!

Well. Not entirely. Perhaps that was what was grating on her heart: the fact that if not for their discovery, this conversation would not be occurring. Samuel would not wish to marry her—he had no wish to marry her.

The thought strengthened her resolve. "You deserve to marry well, to marry within your station!"

"I suppose so, but that is of little consequence," said Samuel dryly. "I will marry you."

"Samuel—why do you keep saying that?" Lulu breathed.

Her pulse was fluttering, inconsistent and painful. He could not seriously be thinking of going through with it. Surely he just said that to Lady Romeril to keep her quiet?

"Because you do not understand!" he said with a dry laugh. "How could you? Lulu, this is the only thing that will save my reputation."

She stared. *No. Surely not. Surely it was the woman's—*

"I am a duke, there are certain things expected of me, and comporting myself according to Society's rules is one of them," Samuel said with a sigh. "You think I would be welcome anywhere if I did not do what was expected? Do you think anyone will respect me if I do not show you, the woman I have ruined, the ultimate respect?"

Lulu's heart was in her mouth. Every word he was saying made sense—and perhaps if they were speaking about two other people, people wholly unconnected to her, she would agree with him.

But this was their lives they were talking about! Irrevocable changes to who they were, what they could do with their futures!

"You wouldn't allow my reputation to be destroyed, would you?"

Lulu started. She had hardly noticed Samuel move to her, standing only feet away.

Instinct pushed her forward. "You're saying you would marry me out of duty?"

She hated how her words quivered, but she had to know.

A wry smile slipped across Samuel's face. "Not purely. I have to admit, the moment we shared, pushed against that column has shown me that there will be . . . compensations."

Lulu's cheeks burned, but she did not look away. "I-I suppose so."

And she could not deny, being married to a duke would certainly be an interesting way to escape the mess she had managed to find herself in.

Lulu swallowed. *That was not why she was doing this,* she told herself firmly. She truly liked Samuel. Admired him. Desired him, certainly. What was all that, if not love?

The fact he could remove her from Mr. Gregory and Mr. Gillingham's blackmail . . .

Well. That was just a convenient coincidence.

"You are a kind man," Lulu said hesitantly.

Samuel snorted as he took her hands. "God, don't talk to me like I'm an archbishop!"

"And handsome, I suppose," she said, a smile tugging at the corners of her lips.

His eyes sparkled. "Could still be an archbishop."

"And you kiss like the devil—"

"That's better!"

"And you're sure?" Lulu said, her voice lowering, trembling at the importance of her words. "You are truly sure you wish to marry me— to restore your reputation, and . . . and enjoy a few compensations?"

What answer she wished for, Lulu hardly knew. How they had managed to get into this situation, she could not understand. But as she stood here, holding Samuel's hands tight, she knew if she made vows to him, she would never break them. Here was a good man, a joyful man. One whose curiosity had certainly managed to land him into a mess, but a man who would do the honorable thing to escape it, rather than abandon her to her fate.

Samuel smiled, and Lulu's stomach turned over as warmth pooled between her legs.

"Lulu Finch," Samuel said softly. "I will marry you."

CHAPTER THIRTEEN

2 May 1811

"OUCH!" SAMUEL GLARED at his own thumb. "What is that doing there?"

"I did say, Your Grace, that the barrel knot is far more difficult than it looks," said his valet reprovingly. "If you would just wait—"

"I can tie my own cravat, man!" Samuel snapped, looking at the monstrosity around his neck which rather suggested the opposite. "I just need to—how on earth did I manage to tie my own thumb into it?"

"Lack of practice, Your Grace," Morris muttered.

At least, that's what Samuel thought he said, but he was hardly sure. His mind had been whirling from the moment he'd awoken that morning. The instant the light had hit his eyes, he had looked at his ceiling and realized it was *today*.

"Truly, Your Grace, I am almost finished with—"

"You worry about getting my collar points nice and sharp, I'll worry about the damned cravat," said Samuel with what he hoped was a grin. "I just need a looking glass, that's all."

The dressing room was bathed with light. His valet had helped him into his breeches and shirt minutes ago, and his waistcoat was carefully laid on a chair. His collar was being carefully prepared by

Morris, and Samuel was determined to do something with his hands while he waited.

He couldn't just stand here, knowing that at any moment . . .

Samuel swallowed. He had an hour yet. Maybe just over an hour before he was expected in the church.

The church. Where he would be getting married.

"Have a care, Your Grace!"

Arms flailing, Samuel managed to prevent himself from tripping over his own boots, carefully polished last night by his valet.

"Who left those there?" he managed to mutter as he approached the looking glass.

"You did," came the muttered comment from his servant.

Repressing a smile and reminding himself to give the poor man a raise, Samuel looked at his reflection. Yes, this would be much easier. A man needed a looking glass to tie a cravat, if he'd said it once, he'd said it a hundred times.

"Ah," said Samuel helplessly.

Yes, well, that he had not considered. Though it was significantly easier to see his hands, it was impossible to work out what he should be doing with them. Whenever Samuel moved his left hand, the blasted right hand moved. When he wanted to move the cravat closer to him, the dratted thing moved farther away.

"God in his—"

"I really will be done momentarily, Your Grace. Why don't you sit in the window seat and wait for me?"

Samuel swallowed the rejoinder he wished to make—namely, that he was not a child and did not need to be told to sit as though he were one. He dropped the cravat on the floor and walked over to the window seat. He sat.

The whole of Edinburgh seemed to be on the move. *Half of them,* Samuel thought dryly, *were attending his own wedding.*

His wedding. It was a startling thought.

True, he had assumed that one day he would be married. One day. A long way off.

He was still young, after all, and there would be plenty of time to create a few heirs and spares by the time he turned fifty. That was what his father had done, and it hadn't hurt the line of succession.

But Samuel knew this was more than an advantageous marriage to a good dowry. Or perhaps he should say it was less. This was a marriage of convenience. A marriage to avoid scandal—though what actual difference it would make, he was not sure. He had still read about his and Lulu's shocking encounter in no fewer than three newspapers.

Samuel shook his head ruefully as he watched the carriages meander by beneath him. *Married.* In just a few short hours, he would be married. And to a woman he would never have suspected would accept him, after the fight she put up.

"A marriage of convenience is the only way to—"

"Absolutely not. Samuel, no!"

It was because she was conscious of his position, he tried to tell himself. *Nothing to do with not actually wanting to marry him.*

If only they'd had more time to converse. Once they had agreed to go ahead with the blasted thing, Lulu had slipped home. He, on the other hand, had been forced to enter Lady Romeril's ballroom and smile painfully as he accepted the pointed congratulations of Society.

He wasn't sure what was worse. Having to walk across Edinburgh in the dark, alone, or having to listen to the Duke of Axwick critique him for getting himself into such a mess.

"There," came a self-satisfied voice. "The perfect collar points."

Samuel looked up to see his valet holding the carefully starched material. Precisely what made them perfect, he could not tell. But it made the man happy.

"Marvelous," he said brightly, trying to make up for the cravat catastrophe. "Any chance you could help me with—"

"Yes, I will tie your cravat in but a moment," said Morris with a wry eyebrow raised. "But first, let us attach the collar points."

Samuel wasn't certain what "us" truly meant. He just stood there while his valet buttoned on the starch that felt sharp enough to cut him.

"You appear, if I may say so Your Grace, a little nervous."

Samuel shrugged, disrupting the tying of the cravat and causing his valet to sniff. "I suppose I am."

"I do not see why," said Morris, eyes focused on the complex knot he was creating in the soft silk. "You are marrying a beautiful woman."

A slow grin crept across Samuel's face. "I am, I suppose."

Yes, Lulu was beautiful. And bold. And mysterious. There was still so much he did not know about her—*though*, Samuel mused, *that was rather common in his circles*. Why, Miss Ashbrooke had once threatened to act as matchmaker, a dreadful prospect. But it did happen that way. Lords and ladies, introduced at a ball, their engagement announced merely days later.

Perhaps what he was doing was not so very radical after all.

"I suppose it does not matter so very much if she has no fortune, no title, or family to speak of," his valet said lightly, finishing off the cravat knot with a flourish.

Samuel stepped away from the man, thunder raging through his heart. "And what precisely is that supposed to mean?"

The look on the man's face was truly terrified, but it was nothing to how afraid the idiot should feel.

Sparks crackled in Samuel's fists as they clenched. What on earth did the man think he was saying? How dare he speak of his future duchess like that—like she was a woman he had just picked off the street!

"I-I just meant—she comes from no noble family, Your Grace, you cannot deny—"

"I will thank you to desist speaking of my wife's heritage," Samuel said, as calmly as he could manage. *Dear God, the man was fortunate he was not standing closer.* "In fact, I believe I would like you to desist working for a few days. Take it off. Paid. Stay out of my sight."

The words echoed in the dressing room. The valet's face was pale. "Your Grace—"

"Out!" barked Samuel, pushed beyond all endurance.

The servant scampered out of the room leaving his master alone, with a perfectly tied cravat knot and an even more intricate knot in his stomach.

Well, Morris was probably not the only man who was saying these things, Samuel thought dully as he pulled on his waistcoat alone. He could not pretend he did not know what half the town thought. They probably saw nothing but a beautiful woman who had surely hoodwinked that foolish duke with her beauty, poor sod.

Only he knew how much more there was to Lulu's character. Her charm. The depths of her feeling and understanding. Samuel knew Lulu, knew her heart, her worth. But in their eyes, she was just a woman.

He snorted as he pulled on his coat. *Just a woman!*

He may not have expected things to end this way. He could never have known his curiosity would lead him down this particular road. But if there was one thing Samuel knew, it was that he was fortunate to be marrying Lulu Finch.

"Your Grace!" spluttered his butler as Samuel half ran down the staircase. "Is anything amiss? I just saw Morris, and he—"

"I'm going out," declared Samuel, heart racing but knowing this was the right decision. "I'll see you at the church."

"At the—Your Grace—"

Samuel did not wait to hear the rest of his butler's speech. He was sure it would be perfectly reasonable: the wedding was in less than an hour, and he was expected at the church in the next ten minutes. It would be irresponsible not to be there. The whole of Society was expecting him!

Which was why it made little sense that he was striding along the streets of Edinburgh to Stewart Buildings.

"You!" said the older woman as she stepped out of the front door. "I did not think I would see you again."

"Samuel!"

Samuel's heart softened.

How she did it, he did not know. Why she had such an effect on him, he would never untangle. But seeing Lulu's wide eyes and astonished expression as she stepped out of her building, the new pelisse he had bought her wrapped around her shoulders, Samuel knew beyond a shadow of a doubt that he was doing the right thing.

Their marriage may be one of convenience—but it would soon become more.

"Samuel Dellamore, you are not supposed to see me before the wedding!" Lulu exclaimed under her breath, cheeks pinking. "What do you—"

"I couldn't wait, I had to see you," Samuel said, words spilling out as he pulled her along the street, away from the prying ears of her neighbor. "You are well?"

"Well?" Lulu repeated. "I don't know."

Samuel's heart skipped a beat. There was something all too knowing about that look.

"You're not having second thoughts, are you?" she said warily.

Joy rushed through Samuel's chest. "Certainly not."

"Then—then why are you—"

"I told you, I had to see you," he said impulsively. "I just had to."

When had words ever not been enough to fully express himself? When had it become so difficult to reach into his own heart and read the words written there?

Perhaps when they had become a different language. Perhaps the moment he had spotted Lulu across the crowded Assembly Rooms, unadorned and unafraid, and realized all the words he knew were insufficient to describe her beauty.

Samuel took her hands. "You are certain, aren't you?"

Lulu raised an eyebrow. "Certain that you are absolutely ridiculous for coming here when you know I am supposed to meet you at the altar? Yes."

"No—certain that you are willing to marry me," he replied with a wry smile that belied his nerves.

For she could answer the most dreaded response, could she not?

Samuel was no fool. He had met many a man and wife who had been pushed together by circumstance rather than affection. Couples who had found themselves unfortunately discovered while . . . getting to know each other better. Then realized that they would be getting to know each other a great deal better. Most of them seemed, if not happy, at least resigned to their fate.

His stomach twisted, his soul rebelling. That was not the fate he had ever wished for himself, but it was definitely not worthy of Lulu Finch.

"You're saying you would marry me out of duty?"

When Samuel had spoken to her just two days ago, when they had agreed this was the only way to save his reputation. Well. He had not quite known what he had been saying. Words had spilled out, a medley of desperation and panic, and she had agreed.

It was only in the intervening time, the long hours spent alone in the dark of the night, that Samuel wondered if he had truly done the right thing. Not for himself, but for Lulu. If she wished for a love match—God knew, he felt something, but what it was he could not tell . . .

"You wish to know whether I still want to marry you?" Lulu said, frowning.

Regret tugged at Samuel's heart. "Of course, I should have known you wouldn't want to—I will have you moved to one of my properties, no one will ever know—"

"Did I ask you to cancel my wedding, Samuel Dellamore?" she said with a chuckle. "I can see you've still got a great deal to learn."

There must have been something on his face, something that told her he was far more serious than she had thought.

Lulu's smile faded, and she squeezed his hands. "Samuel, you—we did not expect to be discovered. If you had known that kiss would seal your fate—"

"I probably still would have claimed it," Samuel admitted.

She grinned. "Your curiosity is going to be the death of you."

Lulu had probably not intended to reprove him, but he felt it, nonetheless.

For she was right. His curiosity was usually such an asset, a useful part of his character that meant he pursued information and informants further and faster than anyone else who served the Crown. Samuel, Duke of Chantmarle, was always one to find out the truth.

Yet here, in Edinburgh, his curiosity had been redirected. The traitors walked free, and instead . . .

Instead here he stood, on a Scottish pavement, holding hands with a woman he knew almost nothing about, less than an hour before their wedding.

"As long as I have you," Samuel murmured. "Then my curiosity is welcome to try to kill me off."

Maybe Lulu knew what he was about to do. She certainly did not push him away when he pulled her into his arms, bestowing a none too chaste kiss on her lips. Indeed she responded, her gloved hands pulling him closer. She moaned, setting off all Samuel's desires which he had managed to dampen. Tendrils of passion were growing into vines curling around his heart, taking him prisoner as his fingers grabbed—

"We should probably get to the church," Lulu said breathlessly, pulling away from Samuel just as his fingers were about to cup her buttocks.

He groaned. "Your rooms are closer."

"Samuel!"

"Well, you can't blame a man for trying," he quipped with a grin.

He was a little breathless. Dear God, kissing Lulu was unlike kissing any other woman he'd ever had in his arms. She was more alive, sparking more joy, more desire, than he could have dreamt.

And that was only when they were kissing on the pavement. When they reached their wedding night . . .

"Samuel," said Lulu severely, slipping her arm into his. "You're thinking about—about *that*, aren't you?"

"Couldn't possibly say," Samuel said with a rueful look up at her building before starting to walk toward the church. "But probably."

Her laughter warmed his heart as they passed astonished passersby. Samuel saw the looks on their faces. Though he had never considered himself part of the fashionable set—not like Penshaw—he was, nevertheless, a duke. His face was known. And if the scandal sheets he had perused that morning were anything to go by, the whole of Edinburgh knew of the rapid wedding to save the Duke of Chantmarle's reputation.

Samuel caught the gaze of a staring gentleman and inclined his head imperiously. The man flushed and looked away.

Lulu giggled. "You know, you're never going to live this down."

"I suppose I won't," he replied sheepishly as they turned onto a street, the church now just ahead of them. "But I will live with it. I am just grateful to you."

"To me?"

He glanced at her bemused face, and his heart skipped a beat.

Samuel had spoken the truth: it would be his reputation ruined if he was seen to have taken advantage of a woman without standing by her. But it wasn't just that which propelled him toward this marriage. It was something more, a hope he had not dared to voice, a need he had not understood.

And this wasn't the right time. Not yet. He could explain his feelings, whatever they were, to Lulu when he finally understood them himself. When, if he was fortunate, Lulu would feel as deeply for him as he felt for her.

"Samuel, if anyone should be grateful, it should be me," Lulu said softly as they halted outside the church where, in just a few minutes, they would become man and wife. "You . . . you saw me."

Samuel blinked. "Saw you?"

It did not appear to be a great achievement. Why, any man could—

"You didn't just see me, a woman. You saw me, myself, the person I am," Lulu said, voice breaking. "I've never been—no one has ever . . . I can't explain it. You'll just have to trust me when I say that marrying you may not have been something I could have ever planned"—Samuel chuckled—"but it will be my honor, for the rest of our lives, to be your wife."

Samuel's lungs tightened. The words he could not have expressed—they were there, in Lulu's heart already. "My duchess."

She turned pale. "Oh, Lord, I—"

"Everybody ready?" said a man's voice with a dark sparkle in it.

Samuel looked around. Penshaw was poking his head through the church door.

"Yes, ready," said Lulu softly. "Well, in you go."

These last words were directed at him, but Samuel did not understand. "Where is your—who is giving you away?"

"I'll be waiting at the altar," said Penshaw hastily, disappearing.

Samuel paid no heed to his best man. Not while his future bride looked so abashed.

"I told you before, I have no family," Lulu said gently. "I . . . well, there isn't anyone to walk me up the aisle. I suppose I'll be giving myself away."

And reckless abandon seared through Samuel's heart. *No.*

"We'll walk together," he said firmly.

"Samuel—"

"I don't care," Samuel said fiercely, linking his fingers through hers and marveling at the way it felt so right to be hand in hand with her. "Lulu, I—I will be your husband soon. But honoring you? Serving you? That starts now."

Organ music started to waft through the air, and the noise of several hundred people suddenly rising to their feet crept through the open church door.

Lulu had not taken her gaze away. "You—"

"From now on," said Samuel with a dry laugh, "let's just assume that both of us are determined enough, and stubborn enough, to dig our heels in."

A squeeze of his hand. A gentle laugh. "Well, in that case . . . let's get married."

CHAPTER FOURTEEN

L ULU TOOK A deep breath. She could sense it billowing inside her, from the very depths of her lungs to her shoulders.

Well, this was it. She was a wife. And a wife did certain things a mere woman never did. Things even a mistress would not do—at least, she presumed so. She had no actual knowledge.

Tugging the golden silk shawl closer around her, Lulu pushed open the door.

She had thought the dressing room particularly large. It had been difficult to accept, as the rather stern butler, Fitzhugh, had shown her around the lodgings Samuel had in Edinburgh, that the entire room was just for clothes.

"A dressing room?" Lulu had repeated in wonder.

The butler had sniffed. "As *all* duchesses enjoy, yes, Your Grace."

Lulu had winced at the time, and winced just to recall the moment, albeit hours later.

Was she ever going to acclimatize to this world? To this life, this title she had never expected and had now thrust upon her shoulders?

Large though the duchess's dressing room had been, it was nothing to the ducal bedchamber.

Lulu's lips parted in wonderment as her head tilted back, attempting to take in the high ceiling, the delicate painting of cherubs and clouds above, gold leaf sparkling thanks to the light of the hundreds of candles on the chandelier.

Everywhere she looked was opulence. Velvet chairs, soft curtains that fell in refined folds. The carpet was plush—or at least, she was almost certain it was, because there were so many ornate rugs, she could barely see it.

And there, right in the center of the room . . .

Lulu swallowed. It was fortunate, really, that Samuel had not yet stepped into the large bedchamber. It meant she had a moment to collect herself.

Or uncollect herself, as it were, as she stood at the end of the large four poster.

Thick mahogany trunks extended up from each corner. A dark navy silken bedcover was an expanse of sky. There were more pillows and cushions upon it than she had ever seen in her life, the canopy stretching over it all in the same dark navy silk.

Lulu's heart skipped a beat. That was where, in the next hour, she and Samuel would . . .

She should never have permitted him to believe the incorrect notion that she had been a courtesan.

Bringing her fingers together and twisting them as her mind raced, Lulu wondered if this was the time to tell the truth. Not the whole truth. It would never do to reveal just how dastardly she had been in the past.

A slow smile crept across her lips. But she would never have to live that life again. It was over. She was free.

"Do you like what you see?"

Samuel's warm voice was enough to make Lulu turn around, but—

"Samuel!" she exclaimed.

It was the same Samuel she knew—except different. The Samuel she was accustomed to invariably wore . . . *well, more clothes.*

"What is the matter?" asked Samuel lazily, shutting the door to the duke's dressing room and stepping languidly across the bedchamber.

Fortunately for Lulu, it was a significantly longer distance compared to any private room she had ever been in before, and so she had a moment to catch her breath.

It was insufficient. Samuel was wearing no coat, no waistcoat, no shirt at all. She gazed at his bare chest, tangled wiry hair spreading across his nipples and descending to—

Lulu swallowed. *Thank God the breeches were still on.* Who knew what she would do if he had emerged entirely naked!

"You . . . you don't like what you see?" asked Samuel, almost hesitantly. He stopped about six feet from her, head tilted to one side.

Heat blossomed. How could he ask such a brazen question?

Because, she reminded herself, *he thinks you've done this before.* He has no idea you're an innocent—no idea this is the first time you've even seen a man's torso!

"I . . ." Lulu did not have the words.

Samuel had been handsome enough with clothes on, she was tempted to say with a laugh. But like this! Did she like what she saw? Oh, absolutely—but it was unbecoming for a lady to speak so openly of desire, was it not?

"I . . . it is appropriate, I suppose," was all she could manage.

Yes, appropriate. She was no fool; she knew what was to happen tonight. Their marriage was not complete until it was consummated, everyone knew that. And that meant . . .

For some reason, Samuel's shoulders slumped as he looked about the bedchamber. "Oh. I had hoped you would like the furnishings—I had them altered ever so slightly when we—well, when it was clear we would need to marry."

A sensation of mingled relief and sadness washed through Lulu's heart. "Oh—oh, the furnishings. Yes, very pleasant."

Samuel had not been talking about himself, whether she admired him—but the room. That made more sense, certainly.

But then he had to use that phrase that cut to the very core of her: *"When it was clear we would need to marry . . ."*

Need to. Not want to.

Oh, there was desire between them, of that Lulu was perfectly aware. And truly, how different was their marriage to countless others in the nobility? Matches were made every day without much insight into character, temperament, or integrity. No, it was usually wealth and fortune, position and beauty that dictated a match.

But did Samuel have to reference that in the ducal bedchamber on their wedding night?

"We . . . well," her new husband was saying awkwardly. "We don't have to do this."

Lulu blinked. *This?* "I don't understand."

"Well, you know, this," said Samuel, gesturing vaguely to the bed.

She looked at it. *This?* The bed was made, she saw no reason to make it again—

As understanding rushed through her, heat rushed through her cheeks. "Oh. I see."

It was difficult to push aside the unexpected sense of rejection that surfaced at his words.

Her new husband did not wish to bed her? Was she truly so odious, their marriage so forced, so contrived, that he had no wish to make love to her?

Or, and the thought rocketed through Lulu's stomach most uncomfortably, *was Samuel half-certain this whole thing could be hushed up?* Why, if they did not consummate the marriage, could it be undone somehow?

"Do you?" asked Samuel quietly. "Do you see?"

Lulu hesitated, but this was not the time to be untruthful. If she expected and wanted honesty from Samuel, it was only right she offer it herself. Even if it pained her.

"No," she said, with as determined an air as possible. *Well, she was the new Duchess of Chantmarle, wasn't she?* She was supposed to have a little gumption. "I don't understand why you don't want to—why you don't wish—"

"Well, it's been a busy day," Samuel said bracingly.

Lulu stared. This was not like the Samuel she knew at all. This was the man who had been desperate to kiss her, almost from the very moment that they had first met. She had seen it in his eyes, sensed it in his touch. Known it for certain when he had started to moan he would never get a kiss . . .

"You're killing me every second that I don't kiss you. Damn, I want to kiss you, Lulu."

So why did Samuel now have some strange hesitancy around her? Were the rumors she had heard Mrs. Abernathy mutter true? Did husbands lose all interest in their wives as soon as they became wives merely because they were . . . wives?

"It's been a busy day?" Lulu repeated. "It's been a busy three days, I would say. Three days ago, I wasn't even engaged."

Their shared laughter broke the tension, wherever it had come from. Suddenly a warmth suffused through Lulu and she knew, though how she knew it she could not tell, everything would be well.

As soon as she managed to navigate the complexity of the marital bed.

"You don't regret this, do you?"

Lulu started. The thought had been one she had considered many times, mulling it over in the darkness of her two dingy rooms. Rooms she had packed up swiftly—not that there had been much to pack—and said goodbye to only that morning.

His lopsided grin was nervous. "I suppose I just thought—well, you are moving into a different world now, a different life. One you may not have . . . I don't know."

It appeared Samuel did not know. Lulu could not recall ever seeing such uncertainty on his face. That once proud and determined air, the boyish charm, the roguish banter—they were gone.

Only then did it occur to her. Though Samuel Dellamore, Duke of Chantmarle, was a gentleman, and a duke, and almost certainly experienced in these matters, that did not mean he was not also nervous.

Lulu almost laughed as the thought crossed her mind. *Samuel, nervous?*

But there was nothing else that hesitancy, lopsided smile, or darting gaze could mean.

Warm compassion mingled with affection. This was not just a momentous evening for her: it was for him, too. They were sharing this. No matter what he imagined she had experienced before, and what she was almost sure he had, this encounter was new. Fresh. Intimidating.

Lulu stepped forward, crossing the distance between them. "Samuel."

"Lulu," he said, taking her hands eagerly.

"I know this is a little strange," she confessed with a wry smile. "You never expected to make a common woman your duchess—"

"I wasn't sure, for a moment back there, that you would have me," quipped Samuel, his roguish manner returning.

Lulu squeezed his hand. "This is new. Strange. It would be easy to be nervous—"

"I'm not nervous," said Samuel instantly.

She raised an eyebrow and tried not to giggle at the pink dots on his cheeks.

"Well. Perhaps a tad."

Her heart contracted, just for a moment. She was starting to see a whole new side to Samuel, a part of him she had not even realized was there. What a privilege it was.

"Why not let your curiosity be your guide?" Lulu suggested gently.

The thought had occurred to her from nowhere, but it was a good idea as far as she was concerned. He was the nosiest man she had ever met. Why not lean into that particular characteristic?

Samuel did not look convinced. "What do you—oh."

His inability to continue speaking, if Lulu had to guess, was because she had released her hands from his and splayed them across his chest.

His warm, soft skin. The thumping of his heart beneath his ribcage. The way his whole body tensed then softened as he grew accustomed to her touch.

Lulu discovered her breath was a little short, just as Samuel's quickened.

So. This was what it felt like. A man. Samuel.

"I see," Samuel said, his voice jagged. "Well, in that case . . ."

Lulu lifted her lips as the Duke of Chantmarle leaned to claim a kiss from his bride.

It was sweet at first: respectful, nothing at all like the kiss he had crushed onto her mouth at Lady Romeril's ball. But it soon deepened, the warmth between them accelerating the passion Lulu had known was just lying dormant under the surface.

Her palms were still pressed against Samuel's chest, but his had swept her up, one hand now cupping her buttocks, the other clinging to her waist.

And desire, warmth, hedonistic longing was rising in her as Lulu had never experienced before. She wanted to feel him, know him, touch him. Feel his touch.

She wanted to know what it was to be loved.

"Oh, Lulu," Samuel breathed, abandoning her mouth but only so that he could trail kisses down her jaw and neck.

"Samuel," Lulu whimpered, unable to help herself.

Was this what it was, to be so overwhelmed with desire that you could hardly speak? It was fortunate indeed that Samuel's hand was holding her buttocks, for her knees were weak, her ankles barely able to hold her.

And debauched thoughts, wild ones no woman should ever countenance, were sparking through her mind. What they could share. What they could do to each other . . .

"May I?"

Lulu blinked, desire and lust hazing her sight. When the picture before her cleared, it was to reveal Samuel's hand, which had been on her waist, now holding her gown's ribbon.

He wished to undress her.

All her instincts would have told her, in any other situation, to flee. To run. That her virtue was about to be compromised. That once a gentleman removed one's gown, there was no going back.

But strangely, none of those instincts appeared.

She was with Samuel. She could trust him. They were married!

And what's more, she wanted him to remove it. She wanted to be as free with him as he was with her.

Lulu swallowed and nodded.

"I need to hear you say it," Samuel said in a growl under his breath. "I need to hear you ask me, tell me, permit me to take it off."

Why did those words ripple such teasing anticipation through her very soul?

Lulu's voice was hoarse. "I . . . I want you to take off my gown, Samuel."

He moaned, fingers scrabbling at the ribbon which was swiftly removed and dropped in a liquid pile onto the floor. It joined her shawl which had already fallen from her shoulders—when, she did not know.

It was soon completely obscured by the falling gold silk of her gown. Pools and pools of it, cascading down her body, until—

"Bloody hell, Lulu," Samuel breathed, staring with wide eyes. "You . . . you're not . . ."

Lulu smiled. "No, I'm not."

It had been a split-second decision that morning. Never before had she been tempted—in fact, she wasn't sure if she had even ever considered it before.

But as she had been dressing for her wedding day, something had told her today had to be different. And so . . .

Lulu stood, entirely naked.

"You—you're not . . ." Samuel swallowed. "You're not wearing any stays!"

She shook her head, fighting the impulse to move her hands to cover the most secret parts of her. "N-No. I thought—if it offends you—"

"Offends—offends me? You think seeing such beauty, being trusted with—thunder an' turf!" Samuel spluttered. "Do you mean to tell me you and I stood up in church, and made our vows to each other, and promised all sorts of things in front of the whole of the Edinburgh *ton* . . . and you weren't wearing *anything* under that gown?"

Lulu shook her head again, wondering whether she had made an awful mistake.

It was an outrageous thing to do—and she was a duchess now, she was supposed to—

"Samuel!"

The cry was forced from her as Samuel pulled her roughly into his embrace.

Oh, such an embrace. Lulu had never known such warmth, such blazing heat as when her breasts were pushed up against Samuel's chest. There was something about the intimacy of skin to skin contact, the way he growled with pleasure, the fervor of his kisses. Something changed between them in that instant. An intimacy was exchanged, and it was not one that could ever be taken back.

Lulu gasped as Samuel's hands once again cupped her buttocks— but it was so different, now she was no longer wearing her gown!

Samuel groaned. "God, I can't take this much longer!"

And then she was released. The sudden absence of him, even though she had only just been growing accustomed to his sensual touch, was enough to make Lulu whimper. Why had he cast her off—was he tired of her already?

Her eyes widened.

Samuel was ripping off his boots, fingers scrabbling at the buttons of his breeches, and before she could even fathom what words to say, he had stripped off everything.

Well. Goodness. That was—

"Lulu Dellamore, Duchess of Chantmarle," Samuel said, his breath jagged. "Will you do me the honor of accompanying me to the bed?"

Lulu did not answer in words. Instead she turned, clambered onto the large four poster, and turned to look at him.

Samuel joined her within a heartbeat, and it was sweet ecstasy—ecstasy to have him nestled between her legs and in her arms. His kisses grew wild, his tongue teasing delight from her mouth that she had never known was there. Heat was growing within her, heat Lulu did not understand. It was pooling to her breasts, her lips, between her legs, and all she wanted was more of him, but she did not know how to—

"Samuel!" she cried.

It was not a cry of pain, though Lulu could see how he may have believed it was.

Samuel halted immediately, looking with concerned eyes as his manhood rested half within. "Lulu?"

"Keep going."

She had not intended to be so blunt, but Lulu could barely think as it was, and she craved more of the sensation that had so startled her. Oh, to be filled with him, to know nothing but him within her, to completely give herself over to him—

"Damn, Lulu, you feel wonderful," Samuel moaned as he slid his manhood deeper within her secret place. "God, I love you."

Lulu did not think twice. It was not a word which had been spoken between them before, but of course she loved him. How could she not?

"I love you," she whispered, then moaned. "Oh, Samuel!"

There was a rhythm growing, a rhythm Samuel seemed to know instinctively but then so did her body. A movement in and out of her, a thrusting motion that sparked pleasure across her thighs down to her toes, up to where her nipples tingled.

Lulu held onto Samuel's shoulders, unable to do anything but receive the sensual delights his body was giving her. This was everything, this was surely the pinnacle of—

"Lulu," breathed Samuel, dipping his head and caressing her nipple with his tongue.

She moaned, the pleasure building, a pressure within her so deep she could never have guessed, and as Samuel increased his thrusts, deepening them by tilting her hips—

"Samuel!" Lulu cried.

How could she cry anything else? Her body was exploding, heat pouring through her, pleasure as she had never known cascading through her, and she lost all sense of sight and sound as Samuel thrust heavily into her, moaning her own name as he did so.

And then there was silence. Silence, save for the ragged breaths and the gentle whimpering moans of their love.

When Lulu opened her eyes, Samuel was lying beside her.

"You were correct," he said, breathing heavily.

Lulu had no comprehension of what her handsome husband was saying. "I . . . I was?"

Samuel grinned, and warmth soared through Lulu's heart just as it had roared through her body only seconds ago. "Curiosity. It's rather marvelous, isn't it? Ready to go again?"

CHAPTER FIFTEEN

3 May 1811

A S SAMUEL SLOWLY forced himself from sleep to wakefulness, he tried not to think too hard about the things he had to do that day.

Firstly, he needed to read the mounting paperwork on his desk. Fitzhugh had made an almost cutting remark on how eagerly the duke had been avoiding his paperwork, and that had to stop. Even if he just pushed the whole pile of letters into a fire. That would at least remove the towering stack which was so menacing.

Secondly, and he groaned, eyes still shut at the thought, he needed to meet with a few of his informants. It had been absolutely too long since he had seen Blakely, for starters, and he had been the only one of them so far to actually show anything of interest.

Thirdly, and perhaps he should have started with this one, he needed to reply to that letter from Judge Smee. It was infuriating that the man required such instant replies, but Lord knew the mail coaches were no longer safe. He would have to send one of his own men.

And fourthly—

Samuel was interrupted from this litany of tasks awaiting him by something odd.

A hand. It was warm, and soft, and smaller than his own. It had crept slowly but surely and was now accompanied by what felt to be an entire person.

Samuel opened his eyes.

Lulu smiled as she curled into him, her arm across him and one leg nuzzled up to his. "Good morning."

And it all came rushing back to him. The scandalous discovery of them kissing at Lady Romeril's ball. The hasty proposal that was, eventually, accepted. The rushed preparations Mrs. Winder, his housekeeper, had warned him had aged her at least a decade.

And yesterday. The wedding. And the wedding night.

A slow smile crept across Samuel's face as he brought an arm around his beautiful, and decidedly naked, new bride. "You," he said softly.

Lulu kissed him on the corner of the mouth, and Samuel could have sung for joy.

It certainly wasn't what he had expected. Though Lady Romeril had been spun the tale, along with a few other doyennes of London Society, he had not actually intended to go to Edinburgh in hunt for a wife.

But that did not seem to have mattered. He had found one, and one who would surely keep him on his toes for years to come. And if last night was any indication . . .

"You know, I am quite exhausted," Samuel confessed with a chuckle. "I did not think you would have such stamina!"

"Me, stamina? I was the one attempting to keep up with you!" protested Lulu happily. "You were the one who—"

"Ah, but you let me," said Samuel, teasingly.

By God, she had let him.

Samuel was not an innocent. He was not aware of any dukes, in truth, who reached the age of thirty without knowing the carnal embrace of a woman. Sometimes a man, he had heard. Whatever made a person happy.

But last night had been different. Last night had been . . . intimate, and in a way he had never experienced before. How, he was not sure. He could not have described it to anyone—not that he was going to do such a thing. No, what he and Lulu had shared last night, it was private. For them only.

"It was special," Lulu was saying softly. "I-I cannot explain to you just how special it was, but you must believe me, Samuel. It was the most precious, the most incredible night I have ever known."

Pride rushed through Samuel's veins.

Though he would be loath to admit it, it soothed his ego somewhat to hear her say so.

He was no cad. Samuel was hardly going to point out, in the throes of passion last night, that this was hardly the typical sort of wedding night for a duchess. For Lulu had been most open with him. She had acted as a courtesan in the past—she was no innocent. What she shared with him was, practically, something she had shared with others.

But Samuel swallowed his bitterness now and reminded himself of what his pretty bride had just said. Whatever those other men had been, he was her husband. What the two of them had shared went beyond the mechanical, or the mercantile. It wasn't a transaction between buyer and seller, but a shared experience between two people who . . .

"God, I love you."

"I love you."

Warmth flickered in Samuel's heart before spreading. She loved him, and he certainly loved her. Who could fail to love her?

"It was special for me," he said softly, stroking Lulu's bare shoulder with his thumb. "More special than I could have believed."

Her hand tightened on him, just for a moment. "Good."

This was not how he could have imagined marriage, but the whole thing seemed perfect. A woman he respected and admired. A beautiful and sensual woman in his bed. What else could a man need?

"Well, Duchess," said Samuel with a broad smile. "What shall we do today? I suppose I shall find out so much more about you, now we are living together. No more secrets!"

He chuckled, warm and safe in the knowledge that though he would share almost all his life with his new bride, there were certain things he would keep from her.

For Lulu's own good, of course. What benefit could she gain by being informed of his affairs for the Crown? It would only put her in danger. He was a duke: he was accustomed to danger. But putting Lulu in harm's way? No need for that.

There was something of a knowing look in her eye. "No secrets, you say? You don't think a healthy marriage should involve a little secrecy—a little mystery?"

Samuel chuckled, adoring the way his chest moved with Lulu curled up against it. "Mystery? You know my curious nature, Lulu. You honestly think I could stop once I thought there was something to discover?"

Their laughter brought such joy to his heart, he could hardly imagine more peace.

This was, it appeared, what he had wanted. Samuel could never have articulated it if someone had asked. He had never been one for settling down, and though he knew he would have to eventually, saw no reason to rush into the bonds of marriage.

And now?

Lulu kissed him lightly. "You'd never discover my secrets."

"Oh, is that so?" Samuel teased. "Look, no more secrets. That's an order, as your husband and as your duke."

It was her mischievous nature which made her say it, he was certain. "No new secrets."

"That's not what I said, you vixen!"

"Samuel!"

His fingers had swiftly moved to tickle her, and her burst of laughter and squirming in his arms only made Samuel continue.

Well. And something else . . .

"Goodness," said Lulu, panting. "I did not think—well, after last night, I rather presumed you would be too exhausted to—"

"You know, I don't think I am ever going to be too exhausted," Samuel said, turning Lulu onto her back and nestling between her legs. "In fact . . ."

It took about two hours for them to be fully sated. Breathing heavily as he looked up at the canopy of his four poster, Samuel wondered if they would ever find the strength to leave this place. Paperwork be damned.

Why walk away from such pleasure?

"Lulu," he began. "What do you think about—"

He was interrupted. Not by an elegant riposte from his wife or a gentle knocking at the door. No, his words were drowned out by the largest rumble of a stomach he'd ever heard.

"Dear God," Samuel said as Lulu broke out into peals of laughter. "And here I was, thinking I had satisfied your desires!"

"Of one type of hunger, yes," Lulu said ruefully. "But I am afraid I need to be sustained if you wish to do that again."

It was half on his mind to linger, to move down the bed and show her precisely what he could do to her to distract from her hunger—but even Samuel had to admit, it had been a long time since the wedding breakfast the day before.

"Fine," he groaned, pushing back the bedlinens and getting out of bed. "You drive a hard bargain, Your Grace."

"Only because I barter with the best, Your Grace," said Lulu with a laugh, stepping out of the bed but with the bedlinens wrapped around her.

Samuel fought the urge to pull them away. He would never be able to resist her once he saw her again in all her glory. But there was something rather charming about Lulu's modesty.

Unexpected, too. Samuel had little experience with courtesans—excellent informants, however—but he had supposed Lulu would have lost all shyness about her body years ago.

As it was, she swiftly stepped over to her dressing room and returned with a robe wrapped around her. "I suppose I don't have time to get dressed?"

Samuel shook his head. "Come on—I want to get you fed then back in bed as swiftly as possible."

"Samuel!"

Laughter followed them as they walked, arm in arm, down the stairs of his Edinburgh residence. Samuel had pulled on his breeches and the nearest shirt but padded along the carpet barefoot. Lulu wore only the robe—which he considered more than sufficient. Perhaps even too much so.

But as a footman appeared to open the door to the breakfast room, and three others moved forward to start serving them, Samuel was astonished to see Lulu flush.

"I—goodness, I—"

"What's wrong?" Samuel asked as he sat on a chair pulled out by a footman.

Lulu, on the other hand, stood by the table, cheeks burning and eyes downcast.

Samuel leaned forward inquiringly. *It was most odd. What had got into her?*

"I . . . they . . . I am dressed only in a robe!" hissed Lulu under her breath.

For a moment, he wasn't sure what she was talking about. *They? Who were they?*

"Tea, Your Grace?"

"Yes, thank you," Samuel replied vaguely to the voice by his ear.

Then he blinked. A hand in his livery had reached forward and was pouring tea into his cup. A footman. In fact, there were now five footmen and his butler in the breakfast room, each of them quietly getting along with their allotted tasks.

And there stood Lulu, flushing furiously, in the middle of them. Naked save for a robe.

They.

"Ah," said Samuel helplessly. "I see."

Well, it was not as though he really noticed his servants. He never had. They were just there, keeping the house running, doing his bidding, tidying and cleaning and polishing and mending. Just . . . servants.

Evidently, Lulu was unaccustomed to this rather intrusive situation. And if Samuel attempted to see it from an outsider's perspective, he could see her point. It was rather odd to be wandering about the place, near nude, with six other men.

"Leave," he said in his most commanding tone.

Samuel almost laughed to see Lulu hesitate, unsure whether the directive was for her as the footmen scuttled out. *Dear God, he would have to remind her several times a day, it appeared, that she was a duchess.* The Duchess of Chantmarle.

"Anything else, Your Grace?" Fitzhugh said smoothly by the door.

Samuel waved a hand. "I'll ring if I need you."

"Very good, Your Grace," the butler said, bowing and closing the door behind him.

It was only then that Samuel realized just how empty the breakfast room was without all those servants. *Goodness, they did clutter up the place, didn't they?*

"There," he said aloud. "Better?"

Lulu stepped over, tapped him on the arm, and said, "You could have warned me!"

"Warned you? What, that a duke has servants?" Samuel said fairly.

Well, perhaps unfairly. It was a very different life. He could still recall the rooms Lulu had taken in Edinburgh. Bare. Almost completely devoid of furniture, definitely devoid of comfort. No fire, no warmth. Hardly any food.

He recalled just how eagerly she had eaten when dining at the Royal Arms Hotel.

Samuel's stomach lurched. She had known real want, real poverty. Well, Lulu would never have to suffer through that again.

"Look, I will be your servant," he said aloud to smooth over the awkward moment, rising from his seat. "Here."

Lulu giggled as he pulled out a chair for her. "You will?"

"Oh, I think you'll find I can serve if I want to," Samuel said, privately thinking that if she had any idea how he had served his country, she may not be so swift to laugh. "Now, breakfast! What do you normally have for breakfast?"

The moment the words had left his mouth, he realized what a mistake he had made.

The color in Lulu's cheeks had faded, the embarrassment of standing before so many men in only a robe dissipating. So it was with defiance and only a slight pinkness in her face that she looked up.

"Nothing," she said simply.

"What, nothing? Ever?" Samuel said faintly as he returned to his seat and grasped his teacup for something to do with his hands.

Surely not. A man needed his breakfast—surely a woman could not be much different?

"Rarely," Lulu conceded with a teasing smile lifting the corner of her mouth. "When there is little money, breakfast is a luxury."

Samuel swallowed.

Breakfast, a luxury. It was only now Lulu was his wife, now their lives were starting to truly intertwine, that he was starting to understand just how different their pasts had been.

He had never been one of the richest dukes. The dukedom of Chantmarle was not overly large, and he saw little point in forcing his tenants to hand over the bulk of their earnings. As long as they covered the costs of the land, new tools, and the employment of his steward, Samuel asked for no more. And he had never wanted for anything.

Lulu? She had wanted for everything. No family, no friends to turn to. No option but to offer her body to any man who would pay for the privilege.

And anger, true anger rose. Not at Lulu—heaven forbid! But at the world. It had let her down, allowed her to go unnoticed and to go without breakfast!

"Well, that changes now," Samuel said firmly, pushing aside his bitterness and concentrating on what he could do about the here and now.

Lulu glanced over to the sideboard to the number of platters lined up there. "And breakfast is . . . ?"

"Ah, let me show you!" Rising from his seat once again, Samuel strode over to the sideboard. "Right, let's see, under here we have—Christ in his heaven, that's hot!"

He dropped the lid of the salver with a clatter and immediately brought his fingers to his mouth. The scalding heat only slightly dissipated as he sucked on them.

Lulu shook her head ruefully. "Some servant you are."

"How on earth do the blighters—ah, they wear gloves, of course," said Samuel, half to himself. "Bother."

"Use a napkin," suggested Lulu with just a hint of teasing in her voice. "I'd hate for the fingers of Duke of Chantmarle to be burnt just for the sake of my breakfast."

Shooting her a look which only made her smile more—and Samuel's stomach lurch—he did as he was bid. Picking up a napkin from the table, he returned to the sideboard and this time far more successfully lifted the lid of the first salver.

"Right, fine, here we are. Smoked kippers in this one, and," he moved along the sideboard, "smoked herring here."

"Smoked herring? For breakfast?"

"Very good for you, apparently," Samuel said with a shrug. "Besides, I think smoked herring has been served for breakfast for the Duke of Chantmarle forever."

Lulu stared. "For—Forever?"

Samuel grinned. "As long as I can remember. My father hated them, I recall, but always served them because his father, who hated all fish, served them. Why he did—"

"And so you eat smoked herring for breakfast every day because it has always been served to the Duke of Chantmarle?" Lulu said in wonder.

Samuel shook his head, a twist of uncertainty curling around his heart. "Well . . . no."

Now he came to think about it, it was rather odd. Why did they continue doing it?

His new wife was looking at him as though he was speaking another language. "Well if you don't eat it, who does?"

"Blessed if I know," said Samuel helplessly, feeling foolish. "I never have. Hate the stuff."

For a moment, Lulu stared. Then she burst into peals of laughter. "You are jesting!"

"I . . . well, I am sorry to say that I'm not," said Samuel, dazed at the realization.

Three generations of Dellamores, each Duke of Chantmarle following the other . . . and he had no idea why they did it. Smoked herring for breakfast!

"I hope the servants eat it up," said Lulu with a shake of her head.

Now that was likely, Samuel thought privately. "It's a tradition, I suppose. So, we have scrambled eggs, poached eggs, bacon, potato, chicken—"

"Chicken?"

"You know, I have never thought about these things before," Samuel said, in a mock haughty voice. "And I don't intend to now! Would you like some breakfast or not?"

"Toast please, Your Grace," said Lulu with a mischievous look in her eye. "And two smoked herring."

Samuel almost dropped the salver lid. "Smoked—"

"Just because you don't like it, doesn't mean I don't," she pointed out, lifting the teapot and pouring herself a cup. "Goodness, I'm starving. Smoked herring? Just the thing."

There was so much he had to learn, Samuel thought ruefully. Not only about being a servant—he had dropped the first smoked herring on the floor and had to scoop it up with what looked like a soup ladle, but Lulu laughingly informed him was a poached egg spoon.

No, he had so much to learn about Lulu. About who she was, her likes and dislikes.

It was strange. On the one hand he felt he knew her intimately. Not just her body, though that was something he was very happy to explore on a daily basis. But her. Everything she was.

"You don't know anything about being a servant, do you?" smiled Lulu as Samuel eventually sat, exhausted, opposite her.

Her toast and smoked herring were almost half gone. It had only taken him a few minutes to pile his own plate with bacon, eggs, and tomatoes. The woman truly was starving. Now he came to think about it, apart from the wedding breakfast, had Lulu even eaten yesterday?

"I make a rather rudimentary servant, that is true," he confessed with a laugh. "But then I doubt you would be much better!"

Samuel had intended it to be a quip, but he was startled to see Lulu shoot him a grin.

"Oh, I don't know," she said nonchalantly. "I was once a lady's maid."

It was a good thing he had just placed his teacup back in its saucer, or Samuel would have been liable to spill it over the white linen tablecloth.

"You—you were—why did I not know that?" he spluttered.

Lulu met his gaze across the breakfast table and raised an elegant eyebrow. "We agreed no *new* secrets, did we not? Still, there are a few old ones, I suppose, that I would be willing to share."

Affection suffused Samuel's heart. Of all women he could have been caught kissing by Lady Romeril . . . and it was her. Dear God, he was the luckiest man alive.

CHAPTER SIXTEEN

5 May 1811

LULU HUMMED TO herself as she perused the plate before her.

She really should not get too accustomed to this. Not that there was anything wrong about sitting in a duke's drawing room—her drawing room. Or having elevenses by herself, spring sunshine pouring through the windows. Or eating a huge amount of cake—

Fine, perhaps the cake was excessive. But Lulu had never met a woman like Mrs. Winder, the housekeeper, for baking.

"Really, Mrs. Winder, you must stop!" Lulu said with a smile at luncheon. At least Samuel was with her now, though he planned to go out soon and meet someone of his Edinburgh acquaintance. "You will force me to let out all my gowns, and—"

"Oh, we couldn't have that, Yer Grace!" the housekeeper said in shocked astonishment.

Lulu sighed with relief. The cakes the housekeeper—her house-keeper—kept supplying were absolutely delicious, so moreish she was having difficulty leaving any on the plate for the footmen to clear up at four o'clock each afternoon.

"Oh, we couldn't have you letting your own gowns out," Mrs. Winder continued, scandalized. "You're a duchess! You're the Duchess of Chantmarle—we have a maid for that!"

All too late, Lulu realized the outrage Mrs. Winder was obviously feeling was nothing to do with baking, and everything to do with needlework.

"Ah," she said helplessly. "But—"

"No wife of mine is having her gowns altered because of cake," Samuel said firmly, rising from his seat and bestowing a kiss upon her forehead.

Lulu relaxed. *At least Samuel understood—*

"No, send her to the modiste," he said cheerfully as he reached the door. "Tell her the Duchess of Chantmarle can have whatever she likes."

Lulu's stomach turned. "Have whatever I—"

"Yes, we must ensure you keep yourself in the manner of your dignity, Yer Grace," Mrs. Winder said in a half maternal, half reproving tone. "We can't have Society saying—well."

The housekeeper's cheeks pinked as Samuel left the room. Lulu looked at her hands.

It wasn't rare that she was reminded just how unusual she was. A duchess, and with not a drop of blue blood in her veins! Lulu could hardly imagine what people in Edinburgh were saying. And farther afield—the news of their marriage must have reached London by now.

Lulu shivered. *The very thought of what those scandal sheets could contain!*

"I'll have the afternoon tea spread for you in the drawing room at three o'clock as usual," Mrs. Winder said, attempting to smooth over the awkward moment. "Is there anything else, Yer Grace?"

Not for the first time, Lulu had to remind herself the woman being referred to as "Your Grace" was not some other lady in the room . . . but herself.

"No, thank you," she said softly. "Three o'clock. Excellent."

The strange thing was, Lulu was finding it rather challenging to fill her time. It was only an hour and a half from the end of luncheon to the beginning of afternoon tea. Though Lulu was loath to ever complain about a plentitude of food—not something she had been accustomed to these last few years—it did make things rather awkward.

The most awkward thing, of course, was that she did not seem to be able to conduct her day in the manner she would wish. "Where are you going, Your Grace?" was such a common phrase in her hearing now, Lulu was starting to despair that she might never be permitted to leave the house by herself. No matter which servant asked, politely if a footman or maid, sternly if Fitzhugh the butler, Lulu had to smile weakly and say the only thing she could. "Oh, nowhere."

Nowhere. It was true: she could go absolutely nowhere without, it appeared, an escort!

"But it's perfectly common," Samuel had said fairly only last night, as Lulu had attempted to explain this particular frustration to her husband. "You're a duchess! We can't have you gallivanting all over Edinburgh on your own!"

"But I gallivanted all over Edinburgh on my own but six days ago," Lulu had tried to point out. "It is not as though I am another person—I know my way about perfectly well!"

"It is not a case of navigation, it is a situation of safety," Samuel had said darkly.

Lulu had flushed. *Was it possible he had guessed?*

She was sure Mr. Gregory and Mr. Gillingham were absolutely furious she had managed to slip their clutches. Why, their blackmail was hardly going to work now, was it? No one would believe such terrible things of the new Duchess of Chantmarle or her family.

No, she was free. Free for the first time in years.

But she was determined to give them the last and final payment. She had been attempting it the very first time she had seen Samuel, and she must do it still. She had to close that door to that part of her life.

"Being a duchess, you could be kidnapped and held to ransom," her husband had continued seriously. "No, I am sorry, Lulu. I can't have you wandering about the place, liable to be snatched at any opportunity."

Lulu sighed as she sat in the drawing room the next afternoon and cut herself another slice of cake. *Well, why not?* It was delicious, and she had nothing else to do.

Besides, Samuel had made it perfectly clear she could be any size, any shape, and he would still wish to rip her gowns from her.

A slow smile crept across her lips. Perhaps she would go to the modiste after all. In the few days they had been married, Samuel had managed to destroy two perfectly good gowns. Not that she was complaining.

A noise in the hallway made Lulu look up. There was only one person in this house who walked like that—bold strides that echoed loudly even if he wasn't wearing boots. Only one person in the world.

"Samuel Dellamore, come in here this instant!" Lulu called out with mock severity.

Samuel poked his head round the door, forehead puckered with concern. "Anything amiss?"

"Greatly," Lulu said gravely.

He stepped into the room swiftly. "Dear God, what is it? You are unwell—you are sick. You have received bad news. Mrs. Winder—"

"I am in desperate need of assistance with demolishing this cake," said Lulu airily, gesturing to the mound of chocolate cake which already had two slices cut out of it. "Or I fear Mrs. Winder may serve it to me for breakfast along with my smoked herring."

Samuel snorted as he dropped onto the sofa opposite her plush armchair. "Not a chance! Though my valet warns me that many more afternoon teas with you, and he shall have to remove a tuck to my breeches."

"A true disaster," said Lulu conversationally, cutting him a slice of the cake, which he accepted. "It's a good thing I am so in love with you that I couldn't care less how many tucks need to be removed."

Her heart skipped a beat as Samuel grinned and met her eye.

How was it possible? To meet a man and know, without a shadow of a doubt, he was a good man? To be certain he would never harm her, forsake her, offend her, or rebuke her? To feel safe, for the first time in years, in the presence of another?

Lulu could not understand it—but then, perhaps she did not need to. Perhaps just being with Samuel was enough.

He was munching quite happily on Mrs. Winder's cake. "So, how is the day of the Duchess of Chantmarle going?"

Lulu groaned as she placed her plate on the console table beside her. The console table that was probably worth more than all the money she had ever possessed. Put together.

"I wish you wouldn't call me that," she said.

"What, the Duchess of—"

"You used to just call me Lulu," she pointed out. "A perfectly serviceable name."

"I suppose it is," said Samuel, still grinning. "But you are a duchess."

"And you're a duke," Lulu retorted, her smile utterly irrepressible. "So should I be calling you the Duke of Chantmarle every—"

"Oh Lord, no," he replied as she laughed. "No, I take your point. Fine. How has your day been going, Lulu?"

A smile was enough for now, Lulu could see, as Samuel tucked into his delicious chocolate cake. But it would not be sufficient for long. How could she convince or cajole her husband to permit her to leave the place without multiple servants accompanying her?

Beyond the fact that it was most strange to be never alone, Lulu knew she had to see Mr. Gillingham and Mr. Gregory soon. They would not wait forever. Heaven forbid they take it into their heads to come to the house!

Lulu's stomach twisted painfully as ice slid into her heart.

No, that would never do. She had worked hard to keep that part of her life completely separate from Samuel. He wouldn't understand—or perhaps he would. Maybe one day, she would feel safe enough to explain it to him.

But only when it was over. And it wasn't quite over yet.

"My day has been strangely monotonous," Lulu said aloud. "Or I suppose, not strangely. I shouldn't expect anything less, when forbidden from leaving without—"

Samuel groaned. "Not this again!"

"When are you going to learn that you married a woman, not a porcelain figure?" Lulu said, trying to inject mischievousness in her voice. *If she could only make him see.* "I don't want to spend my life cooped up here!"

"Then go out, take one of the maids with you," Samuel retorted, finishing his cake. "I really must congratulate Mrs. Winder, that was—"

"But you go out without a chaperone," Lulu pointed out.

He snorted at that. "Of course I do! I'm—"

"A man."

Samuel frowned. "A duke. Nothing is going to happen to me."

Lulu swallowed. *Nothing, if she could help it.* Would Mr. Gregory and Mr. Gillingham be foolish enough to attempt something on the life of the man she loved, merely because she was no longer willing to be their little pawn?

Perhaps. Perhaps not.

The fact she did not know was more than sufficient grounds to be determined in getting their final payment to them.

"I am afraid you are going to have far too much to do here, at any rate."

Lulu blinked. *Now that was a nonsense.* "To do here? What on earth could I—"

"You are the new Duchess of Chantmarle, and half of Edinburgh is desperate to meet you," said her husband with a wicked glint in his eye. "Are you ready to face Society?"

Now that was a challenge she had not considered. Lulu sank back in her armchair, both astonished and appalled at the suggestion. "What—you mean, host afternoon tea?"

"Afternoon tea, luncheons, dinners, card parties, music recitals—the lot," said Samuel happily. "You know, I think I'll have a second slice of cake—awfully good, isn't it?"

Lulu did not respond.

Afternoon tea, luncheons, dinners, card parties, music recitals? Surely he was joking. Samuel could not expect her to do so much, host so much, when she was still learning how to permit a footman to place a napkin on her lap? Resisting the urge to push the man's hands away and issue him a sharp slap had been rather difficult.

Lulu knew, deep within her soul, that she could not be expected to be a hostess, in the grandest sense of the word. *Could she?*

"Now hang on a minute," Lulu said firmly as the door to the drawing room opened and Fitzhugh stepped in. "You cannot think I can—"

"Your letters from the afternoon post, Your Grace," interrupted the butler firmly, holding out a silver platter to Samuel upon which lay three letters.

Lulu worked hard to keep her face impassive.

It was because the old man was unaccustomed to change, Samuel had told her. That was why he frequently acted as though she were not there.

"Oh, thank you, Fitzhugh," Samuel said carelessly. "You were saying, Lulu?"

Lulu almost smiled at the grimace that passed across the butler's face. Still, her husband supported her, even if Fitzhugh did not like it.

"I was *saying*, I cannot think why you believe me suitable to host such things," she continued, as the butler left the drawing room and Samuel lazily looked over the letters in his hands. "I've never hosted so much as a riot before, and—"

"Oh no, we can't have a riot," Samuel said vaguely. He was scanning a letter he had opened, then snorted. "No, Lady Romeril would have a fit."

Lulu tried not to smile, but it was impossible. There was something so endearingly charming about the way Samuel could not bear to wait a single second before reading his letters once they were placed in his hands. The thought that he wouldn't know, even for a minute, who had written to him!

The open letter was cast aside, as was a second. Even after only a few days of being his wife, Lulu recognized the handwriting. "Your steward again?"

"The man thinks it vital I know every breath my horses take, and I tell him again and again I simply do not care," said Samuel with a shrug. "My apologies, I know I'm being rude. I'll just read this last one, then you'll have my full attention."

And with that, he turned the final letter over to crack the seal.

Lulu's heart stopped.

When it started again, it was thumping most erratically, causing pain to shudder through her.

She knew that handwriting. Of course she did, it was the handwriting she had dreaded for almost a year.

Mr. Gregory.

"No idea who would be sending me a letter in the afternoon penny post," Samuel was saying airily as he started to unfold the letter.

Everything appeared to be slowing down. Lulu couldn't understand it, but it was taking an age for him to open the letter, yet the additional time did not seem to be giving her any more opportunity to think of a solution.

That Samuel must not be permitted to read whatever Mr. Gregory had written in that letter was beyond doubt. The icy grip around her heart told her that much.

But how she was supposed to stop him, Lulu did not know.

That was perhaps why her instinct overrode all sense.

She grabbed it.

Just in time, Samuel flicked it away. "Now just what do you think you're doing?"

In someone else's mouth, the words might have been a reproof, but Lulu saw to her horror that Samuel was laughing. *Did he think this some sort of game?*

"It's meant for me," she said, her mouth dry. "Honestly, Samuel, I—"

"It says the Duke of Chantmarle on the front, not the Duchess," Samuel said, holding it just out of her reach and chuckling. "Lulu!"

But it was no game. Dark, bitter panic was rising. If Mr. Gregory had written to Samuel, there was nothing positive in that letter. It would only bring her ruin, and pain, and Samuel too.

She had to get that letter.

"Please, Samuel, I—"

"Let me read, then we can discuss how many soirees you will host before we return to London," said Samuel with a grin, pushing aside her hand and lifting the letter to his eyes.

"I'm begging you Samuel—"

But it was too late. Lulu knew it, the moment his name had once again left her mouth. Samuel's gaze had sharpened on the letter before him, his eyes scanning across it, and there was such a look of horror draining into his face that she knew it was too late.

"You . . ." Samuel breathed.

Lulu closed her eyes, just for a moment, as though that could stop what was happening—but it was no use.

"You—is this true?" he demanded, flinging the letter at her.

Lulu clutched at it with trembling hands and read the few lines Mr. Gregory had penned in an untidy scrawl.

It was not pleasant reading.

Your Grace,

I am sorry to inform you that the woman you have taken to wife is a spy—a traitor, in fact. She has been passing secrets from the military barracks at Edinburgh Castle to an informant. Information which has been to the great detriment of the British Army.

Sorry to bring you such dire news—

A friend

A friend indeed. Neither Mr. Gregory nor Mr. Gillingham could ever be described as—

"I said, is this true?" came Samuel's firm voice.

Lulu swallowed as she dropped the letter into her lap and looked up at her husband. The man she loved. The man she trusted, and who had trusted her.

A man whose trust she had evidently somehow betrayed.

"Y-Yes," she said, hating her voice's quiver. She stuck out her chin. "And I did it because—"

"I don't care why you did it, the fact is that you—dear God, this whole time, you were right under my nose!" Samuel exploded, rising from his seat and pacing to the fireplace.

Lulu's heart cracked as she saw how unwilling he was to look at her. Yes, it was a betrayal of her country—but she'd had no choice. And besides, it had occurred months before she had ever met Samuel. Why should he care so much about—

"I've been such a fool," muttered Samuel, leaning against the mantlepiece and hanging his head in abject grief.

Lulu rose, hardly knowing what she was doing but certain if she was close to him, she could make him see. "I didn't want to do it! They—"

"But you did it," snapped Samuel, turning to her with such a glower, Lulu stepped back. "You did it, didn't you? Passed secrets from our army, our country, into French hands? Didn't you?"

His last two words were spoken with such pain, such finality, Lulu did not know how she still managed to stand. "Yes," she breathed.

Samuel groaned, turning away once more—and it was that inability to look at her that cut so deeply into Lulu's heart. She had never betrayed anyone before. She had always protected those she loved—indeed, she had only done this because of love!

Perhaps that would help him understand—maybe then, Samuel would see.

"I thought you were a courtesan!"

Lulu blinked. Oh, of course. Why had she ever let that misunderstanding continue? It was just lie upon lie, that was what she had created.

Samuel's face was pale. "You . . . you weren't, were you?"

She swallowed, hating that she could disappoint him so many times over in just a few minutes. "N-No, I have never been a courtesan. I let you believe that because the truth—"

"So . . . so our wedding night . . ." It appeared Samuel could not even finish his sentence.

Shame rushed through her. "It was my first time. And oh, Samuel, it was wonderful—"

"God in his Heaven—do I know you at all?" said Samuel to the wall. "I don't know a thing about you—despite all my curiosity, you were lying every—"

"I wasn't lying! I never said—you assumed—"

"And you're a traitor," he said dully. "A traitor to everything I believe in. Everything I stand for."

"I did it because—"

"I don't want to hear it," Samuel said dully, not turning around.

Something akin to righteous anger bubbled in Lulu's veins. *How dare he?* Did she not have the right to defend herself?

"My brother was caught in—caught with . . ." Lulu swallowed. "Well, let's just say that the person he was caught kissing furiously in an alley was not someone he could swiftly marry to calm the scandal."

The words rang out in the drawing room. Slowly, almost imperceptibly, her husband turned toward her. "He . . . he was—"

"He wrote me a letter," Lulu said, pushing forward despite the pain, desperate to catch Samuel's eye. "A letter that was intercepted, and two months before he died—"

"You never told me you had a brother," said Samuel slowly.

Lulu tossed her head with impatience. *That was the part he was dwelling on?* "The letter was found, and I have been blackmailed ever since. The scandal—if the news were to get out, my brother's name would be sullied forever!"

Samuel was staring with blank eyes. "But he's dead—your brother, I mean. There is no name to sully."

"I made the agreement with Mr. Gregory and Mr. Gillingham before Malcolm died," Lulu said wretchedly. If she had known her brother would soon succumb to sickness, would she have—no, she could not torture herself by wondering. "I thought, a few letters, what harm could it do?"

For a moment, Samuel had appeared to be softening to her, but his gaze hardened. "You do not know the damage you have done," he said with a clenched jaw. "The efforts I have gone to, all to find—"

"Efforts you have . . ." Lulu breathed, and then she saw. *Of course. It was all so ridiculous.* "You came to Edinburgh to look . . . to look for the person—"

"For the traitor, yes," said Samuel heavily. "Oh God. And I married her."

CHAPTER SEVENTEEN

S AMUEL LOOKED DULLY out across his study.

Well. It had come to this.

What a fool he was. What an idiot. What a blind dullard he was—truly, after all the "pretending" he had done for so many years to lull others into a false sense of security. But he had only fooled himself. Convinced himself he was a judge of character, when in fact . . .

"I made the agreement with Mr. Gregory and Mr. Gillingham before Malcolm died. I thought, a few letters, what harm could it do?"

Samuel sighed heavily and dropped his head into his hands. It ached painfully, throbbing temples mingling with a harsh tightness across his brow.

"Can I get you anything, Your Grace?"

Samuel did not even look up. He did not need to. He knew that voice well enough to recognize it without looking Fitzhugh in the face, and he knew the butler would not be offended by his lack of civility.

"No," he said dully. "Just peace and quiet."

The butler cleared his throat. "That woman—"

Samuel's heart constricted. "The duchess."

He owed her that, at least. No matter how idiotic he had been, he had been well and truly taken in, and he needed to accept that. Lulu would have the title of the Duchess of Chantmarle for the rest of her life.

Even if she would not share that life with him.

Fitzhugh coughed. Even without looking up, it was clear the cough was derogatory. "Indeed. The duchess, as you say, is upstairs. In a *guest* bedchamber. She instructed Mrs. Winder to make up the bed, and I saw no reason to prevent it."

Samuel nodded, stomach twisting painfully. She was an intelligent woman. Lulu must have known, after their blazing row in the drawing room hours ago, that the last thing he would wish was to share a bed.

Besides, it was hardly unusual for people of their caliber. In fact, now he thought about it, he wasn't sure his parents had ever shared a bedchamber. They had always had their own, one beside the other. Perhaps they knew more about marriage than he had ever credited them.

"Fine," Samuel said listlessly.

"She has given instruction that her dinner is to be taken up to her."

Samuel snorted. Well, perhaps he was seeing more of Lulu's true personality, now that the truth was out.

Food. It was always about food. No wonder she had thought to seduce him; after going hungry for so much of her life, he was the very tangible offer of a goldmine. Was that all it was, for her? The opportunity to live well and in relative comfort for the rest of her life? People had married for less.

"And she has also ordered," continued the butler, sniffing at his last word. "Ordered, mark you, that no one is to disturb her."

"Fine," Samuel repeated. There was no energy in his words, no fire in his chest. All had been expulsed in his argument with Lulu that afternoon.

To think, a man could walk into his own drawing room and expect nothing save an innocent slice of cake and be faced with that.

She has been passing secrets from the military barracks at Edinburgh Castle to an informant.

Samuel sighed heavily. "That will be all, Fitzhugh."

"But—"

"I said that will be all, damn it!" He had not intended to speak so harshly. It was frustration with Lulu, with the whole damned situation, that poured from his mouth.

But it wasn't the butler's fault.

Samuel looked up. "Fitzhugh—"

The study was empty. He had not even noticed the door closing—now that was a sign of an impressive butler.

Samuel leaned back in his chair and allowed the loathing he had been attempting to keep at bay overwhelm him. The trouble was, try as he might, he couldn't loathe Lulu.

If even half her story was true, she had been faced with a difficult situation. Though she had not gone into the details, Samuel was not ignorant enough of the ways of the world to guess what she had meant.

"Well, let's just say that the person he was caught kissing furiously in an alley was not someone he could swiftly marry to calm the scandal."

Her brother had been kissing a man, and the scandal which would have rushed through Edinburgh would indeed have been the end of their good name. The name of Finch would have been destroyed. And so instead, she had decided to ruin the name of Chantmarle.

But how could he have been so reckless in his actions?

Samuel stared, unseeing, across his study to the opposite wall, where a bookcase kept all the dukedom's accounts from the last century.

That was the trouble, wasn't it? It wasn't as though Lulu had sought him out, hunted him down, attempted to ensure she caught him. No, it was his fault. All him. His ruddy curiosity, his inability to leave a mystery unsolved. That was what had brought him here. If he'd just listened to her, the first time they had met . . .

"I'm warning you. It's not a good idea to get too close to me."

"I wouldn't say that. In fact, I am rather enjoying it."

Samuel sighed. Yes, it was his own curiosity which had brought him here. Now he was married to a liar.

Worse than a liar. A traitor!

He winced. He would have to write to Judge Smee at some point. The man would be delighted to hear the Duke of Chantmarle had discovered the breach. Samuel would have to consider just how he would manage to explain the complex situation without revealing it was the duchess herself who was the miscreant.

A door slammed somewhere below. Samuel hardly heard it. His mind was spinning.

He had come to Edinburgh unencumbered with wife, excited, ready to hunt the traitor. And where was he now? Married to the very woman who was destroying everything he had worked toward.

Well, Samuel thought, *there was nothing for it.* Judge Smee was waiting for his report, and there was no putting it off.

Pulling a piece of paper toward him, he carefully dipped a pen in the inkwell as rapid footsteps echoed down the corridor, along with a voice that was most irate.

"—simply cannot barge in here and—"

The door to the study burst open.

For a moment, just a moment, Samuel thought—hoped—it would be Lulu. That she had an explanation, that it was all a misunderstanding. That she was covering for someone. That she had nothing to do with it at all.

As pleasing and unlikely as that would be, however, it was not Lulu standing in the doorway, out of breath and studiously ignoring the berating of his butler.

It wasn't even a woman.

"Vaughn!" said Samuel, genuinely amazed. "What the devil are—"

"A doctor," said Daniel Vaughn, breathing heavily and pushing his dark hair from his eyes. "I came as quickly as I could, I didn't know anyone else in this godforsaken town to ask. I need a doctor, one who can be trusted."

Samuel stared, utterly dumbfounded.

What on earth was the younger brother of the Duke of Thornfalcone doing here? Not here in his study, or even his home, but in Edinburgh. Weren't the two brothers—

"Chantmarle?" Vaughn stepped into the room, still ignoring the butler's protestations.

"—His Grace's private study, you were clearly not invited—"

"Please, Chantmarle, I am begging you—just a recommendation, I can pay the bill myself," said Vaughn desperately. Mud spattered his heels and breeches. Water dripped from his shoulders. He had run through the rain. "A doctor, man!"

Samuel shook his head as though ridding water from his own ears. "A doctor."

He truly was the dullard he had thought he was aping, he thought privately. Christ and all his saints, when was he going to wake up?

"Fitzhugh, send for Doctor Harford," Samuel said hastily. "And for Doctor Walsingham, if he is in town. The last I heard he was still in London caring for—"

"Oh, I would not dare to hope Doctor Walsingham could be in Edinburgh," said Vaughn faintly. "But this other man, this Doctor Harford, you trust him?"

"With my life," said Samuel with a shrug. His shrug faded as he saw the look on his friend's face. "By Jove, it's as serious as all that?"

"Please send for Doctor Harford at once, to the Thornfalcone residence, and tell him he will be rewarded most handsomely," said Vaughn to the butler. "Swiftly, man!"

Though evidently unappreciative of being spoken to in such a way, Samuel could see his butler was conscious of the sense of urgency in the man's voice. This was no time to quibble about niceties.

"At once, sir, Your Grace," said Fitzhugh with a bow of his head.

And then he was gone.

Samuel watched with horror as Vaughn, his duty seemingly done, seemed to waver on his feet. The man slid against the bookcase, eyes closed.

"Christ alive man!"

Rushing forward, Samuel helped his old friend into the chair on the other side of his desk. Fortunately, his father had been rather a reprobate. The hidden drinks cabinet in the other bookcase was kept well stocked thanks to Fitzhugh's love of tradition. Samuel had never needed to plumb its depths before—*though*, he thought wryly as he poured a large measure of brandy into a glass then repeated the action with another, *he had never needed it before.*

Pushing a glass into his friend's hand, Samuel tried to smile. "Buck up there, old thing. Get that down you. It'll help."

For a moment, he thought Vaughn too exhausted by whatever ordeal he had undergone to even lift the glass. But with his eyes half open and bleary, the man then raised it to his lips and drank half his glass at once.

It was good stuff. Samuel's eyes nearly watered as he sipped at his own glass, sitting heavily in his own seat and looking at the man before him.

He was the younger brother of the Duke of Thornfalcone and one of the few younger brothers of dukes in the land who did not have a title of his own. Both Daniel and his brother, David, had explained it to him once but he hadn't truly understood it. His own brother was an earl, as were most younger brothers.

But a title would not aid Vaughn in whatever he had been battling, as far as Samuel could see.

"Well, I know the doctor isn't for you, or you would have request-ed he be brought here," said Samuel, trying to inject jollity into his voice. He had never felt less jolly. "What's the problem?"

He tried not to think of Lulu as he spoke. Lulu, upstairs and alone. Lulu, under him as she called his name, her eyelashes fluttering as he pleasured her. Lulu, betraying the country . . .

"It's for my brother," said Vaughn heavily. "God save him."

Samuel swallowed. *Well, there was always someone to remind you that perhaps the battle you were facing was not the worst in the world.*

"You believe his life to be in danger?"

"Yes—no. I don't know," Vaughn sighed. "Can a man be healed once he has passed the point of saving? Once his morals have led him to such sickness . . ."

Samuel was no medical man. He had attempted to sit in on a medical lecture once while at university. The stench of the lecture hall itself had been enough to force him away.

But there appeared to be more here than met the eye. Vaughn looked exhausted, as though he had been carrying a great burden for a long time.

The rumors were true, then.

"He is near the end?" Samuel said quietly. "The pox?"

Vaughn winced. "I try not to speak of it."

"Of course, naturally, I just—"

"But it is no great secret," Vaughn continued heavily. "If he does die, if this Doctor Harford of yours is unable to save him . . ."

His voice trailed away, and he lifted the brandy glass which, Samuel saw, was already nearly empty.

That was something he could not have predicted. The Duke of Thornfalcone was a towering personality, a man the likes of which the *ton* had never seen before, and thankfully would never see again.

The idea that he could soon be gone, his brother taking his place . . .

"If you wish to talk about it," Samuel said awkwardly. *Blast it, this wasn't what gentlemen did, but it couldn't be plainer that the man was in pain.* "I am not a great conversationalist, but I have a willing ear."

Vaughn smiled ruefully. "I wouldn't wish to impose, old chap. After all, it's not your problem. I am sure you have enough of your own."

It was on the tip of his tongue to respond that he certainly did, but

Samuel managed to keep the comment within. What good could come from spilling out that secret to another? No, this was a private shame. One which no one else would have to suffer, if he had anything to do with it.

"Besides, you're a newlywed! I was honored to be invited to the wedding, I am just sorry my brother and I could not attend," added Vaughn with a bracing smile. "I hear only good things about that wife of yours. Shouldn't you be with her, enjoying the . . . the fruits of tender affection?"

The man meant well. Samuel knew Daniel Vaughn was not one to enjoy the pain of another. The poor thing had no idea.

Yet that did not halt the agonizing pain from seeping through him.

Yes, he should be with his wife. They should be happy together, enjoying these early days of marriage in which everything was good, and all they could do was discover new pleasantries and share new pleasures.

And here he was, wondering how on earth to write to his friend in London that his wife was a traitor—*the very traitor he had been sent to find!*—while sitting with a man whose brother appeared to be dying.

Not the honeymoon he had expected.

"Chantmarle?"

"I beg your pardon?" Samuel said, blinking. The study before him came back into view, along with his friend. "I do apologize, I was just thinking of—"

"Please, do not apologize for losing yourself in thoughts of your wife," said Vaughn with a bracing smile. "That's as it should be."

Samuel hesitated, but he had to tell someone. He could not bear this weight, this burden upon him. He could not tramp upstairs to the ducal bedchamber, empty of the beautiful bride who had filled it every night since they were married.

And Vaughn was a good sort. They'd known each other since they were boys. *And besides,* Samuel tried to convince himself, *the man would be a duke soon, by all accounts.* If there could not be secrets and honor between dukes, what hope was there?

"I need to tell you something," Samuel blurted out.

Vaughn frowned. "Something?"

Samuel sighed, and wished to goodness he had nothing but good secrets. That was the lot of a man who served the Crown of course, but no secret had ever cut so close to home.

"Something," he conceded. "Something terrible."

Vaughn's eyes widened. "Heaven help us—what on earth—"

"It's Lulu—I mean, Lucy," Samuel corrected hastily. "My wife."

A shadow swiftly rushed across his friend's face and his heart sank. Dear God, was it possible . . . was it possible Vaughn already knew? That he, Samuel, had been the only man in Edinburgh not to know?

"I thought you may wish to talk to someone about this," said Vaughn awkwardly. "I'm not sure I am the best one, of course, not being a married man—"

"What has marriage got to do with treachery?" Samuel said helplessly.

He threw back his glass and finished his brandy, its scalding heat burning his throat and preventing tears from prickling in the corners of his eyes. How would he ever look the world in the face again?

"Treachery?" Vaughn stared. "I wouldn't call defending her brother's honor treachery."

Samuel stared. *What on earth . . .* "What the devil do you mean?"

It did not seem possible that Vaughn, of all people, should be aware of the truth of Lulu's betrayal. The Vaughn brothers weren't even supposed to be in Edinburgh, as far as he had known! The last Samuel had heard, they were for Brighton. So how—

"Look, it's an open secret, you understand?" Vaughn said awkwardly. "Most of Edinburgh Society know it, even if we don't speak of it."

Samuel's mouth fell open. How was it possible he had been in

Edinburgh for weeks, and never heard about this? Why had no one warned him?

"You cannot be serious," he said slowly.

Vaughn shifted uncomfortably in his chair. "Look, it was a long time ago—and the poor man hadn't hurt anyone, had he? To be honest, I don't see the problem. Two people, two adults of course, who consent to—"

The man wasn't making any sense. Samuel stared, utterly befuddled. Perhaps he'd had more brandy than he thought.

"What are you talking about?" he said, interrupting Vaughn's words.

The man frowned. "Why, Miss Finch's brother—I do apologize, the duchess's brother. It's well known, even if no one speaks of it out of respect to Miss Finch, that he was caught . . . even I know that, and I only heard last spring when I was visiting a relative. You mean you did not know?"

Samuel laughed darkly. "No, but strangely enough, that wasn't what I was referring to. No, I was thinking more of the military secrets she's been sharing with the French."

Vaughn dropped his glass. It shattered on the hardwood floor. "Christ, I beg your—"

It took but five minutes to clear up the glass as best they could, but an additional ten to fully explain the story.

Samuel sighed as he leaned back. "So there you have it. My wife is a traitor."

"Is she?"

Vaughn was frowning, as though he had been presented with a complex puzzle.

"What the devil do you mean, is she?" snapped Samuel, pushed beyond all endurance. "The woman—"

"Is not a traitor, at least not in my book," Vaughn said slowly. "No, hear me out. She had no wish to share this information, she was blackmailed, wasn't she?"

Samuel scowled. "So she says. Over a brother."

"I've confirmed that part of her story," said Vaughn fairly, as though he was sufficient.

Stomach twisting, Samuel nodded briefly. He could not even bear to say aloud that his friend was right. Because if he was—

"It sounds to me like the duchess didn't think much harm would come from passing on those messages," continued Vaughn, irritatingly calm. "Alone, no one to turn to . . ."

His voice trailed off as he met Samuel's eye, who had been carefully avoiding him for a full minute.

Oh, blast. It all sounded so reasonable, when put like that.

"You think . . . you think I should forgive her?" Samuel asked stupidly.

Vaughn sighed heavily. "I'm not sure. I suppose the first question you have to answer is, has she done anything tangible to offend you?"

CHAPTER EIGHTEEN

6 May 1811

L ULU KEPT HER voice as steady as she could make it. "I must say, I appreciate you seeing me at such short notice, Mr. Finlay."

The man shuffled papers on his desk with a sickly smile. "Not at all, Your Grace. Not at all."

Smiling at a man who did not deserve it had never been something Lulu had struggled with. All women could do it. It was a certain twist of the lips, a forcing in the eyes, the need to make the man before you truly believe that you were happy to see him. It had never failed her.

Never until now had it been so awfully difficult.

But Lulu tried. She really did, despite the fatigue in her shoulders, the angry throbbing in her head which had not let up since she'd lifted her it from her pillow that morning. That she had not slept probably did not help.

"Thank you, Mr. Finlay," she said aloud, injecting as much warmth into the words as possible. "That is most kind."

The trouble was, it was kind. That was why it was so frustrating that she sounded so insincere.

The office she was sitting in was large, airy, and bright. The wide bay windows allowed sunlight to stream through onto the little cluster of chairs and sofas arranged around a magnificent golden yellow rug, and just to the side was a desk flanked with two large cabinets.

Lulu had been impressed—but then, the recommendation had come from Fitzhugh, the butler, who she was sure would want to send her to someone who knew his business well. Fitzhugh's direction to her that morning had been very precise.

"You leave here—you are leaving here, aren't you? Excellent, so take a left from the front door, straight along the road until you reach Marchant Street, then turn right. A second left takes you onto Union Street, and you'll see the sign on your right."

"I'm not usually—I mean, His Grace likes me to be accompanied whenever I—"

"I shall see to that. Just go."

She'd been worried she would struggle to find the lawyer's office, but it was hard to miss. Lulu wasn't sure whether the Finlays had something in particular to prove, but the large gilt bronze sign outside the office proudly proclaimed: *Finlay, Finlay, Finlay, and Sons Ltd.*

Lulu had blinked, almost dazzled by the reflection of the sun.

Goodness, they were so important that there were three of them?

She had been ushered into the office by a flushing footman then by a bowing clerk who looked just as dazzled as she had felt outside. It was only when Lulu had been carefully seated in an armchair in Mr. Finlay's office did she realize, with a sinking heart, why.

"Such an honor to receive a visit from nobility," Mr. Finlay was saying. "If I can be of any assistance, I would be greatly honored . . ."

Of course he would. Lulu's shoulders slumped as she realized just why the bowing, scraping footmen had been so eager that she see Mr. Finlay straight away.

What lawyer in Edinburgh would turn away a duchess for a client?

"—helped many fine people in my time, so I am sure whatever service it is you are looking for, Your Grace, we can help—"

Though it was on the tip of her tongue to ask which one he was, the first, second, or third Finlay emblazoned on the front door of their office, Lulu managed to hold her tongue. Aside from it being far too rude to say aloud, she needed him.

The Finlays were the only ones who could help her now.

"So," said Mr. Finlay, after his long monologue that Lulu had barely heard. "You grace us with your visit today, Your Grace, ahaha, no pun intended, because . . . ?"

His voice trailed off in what he evidently thought was a tactful manner.

Heat scalded Lulu's cheeks as she attempted to collect herself. This needed to be done delicately. She would have to trust, naturally, that the man could be discreet, but even so. She couldn't just come out with it. The last thing she should say was—

"I want a divorce," Lulu blurted out.

It was the wrong thing to say. Mr. Finlay's bushy eyebrows rose so high, they were almost lost in the ridiculous looking legal wig the poor man was wearing. It looked most uncomfortable to Lulu, but nothing like the discomfort he was clearly now feeling.

"Ah," said Mr. Finlay awkwardly.

Lulu's stomach twisted. She probably should not have been so blunt—but what else was there to say?

She could no longer force herself onto Samuel—onto His Grace, the Duke of Chantmarle. That was how she needed to remember him.

Pain shot through her heart, but Lulu did her best to push it away. It was what was best for Samuel. He would see that, one day. Society may deride him, but that would be temporary. It would be nothing to the scandal once they all discovered her true actions.

"D-Divorce?" stammered Mr. Finlay, slowly sitting on the sofa opposite her and wiping his brow with a handkerchief. "Forgive me, Your Grace—"

"Please, don't call me that," said Lulu.

The sooner she grew accustomed to being plain old Miss Finch again, the better.

Mr. Finlay swallowed. Obviously that was a step too far. "Forgive me if I have recalled this inaccurately, but by my reckoning . . . I mean to say, you were only married to the Duke of Chantmarle a week ago."

Lulu tried to smile. "Yes, that's right."

She was banking on that. Such a short time, she had argued in her mind all night long. Surely any lawyer would understand she had made a mistake—a big one—and recognized it swiftly enough. Divorce was not so difficult in that circumstance, was it?

"I suppose then you will actually be wishing for . . . for an annulment," the lawyer managed.

Lulu frowned. "An annulment?"

She had heard the term before but never been entirely sure what it consisted of. Was that a sort of divorce only available to the wealthy and titled?

"Yes, an annulment," the man continued. "It—well, a divorce ends a marriage, but an annulment says in legal terms that the marriage never happened at all."

Lulu's heart skipped a beat. A week ago she would have thought the idea monstrous, but now—now, did she have much choice?

"Well, that sounds like just the thing," she managed to say. "Yes, I would like an annulment, please."

Mr. Finlay cleared his throat. "Goodness, I wish my wife were . . . Your Grace, an annulment can be offered to a couple if the marriage has not been . . . if it wasn't . . ."

Lulu leaned forward, eager to hear the rest of the sentence. If the marriage had not been what?

But it appeared the lawyer found the annulment itself a difficult thing to stomach. Swallowing hard, and perspiring even harder, the man wiped his brow again, then he wrung the handkerchief in his hand.

" . . . if the marriage has not been . . . consummated," he whispered.

Lulu immediately leaned back and tried not to notice just how her cheeks burned.

Not consummated? Oh, bother. The marriage had been consummated, several times.

He tried valiantly to continue. "And if it has—"

"I am afraid it has," said Lulu, flushing furiously. *Oh, if only there were lady lawyers!* Then at least she would be able to talk about this without boiling like a lobster! "Does that mean an annulment—"

"Completely out of the question, I am afraid," Mr. Finlay said, almost in relief that the conversation about an annulment was formally over. "Now, a divorce will be tricky. Scottish laws and English laws, very different. You yourself are English yes, you and your husband—but a Scottish wedding. Unless we can secure a Scottish divorce, it will leave the duke unable to marry directly, you see, and he will need to pay you a pension . . ."

The man droned on as Lulu stared in horror.

Was it truly that difficult? She had always imagined a wealthy man, a noble man, one with such charm and standing in Society could procure a divorce as others bought a horse. With a little money, to be sure, and a little effort. But the idea it would involve so many problems?

It had never occurred to her.

The lawyer was still rattling away. "But if that is what you and the duke decide—"

Lulu swallowed. She couldn't make this decision now, not after discovering the complexity of the thing. She would need to think about it, consider other options to release Samuel from the burden of being married to her.

"I think I will need to consider this further," she said quietly, rising to her feet.

Mr. Finlay rose immediately, relief apparent on his face. "Of course, of course, Your Grace. My door is always open, come for any additional advice at all."

He was very kind, very well meaning, and excruciatingly embarrassed, Lulu could see as Mr. Finlay waved her off at the door. No, she could not return there. Not if she wanted to be able to hold her head high.

The spring air was crisp and bright, the scent of flowers dancing along it. Lulu leaned against the wall and closed her eyes for a minute, trying desperately to think.

She needed to end her connection with Samuel, that was obvious. She had caused him such pain—such agony. The words he had uttered, they rolled around her mind time and time again, inflicting pain with every remembrance.

"You came to Edinburgh to look . . . to look for the person—"

"For the traitor, yes. Oh God. And I married her."

Lulu swallowed and opened her eyes, gripping the reticule her lady's maid had chosen.

There was something she could do—something she had believed impossible before she had been wed, but now the comforting weight of the reticule reminded her that had changed.

She had placed the two pounds she had carefully saved into the reticule days ago, desperate for a chance to leave the house alone, but Mrs. Winder and Samuel combined had made that almost impossible.

Until now.

Lulu tried to smile. Well, the butler may have it in for her, but he had permitted her the first opportunity she'd had to leave Dellamore House without a chaperone. This was her chance to end this blackmail, once and for all.

It was only when she stepped onto Union Street, however, where Mr. Gregory and Mr. Gillingham conducted most of their affairs, that she became suddenly conscious of what she was doing. It would hardly do if someone saw the newly minted Duchess of Chantmarle going to meet such ruffians. The scandal! The outrage would be immediate, and she would have no recourse to defend herself. Samuel would know . . .

Lulu blinked and halted, leaning against a wall as her legs quavered.

No, it wasn't possible. It was a trick of the light. One gentleman looked very much like any other at a distance. It was easy to be mistaken, to see something that wasn't there.

They must use the same tailor, Lulu told herself firmly as she peered across the street at the man who had just stepped out of Mr. Gillingham and Mr. Gregory's residence. That must be the reason for the intense similarity between the man before her and Samuel.

But as the man turned to glance to his left, Lulu's breath caught in her throat.

It was him.

She put out a hand to the cold brick wall beside her but even its cooling effect was insufficient to calm her. Heart beating wildly, stomach lurching, Lulu stared as Mr. Gillingham also emerged from the building and carefully shook Samuel's hand.

Shook Samuel's hand?

Lulu could not understand it. Everything she believed was crumbling around her.

Did Samuel know Gillingham and Gregory? Was that why he had no compunction in approaching her at the Assembly Rooms? But how was he involved with them? The blackguards had no acquaintances, only associates. Only people just as tangled in wrongdoing as them.

An awful thought rushed through her mind that she could not ignore. Was it possible . . . oh God, was it possible Samuel had been involved with them from the very start?

She had to get away.

The thought flashed scarlet in her mind. Lulu knew she had to follow that instinct, and at once. The last thing she needed was to be spotted here by either of them. She had to get away, return—well, not home, for Samuel's residence could never be home. But certainly she must remove herself from this street, where at any moment—

Samuel turned and his gaze locked on hers.

Lulu gasped. Her visceral reaction surprised her, roaring through her veins like wildfire. Pain, and shame, and anger. It was a heady cocktail that would surely end in tears.

But of course, Samuel would not be so foolish as to—

"No," Lulu breathed.

After saying a final short word to Mr. Gillingham, Samuel turned to her and started to cross the road.

What did he think he was doing? What could possibly be gained by—

"You are alone," said Samuel curtly as he reached her.

Lulu swallowed, mouth dry, throat hoarse, and bit down the retort she wished to make. *Yes, I am alone. I have always been alone. Even married to you, I was alone.*

"What was Mrs. Winder thinking, allowing you to—"

"Mrs. Winder is not my keeper," Lulu managed to say, highly conscious of the other people passing them on the pavement.

Oh, did this argument have to be this public? Perhaps it was a blessing. Perhaps it would prevent them from losing their tempers and disgracing his name once again.

"I told you before," Samuel said stiffly. "I'd prefer it if you were in company all—"

"What, afraid I will transport another secret to the French?" Lulu exclaimed, unable to hold in the bitterness and the pain. "Afraid I will disgrace you once again?"

Samuel's eyes flashed, his whole face contorting with pain. It was a pain mirrored in her. Oh, she had never intended to hurt him, and yet all she seemed able to do was injure!

Perhaps she should have spoken to another lawyer. Perhaps it would be better, easier, kinder even to leave Samuel Dellamore, Duke of Chantmarle, behind. Being married to him was surely a cruelty. Did that not make divorce a kindness?

"Lulu," Samuel growled, dropping his voice and taking a step closer to her.

Lulu instinctively took a step back—at least, she would have done if there were not a very inconvenient wall in the way.

"Samuel," she breathed.

And for some reason, that appeared to have an effect on him that was most unexpected. The darkness in his eyes disappeared, melting into—that could not be affection. He could not still care for her after everything she had revealed!

"Samuel!"

Lulu had not intended to shout his name, but she had been much provoked. Samuel had suddenly grasped her arm and pulled her, without a word, along the street and into an alley.

The alley was dark and damp. There were only about three feet between the two walls, and the dead end to her left meant it was quiet. The noise of the street had disappeared as swiftly as though someone had removed it from Edinburgh completely.

Lulu's lungs hurt. She'd not taken a full breath in quite some time.

"S-Samuel," she stammered, trying to pull her arm free of his grip. "Why are you—"

"I ask you to travel with someone as I care for your safety. And—"

"Care about my safety? Care about me shaming you, that's what you mean," Lulu said, finally wrenching her arm from his grip. "I saw you, with Mr. Gillingham!"

She had not thought to say the words here, in a dank alley, but she could wait no longer. What had Samuel been doing, consorting with such ruffians?

Samuel's eyes softened. "Yes, you saw."

"I-I did," Lulu said, hating her voice shook at that moment. "How long have you been seeing them? Have you worked together—what is going on?"

There was a desperate edge to her voice she could not control. Lulu did not understand, her mind overswept with confusion and longing.

Longing for things to be right between her and Samuel again.

They'd had moments of true happiness, true joy, but she had laid the foundations for their destruction long before she had even met him.

Samuel took a deep breath. "I wish you would trust me, Lulu."

"How can I?" she asked, blinking back tears. "When I myself am so untrustworthy."

"Damn it—"

Lulu gasped. Samuel crushed his lips to hers, hands pulling her into a rough embrace.

The kiss was unexpected, but so too was the genuine fervor of his affection. Try as she might, Lulu could not resist. She had craved him—and been pained by the lack of his touch—the moment the truth had slipped from her lips, the moment he realized she was the traitor he had been looking for.

The moment she had known herself separated, irrevocably, from him forever.

Lulu clung to him, parting her lips and deepening the kiss. She knew this would be their last, knew she would have this as her parting memory. So she poured into it all her hopes never to be realized, all her dreams which she'd never see, and her deep affection for the man who had loved her, even if imperfectly.

When the kiss finally ended, she expected Samuel to pull away— but he kept her in his arms and instead pressed his forehead against hers.

"I met with Mr. Gillingham today," he said in a jagged voice. "And paid your debt."

Lulu could not take in the words. She was too overcome by his scent, his warm hands around her, the blazing heat of his kiss still tingling on her lips.

"Lulu, I paid your debt," Samuel repeated quietly, his forehead still pressed against hers. "You don't have to live under the pain of that blackmail anymore. You . . . you're free."

It could not be true. Lulu had dreamt of the moment when she would be free of Mr. Gregory and Mr. Gillingham's power for months. The weight of the two pounds she had so carefully collected was heavy on her arm in her reticule.

"You . . . you paid them?" Lulu breathed. "But . . . you were so angry with me—"

"I think I was more angry at myself," Samuel said in a low, rueful voice. "Angry I hadn't seen the danger you were in. Angry you'd had to face that challenge alone. Angry you . . . you had not felt able to tell me. That you hadn't come to me."

Lulu swallowed, confusion and pain mingling in her heart but softened by hope.

Was it possible—could it be true?

"So . . . so you aren't angry at me?" she repeated. "With my sharing secrets, with—"

"Do I wish it hadn't happened? Of course," Samuel said with a dry chuckle. His breath was warm on her face. "But am I going to hold you accountable for things you did, decisions you made before we even met?" He stole a brief but searing kiss. "No."

Lulu sagged in his arms, the burden of the last few years finally lifted. She did not have to live in fear. She was free—more than that, she had a husband by her side who had heard the very worst of her and was still here.

"I do love you," she began.

Samuel snorted a gentle laugh. "I should think so!"

Lulu tapped him on the arm. "Not because of what you've done! Grateful as I am, it is because you have forgiven me, loved me, want to keep choosing to love me, that I love you. You . . . you're everything to me, Samuel."

"And you're everything to me," Samuel whispered, his grip tightening. "Lulu, I've spent my whole life being curious about the world, about people, but you have made me curious about myself. About the sort of man I want to be—the sort of husband I could be. And I'll never stop striving to be better, to give you better."

"Well in that case, you may wish to prepare yourself for a scandal," murmured Lulu, excitement rushing through her heart.

She almost laughed as she saw Samuel's eyes widen. "Dear God, what now?"

"Well, if I am not very much mistaken," she said quietly, grinning and not taking her gaze from his as her hand crept down to the growing bulge in his breeches. "We are about to explore what better ways we could get to know each other right here . . ."

CHAPTER NINETEEN

13 May 1811

"READY?"

Samuel could hardly keep the excitement from his voice. Every syllable seemed to quiver with it. The hope she would be impressed. The knowledge she would be, merely to please him. His pleasure in her wanting to please him . . .

Was this how all marriages were? Did everyone experience this shared excitement and terror that one's spouse may one day be sad? Did everyone battle against their instincts to solve every problem for their beloved, protect them from all harm, keep them safe and happy? Surely he could not be the only one.

"As ready as I will ever be," said Lulu dryly with a mischievous glint in her eye. "You know, I cannot believe we came all this way for this!"

Samuel swallowed his anticipation. "You do not wish to visit the homes of the fabulously wealthy?"

Lulu rolled her eyes. "I just don't understand why we had to apply to the housekeeper. You're a duke!"

"You're a duchess," he pointed out, clambering down from the carriage and offering a hand.

"Exactly!" Lulu said, her cheeks pinking at the reminder of her new status. "You'd think, wouldn't you, we would be receiving an invitation rather than asking . . . my goodness."

"My goodness" was about right, in Samuel's estimation. He had always been impressed by the visage of Brierwell Hall. The towering spires, the way the place simultaneously loomed and was welcoming. Perhaps it was the gray weathered stone. Perhaps it was the warm windows, dazzling in the late afternoon sun, which gave the place a glow.

Whatever it was, he had never received anything but a warm welcome at Brierwell Hall.

"I have always wanted to visit the homes of the good and the great," Lulu said, shyly as she peered up at the Hall. "I mean, this is your world. A world you grew up in, but for me . . ."

Her voice trailed away. Samuel's chest swelled with pride. *It was all going perfectly.*

"When you said that you wanted to take me on an excursion, I could not have imagined this," said Lulu in a stronger voice. "I mean, the gardens alone look magnificent!"

They were indeed, and Samuel saw no need to argue with her. The gardens were immaculate: elegantly trimmed hedges with yew trees flanking the main gates, an avenue of oaks they had already driven down, and here by the house, early roses.

"Well, whoever lives here is certainly fortunate," Lulu said, slipping her hand into Samuel's arm. "Who did you say it was again?"

Samuel swallowed. Deception was all par for the course when working for the Crown, but he rarely kept anything important a secret from those he truly cared about and respected.

Still. It would be worth it.

"I didn't," he said airily. "A nobleman, he's rarely here."

Lulu snorted as she stepped forward, her eagerness tugging on his arm. "More fool him, I say. He truly must be a dullard if he willingly chooses to leave this magnificence."

"Yes, I suppose he is," Samuel said quietly under his breath as they stepped up the sweep of stairs to the front door. "A complete dullard."

"Though I suppose if you grew up here, saw it every day," Lulu said, evidently attempting to be fair to the unnamed gentleman she was happily critiquing, "I would guess he doesn't see . . . doesn't see . . . How could anyone leave this?"

Her head was tilted back as she attempted to take in the splendor of the place.

Samuel mimicked her. *She was right. How could anyone leave this?*

The ceiling was covered by a striking painting of the gods of the Greek pantheon. There was Poseidon in the sea, Hera, Hestia and Demeter, Hades in the depths of hell, Zeus in the clouds. The whole piece was finished off by a frame of gold, glittering in the afternoon sun.

Lulu breathed out slowly. "And this is just his entrance hall!"

"Oh, I believe many people with houses this large put much of their money in the entrance hall," Samuel said as calmly as he could manage. "Designed to impress, you know. That way, anyone who merely visits the hall and perhaps the drawing room can go away singing the praises of the house without seeing—"

"The dusty corridors and the damp bedchambers?" quipped Lulu with a smile. "No, you cannot convince me the rest of this place does not live up to this."

She continued gazing around in evident wonder.

Warmth suffused Samuel's heart. It had been a gamble. An idea he would not have conceived of unless he had met someone like Lulu. Someone who adored intrigue, and a mite of danger. But most of all, wanted to be loved.

"Where to next?"

Samuel blinked. Lulu was looking expectant. "Well, I suppose we just wander . . ."

So wander they did. Though his wife did mention a few times that she found it strange the housekeeper had not come out to guide them, she and Samuel made the best of it.

They found not one, but two drawing rooms, one on the east side of the house to catch the winter sun and one on the west side to keep cool in summer.

"Such extravagance!" laughed Lulu, trailing a finger along a console table made of marble. "Do you think they have a different bedchamber for each month of the year?"

Samuel swallowed his answer. She would not believe him.

After that they found the dining room, a resplendent room mainly in red, with velvet on the floor, silk on the walls, and gold gilt again on the ceiling.

"It's as though they had a goldmine and didn't know what to do with it."

Samuel bit his lip and shrugged. "Maybe."

It was when they stepped into the Orangery, however, that Lulu truly started to gush. "Look at these trees! How do they do it, I wonder? I've never seen an orange before, do you think they—"

"Never seen an orange before?" Samuel interrupted, incredulous.

It was astonishing to hear—and yet, perhaps not.

Lulu had a wry smile. "Sometimes you forget, I think, just how easy it is to live when one is poor. You have to sacrifice the essentials of course, like oranges—"

Samuel snorted.

His wife was grinning. "But we get by. Come now, Samuel. You aren't impressed? You have barely said two words of praise for this place, and I'm sure you've never seen better!"

Samuel's stomach lurched. Standing as she was, gesturing at the plants around her, Lulu presented a picture of perfection.

The white of the limestone floor. The terracotta pots, bursting with life as the dark green leaves and the orange of the fruit seemed to grow right before his eyes. Lulu, standing between them. Her gold and black piped gown—his favorite—fit perfectly.

"I have truly never seen better," he said honestly.

She caught his meaning—at least, she appeared to. Pink dots appeared in Lulu's cheeks. "I meant the house."

"So did I," Samuel quipped. "I cannot possibly fathom what else you think I could have meant."

Lulu's teasing smile made his heart skip a beat. This had been a good idea, then. After all, she had not—

"Admit it, this place is far finer than anything you have ever lived in," said Lulu with a mischievous grin, turning away and peering into an orange tree.

"I think I would say that I grew up in a place just as nice as this," Samuel said honestly.

His heart was beating faster. Had it been a mistake? Had he overplayed his hand? Would Lulu appreciate the jest, or would she perhaps find it underhanded? His shoulders tightened, just for a moment. The last thing he wanted was for Lulu to feel as though there were others plotting around her. Perhaps this was a mistake. They could leave now, he would never have to explain—

"Surely not!" Lulu protested, turning to fix him with a stern air. "As nice as this?"

"Exactly as nice as this," said Samuel softly with a wry smile.

"Exactly as . . ." Lulu's voice faded as her eyes widened. "Samuel Dellamore, is this your house?"

"Maybe?" shrugged Samuel with a wide grin, shoulders relaxing as he saw astonishment, not hurt, in Lulu's face.

"But—but—I've been going around it praising it to the hilt!" spluttered Lulu with a laugh. "You said you had to apply to the housekeeper—"

"Of course I did!" Samuel stepped forward and lowered his voice into a mock whisper. "You think I would dare come to my own Scottish residence without the approval of Mrs. Winder? The audacity!"

Their laughter filled the Orangery and Samuel knew he would never be happier than this. How could he be? This was everything he wanted. No, it was more than that. He had never known he wished for such a connection, for a bride. A wife! A woman by his side at almost all moments, someone who understood him and yet was willing to learn.

His affection soared through him. He would never find someone else like Lulu, and he knew it. All he had to do now was prove himself to her. Every day.

"You are an absolute cad," said Lulu, tapping him lightly on the arm but grinning all the while. "I can't believe you almost made a complete fool of me!"

"I am just relieved you like the place," Samuel teased. "Imagine what I would have done if you had stepped out of that carriage and pronounced the place unpleasant!"

Lulu groaned as he laughed harder. "You cocksure rogue!"

"Guilty as charged," he admitted freely as they strode to a sofa placed near the glass wall of the Orangery. "Does this mean, however, that you have forgiven me?"

"Hmmm," considered Lulu as she sat, curling into his arm. "I will think about it."

Samuel's heart swelled.

It had been a gamble, but he could think of no better way to introduce Lulu to his Scottish home—their Scottish home—than this. Brierwell Hall. If she had truly not liked it, well, that was no matter. They had plenty of other homes. One of those would do.

But he needed to know her true opinion, without her judgment being clouded by trying to please him. That was the greatest difficulty at the moment. The pair were so eager each to make the other happy, it was starting to become impossible to know if they were giving true opinions or just saying what they thought the other wanted to hear.

That would fade, Samuel was sure. But this was a swift way to make sure.

"I cannot believe it." Lulu's voice was so soft, he almost missed her words.

Kissing her head, he murmured, "Cannot believe what?"

"This," she said, squeezing his hand. "You. Me. This place."

"I admit, I can hardly believe that I have you."

Her disbelief in his words not in a verbal reply, but in the way she scoffed.

"I mean it!" Samuel protested with a laugh. "I have shown you jewels, and gold gilt ceilings, and diamond chandeliers, and Rembrandts—"

"What's a Rembrandt?"

"—and not even the whole place combined is more precious than you," Samuel said with a wry smile. There would be time for art history later. This moment, this was important. "I hope you believe that, Lulu—or that you can believe it in time."

His wife tilted her head to meet his eye, and he saw within it a desperate wish to believe it was true. Perhaps that was enough for now.

"I just can't believe you have forgiven me," Lulu whispered. "I know you have, but . . . it doesn't seem real."

Samuel's gut lurched.

That was the one dark spot in their past. The blackmail. The letter he had paid a hefty three pounds to procure. The treachery Lulu had entered into, just to keep the publication of her brother's letter at bay.

She had done much for him, this Malcolm. Many sisters would only do half as much for their brother if he lived, let alone to protect the memory of one who was gone.

And she had suffered. Samuel could see that—had seen it in the way Lulu had lived. Even saving her pennies to the point of poverty, she had not had sufficient funds to buy her way out of trouble. So she had been forced to . . . well.

Samuel sighed. "If I had been paying attention, I would have spotted the signs."

Lulu wrinkled her nose. "The signs?"

He shrugged. "I am a servant of the Crown, I have seen them countless times. Your association with ruffians, your appearance in places like the McBarland's gaming hell—"

"Yes, I was surprised I was able to distract you from that," she murmured.

Samuel's loins warmed at the mere memory of Lulu in that place. He had not noticed then, as he did now, just how swiftly he had been distracted by Lulu's presence. To his own detriment, in the short term.

"If I had put the clues together, I would have realized you were unwillingly tangled up in all this," Samuel said. "I would have been able to speak to you, help you—"

"I probably would have lied," Lulu said ruefully.

Samuel raised an eyebrow. "You would?"

"I did not know if I could trust you or not!" she pointed out with raised eyebrows. "You think I had gone that long without considering taking someone else into my confidence?"

It was a fair point, and not one Samuel had considered.

"No, I knew anyone I confided in would be just as much at risk as I was," Lulu was saying. "I wouldn't do that to you. I couldn't risk . . . you were important."

Samuel swallowed. "Even then?"

"Even then."

They sat for a few minutes in silence as Samuel wrestled with whether this was the right time to share the information that Judge Smee had sent from London. He had to someday, he knew. It would be cruel to allow Lulu to continue under such a misapprehension.

But was now the best time?

Lulu sighed. "I just . . . I will never escape the guilt."

"Guilt?"

"The harm I have caused by my actions." Her voice was soft, almost inaudible. "All that information I shared, the damage it has surely done to those brave fighters in France."

Her voice trailed off. She gripped Samuel's arm. It was the sign he needed.

"Lulu," he said gently. "I received a letter from London. A letter from a man—"

"I don't want to hear it," Lulu said quietly. "I cannot bear to hear any news of the consequences of my actions," she continued in a pained voice. "I am sure my imagination can fill the gaps."

Of course. She believed he had bad news for her—she would expect to hear what harm had come from what she had done, not hope.

Samuel cleared his throat. "I think you'll want to hear this. Aren't you curious?"

Lulu met his gaze and he saw the pain within. The regret. The certainty that what she had done was truly terrible, that she could never be fully forgiven for her betrayal.

"Lulu, the information you shared—it was all false," he said, as gently as he could.

She stiffened beside him on the sofa. "F-False?"

He nodded, trying to consider the best way to explain. Judge Smee had been harsh in his condemnation, despite the fresh revelations. He did not know Lulu as Samuel did.

"It was discovered, after the very first message, that there was one in the encampment at Edinburgh Castle sharing secrets," Samuel explained gently. "They discovered who it was within a day. Everything that man shared with you, everything you told the French . . . it was false information. Designed to keep the French interested. It didn't—you didn't do any harm."

He watched the dawning realization of what he was saying brighten Lulu's face. She seemed to come to life right before him, the parts of her which had died returning to full vigor.

"I . . . you mean, I did no harm by passing on the information?" she breathed.

Samuel shook his head. "If anything, you did us a great service."

"A great—"

"You helped uncover a traitor in the encampment, and allowed us to continuously distract the French," he pointed out kindly. "Don't you see? The army didn't tell us in London the full story, they wanted us to hunt out the go between—"

"Me," Lulu said faintly.

Samuel nodded. "But they were never truly worried, because they had stopped the betrayal at the source. You acted to best protect yourself, and you don't have to blame yourself for anything, anymore. Your actions did no harm."

For a moment, he watched as Lulu attempted to take it all in. It was a great deal of information. He himself had found it astonishing when he had read Judge Smee's letter.

Lulu sagged with relief against the sofa. "You . . . you are sure?"

"Certain," Samuel said with a smile. "I am proud of you, you know."

She managed to laugh at that, and a little of the Lulu he knew returned. "Why, because I didn't actually manage to do anything that I intended?"

"Because you felt guilty," Samuel said, kissing her on the forehead and wishing she could see herself as he saw her. "Because though you were pushed into an impossible situation, you felt remorseful. That says far more about you than the people who forced you into it."

Lulu took a deep breath. "With that in mind, I must see the rest of the house."

"Curious?"

She nudged him in the ribs. "We have endured enough "curiosity" for a lifetime!"

He groaned, clutching his ribs as though she had done him a great injury. "Oh, we'll have the rest of our lives to explore the house. I'm more interested in exploring you."

"Samuel!"

"Well, it's my house," he said fairly. "Our house. No one is going to disturb us here . . ."

EPILOGUE

18 June 1811

"OH, MY DEAR, you simply must attend—"

"No, I have the duchess coming to me on the twenty first, you must be patient—"

"How can she, when I believe she already promised attendance at my ball!"

Lulu smiled weakly as her stomach lurched and the doyennes of London Society happily argued around her. About her. Over her.

It was like a dream. As though the Scottish manor were not enough, Samuel had informed her only the day before their journey to London was completed that he owned not only a townhouse in the capital, but some sort of castle in Cheshire and "a pile" in Devon. Lulu had been forced to ask Mrs. Winder for a map. Even then it had taken her a while to find it.

Cheshire! Scotland! Devon! London!

It was certainly a very different life from the one she had originally thought her future would contain.

Not that she was complaining. Even if she was about to be torn apart by these ladies.

"I think you will find that I have precedence in this matter," said Lady Romeril icily. "It was, after all, under my guidance that His

Grace, the Duke of Chantmarle was able to find such a *suitable* bride in the first place."

She affixed Lulu with a glare.

Lulu smiled and curtseyed demurely, but she was sure to meet Lady Romeril's eyes once more with just a hint of silent rebellion. She was indebted to Lady Romeril, it was true. But perhaps not quite in the way the older woman thought.

"There, that's settled," said Lady Romeril with a supremely satisfied voice. "I suppose she will come to you, Mrs. Marnion, a few days later. After that—"

"Thank you, Lady Romeril," said Lulu sweetly. "I am grateful for your guidance and support in Edinburgh, but I believe your support can stay there. I am the Duchess of Chantmarle. I am able to accept my own invitations—or decline them, I suppose. If I wish."

The scandalized look on Lady Romeril was quite worth the bold statement, but Lulu would have made it no matter who she'd been faced with.

She'd had enough of being controlled by others. Enough of being told what she should do, and how she needed to act to survive.

That ended. Now.

Lady Romeril raised an imperious eyebrow. "My word. Stepping into the role of duchess with both feet, are we? Killing off the old and on with the new?"

Lulu swallowed, forcing down the nausea which had plagued her all morning. She was not sure just how much Lady Romeril knew about her past. Far too much, it appeared.

"Just so," she said with a smile as light and carefree as she could make it. "Now if you will excuse me, ladies, I must mingle with my other guests. I cannot let it be said that the Duchess of Chantmarle plays favorites this early in her marriage."

Lulu stepped away as the titters of the ladies she had been conversing with rose in the large drawing room.

When Samuel had suggested they host a wedding reception upon their arrival at the townhouse, Lulu had initially thought him ridiculous.

"A wedding reception? We've already had a wedding reception," she had pointed out.

"In Edinburgh," he said fairly. "Not London—more than half my acquaintance is here."

And so Lulu had agreed. Something small, she had impressed upon her new husband. Nothing too ostentatious.

Which did not explain why there appeared to be several hundred people clogging the stairwell.

"Ah, Your Grace!"

"Your Grace, how wonderful to—"

"Is that her?"

Lulu smiled as she descended the wide sweeping staircase in search of her husband. They had been forced to open the smoking room and the morning room to accommodate the large number of guests. Something that Fitzhugh—

"Ah, Your Grace," came the dry tones of the butler.

Lulu hesitated, then halted in the corridor. It was quieter here, almost all the guests had made their way upstairs to the drawing room. It was just her and Fitzhugh.

Wonderful.

"I wished, if it is not too much of an inconvenience, to have a moment of your time, Your Grace," said the butler darkly.

Lulu braced herself. *This could not be good.* "Of course, Fitzhugh." She almost continued with *What is it?* when the man did not appear to wish to speak. Which was most strange as he had been the one to accost her.

Finally, the butler swallowed and drew himself up stiffly. "I wish to apologize. I—"

Lulu blinked. "I beg your pardon?"

Fitzhugh affixed her with a stern look. "Please, Your Grace. Allow me to—"

"Yes, yes, right," she said hastily, raising her hands in mock surrender and pressing her lips together firmly.

Surely she was dreaming. *Fitzhugh did not go around apologizing!*

But it appeared that now, he did. "You will understand and appreciate, I am sure, that I was . . . suspicious of a woman of your rank— our rank, I may say—marrying His Grace."

Lulu nodded, hoping that was sufficient to demonstrate her understanding but simultaneously not interrupting.

It appeared it was. "I see now that you make His Grace truly happy, and that is all that anyone who knows him would wish," continued the butler in rigid, clipped tones. "I misjudged you. Given the gossip about you, I thought you would destroy his reputation—"

"Ah," said Lulu helplessly.

"—but if anything, I do believe you have improved it," said Fitzhugh with a hint of a smile. "The man comports himself like an idiot. On purpose, I am given to understand."

Lulu forced down a smile. "I am given to understand that also."

The man nodded. "As long as *we* understand each other."

Lulu could hardly believe it. This stiff, stern servant who had made her feel so isolated, who had himself pointed her in the direction of a lawyer as she sought a divorce . . . apologizing? Admitting he was wrong?

Well, not entirely. But it was halfway there.

"Thank you, Mr. Fitzhugh," said Lulu softly, adding the honorific and seeing immediately it was the right decision as he swelled with pride. "I hope to continue impressing you, and of course, serving His Grace in any way that I can. We share that, I think."

The butler nodded, and without another word, stepped along the corridor.

Lulu stood there for a moment in genuine shock. *Well!* You could have knocked her down with a feather. That was certainly not what she had expected from the gruff older man.

When she entered the morning room, it was to see her husband standing with a man she did not recognize. He had close-cropped dark hair, a heavy expression, and a commanding presence.

Samuel looked around. "Ah, there she is! Come here, Lulu."

Lulu flushed as she approached the two gentlemen. Try as she might, she had been unable to convince Samuel to only call her that pet name in private. He just could not help it.

"Your Grace," bowed the stranger.

"This is Daniel Vaughn, Lulu," said Samuel happily. "Vaughn, my wife, Lucy."

Grateful he had at least introduced her by her proper name, even if it was strange to hear it in his mouth, Lulu smiled at her guest. "You are very welcome, Mr. Vaughn."

Mr. Vaughn smiled. "And I am very grateful to be so welcomed, Your Grace. It is a . . . well, a pleasant distraction. At the moment."

Now she came to look at him, Lulu could see the man looked unwell. Oh, nothing serious. A drawn look around the eyes, a heaviness across the shoulders. He seemed to be a man who was overly tired, or tired of something—she could not tell which.

"Vaughn," she repeated. "I believe there are two Vaughn brothers, are there not?"

Immediately, Lulu saw she had made a mistake but didn't know what it was. Samuel's eyes had widened and the others in the morning room swiftly left, closing the door with a snap.

Lulu looked at the two gentlemen who remained. "I—I am sorry, I did not intend—"

"It is quite all right, Your Grace," Mr. Vaughn said with significant reserve. "My brother is the elder. The Duke of Thornfalcone."

"Not that you'd know it to look at them," Samuel quipped.

Lulu shot him a look. Why on earth was her husband being so

cruel about Mr. Vaughn's appearance? No younger son, surely, would like to be jested that he looked older than his sibling!

But for some reason, Mr. Vaughn chuckled. "Your poor wife, Chantmarle, she doesn't know what you mean. I am a twin, Your Grace," he said to the bewildered Lulu. "We're identical twins."

"Identical twins?" she repeated. "Goodness."

It was the sort of thing one read about in stories, not met in a morning room.

"And how is your brother?" Samuel was saying.

Mr. Vaughn winced, though why Lulu had no idea. "You know, I think I'd rather not talk about it. Not now, not today. Soon I'll come by for a visit, and we can talk then."

Lulu hid her smile. There were still plenty of Samuel's friends and acquaintances who were uncertain of her, and most of the others still preferred to meet with her husband in private.

She could not blame them. A woman of no name, no family, no connections? No fortune, dowry, or expectancy of inheritance? No title? Where had the Duke of Chantmarle found her?

But this appeared to be different. Mr. Vaughn was not being rude in cutting her from the conversation, Lulu was certain. No, this was a private pain, one he had no wish to share.

Now that, she could quite understand.

"In that case, we will not speak of it," said Samuel happily. "Not on a day when we are celebrating! Which reminds me, have you heard about old Gilroyd? Man has made the most ridiculous vow . . ."

Lulu allowed the conversation to wash over her for a few minutes. She had never heard of Mr. Gilroyd, let alone met him—though now she came to think about it, she supposed it was possible the man was also a duke. Samuel did not really seem to differentiate. It was one of the things she adored about him.

Affection for him expanded, filling her completely. It did not seem possible that she had found a man like this in the whole world—let alone that she had convinced him to love her. Though as she recalled, it had been Samuel who had begged her to marry him . . .

"*A marriage of convenience is the only way to—*"

"*Absolutely not. Samuel, no!*"

"—and why did you not marry in London, Your Grace?" Mr. Vaughn asked politely.

It was because she was thinking of such wicked and lustful things, Lulu told herself later. That was why she responded so boldly.

"Why, because Samuel simply couldn't keep his hands off me," Lulu replied with a smile.

That smile faded as her cheeks burned. *Dear God, what had she said?*

But though Mr. Vaughn was evidently surprised by her direct response, he laughed with Samuel. "Dear me, how refreshing to meet a woman who speaks openly!"

"Perhaps a little too openly," Lulu said ruefully as her stomach lurched.

"Well, much as I would love to stay and hear all about it, I have to be back to meet with Doctor Walsingham," Mr. Vaughn said, and he truly sounded regretful.

"A drink in a few days' time, Vaughn?" Samuel called after him.

"Count on it," said Mr. Vaughn with a nod to them both.

And then they were alone.

Lulu groaned. "I cannot believe I just said that! Aloud! With my mouth!"

"Neither can I," chuckled Samuel, shaking his head. "My word, I think you frightened him away!"

She groaned again, dropping her head into her hands. Here she had been, determined to make a good impression on the people of London—to impress Samuel's friends, most of all. And what had she done?

"Do you think he will tell anyone?" she said, peeking out from between her fingers. "Will I read about that in the gossip pages tomorrow?"

"Oh, never fear, Vaughn is far too noble for all that," Samuel said cheerfully. "Besides, you spoke nothing but the truth. I was far too curious to taste your lips, wasn't I?"

Lulu shivered as she recalled that moment. That heady tension, the growing desire both of them had attempted to ignore. The opportunity at Lady Romeril's ball, the sudden shock of Samuel's crushing kiss on her lips, and the knowledge—oh, the sincere knowledge that she wanted to feel his kiss every day for the rest of her life.

"Lulu?"

She blinked.

Samuel was looking at her, face full of concern. "Are you quite well?"

"Oh, perfectly well," said Lulu with a bracing smile even as her stomach lurched. *No, she could overcome it this time.*

It would be a great shame, after all, to destroy a perfectly good rug. Though that did not mean she had to quell everything. Why not, in this moment, with all their guests upstairs in the drawing room happily entertaining themselves, reveal the truth?

"Although," she said slowly, "I must say I have been surprised at your lack of curiosity since we arrived in London."

Samuel frowned, his handsome forehead crinkling. "Lack of curiosity?"

Excitement was rushing through Lulu's body, intermingling with the nausea that was ever present at the moment. "I mean, you haven't wondered why I haven't been myself?"

"Yourself?" Samuel appeared to be completely lost. "Well, the journey was difficult for you. You felt so unwell, I felt so sorry for you—"

"And you weren't curious about other things?" Lulu prompted.

Surely the man could not be this dense!

But then, were gentlemen taught about such things? Was this one of the areas where she was fully informed, and it was Samuel who would need to be told?

"I've learned my lesson," said Samuel repentantly, shaking his head. "Curiosity could kill a duke! Especially when it comes to you!"

"Well, that would indeed be a great shame," said Lulu, beaming. "But then, as it appears there could be an heir on the way, I am not so concerned about the Chantmarle line."

It took a moment. *Samuel was, perhaps, not as sharp as he thought,* Lulu could not help but think with a giggle. *Had she not been obvious enough?*

And then Samuel swept her into a tight embrace that knocked the very wind out of her. He clutched her tight, one arm completely around her waist and the other cradling her head, as though at any moment she could fall apart into pieces.

"You're not," he breathed, deep emotion in his voice.

"Being strangled?" Lulu choked. "Yes!"

Samuel swiftly released her, but within a heartbeat he had grabbed both her arms. "You—you are—you're not with—"

"I am indeed," said Lulu with a shy smile. It felt so strange, saying it aloud. Well, almost saying it aloud. *This was the time.* "I . . . I am with child."

Samuel burst into whoops and embraced her again, though thankfully this time with less vigor. "A child! A child, Lulu—part of you, and part of me!"

"Hopefully a lot more you than me," Lulu said sheepishly.

A child. A new beginning. A fresh start. A chance to make good all the mistakes she had made.

"What—oh, no, they've got to be a tiny you," Samuel was saying, his cheeks flushed and his eyes wide with excitement. "A little you! Oh, Lulu . . ."

His kiss was fervent but reverential, sparking desire but also confirming his devotion. Lulu leaned into it, desperate for every heartbeat.

When they broke apart, she was astonished to see sparkling tears. "Samuel!"

"Well—a child!" Samuel said, his voice breaking. "Oh, Lulu. A whole new adventure."

"One we can take together," said Lulu, heart singing as she slipped her hand into his. "Together."

About Emily E K Murdoch

If you love falling in love, then you've come to the right place.

I am a historian and writer and have a varied career to date: from examining medieval manuscripts to designing museum exhibitions, to working as a researcher for the BBC to working for the National Trust.

My books range from England 1050 to Texas 1848, and I can't wait for you to fall in love with my heroes and heroines!

Follow me on twitter and instagram @emilyekmurdoch, find me on facebook at facebook.com/theemilyekmurdoch, and read my blog at www.emilyekmurdoch.com.

Made in United States
Orlando, FL
23 December 2023

41058571R00127

Keto Diet For Weight Loss

The Essential Guide With Easy, Tasty and Healthy Everyday Ketogenic Recipes for Beginners and Advanced

Chloe Roberts

Disclaimer Notice:

Please note the information contained within this document is for educational and entertainment purposes only. All effort has been executed to present accurate, up to date, and reliable, complete information. No warranties of any kind are declared or implied. Readers acknowledge that the author is not engaging in the rendering of legal, financial, medical or professional advice. The content within this book has been derived from various sources. Please consult a licensed professional before attempting any techniques outlined in this book.

By reading this document, the reader agrees that under no circumstances is the author responsible for any losses, direct or indirect, which are incurred as a result of the use of information contained within this document, including, but not limited to, errors, omissions, or inaccuracies.

Table of Content

Introduction

Thank you for purchasing **Keto Diet For Weight Loss: The Essential Guide With Easy, Tasty and Healthy Everyday Ketogenic Recipes for Beginners and Advanced**

The ketogenic diet is a dietary regimen that drastically reduces carbohydrates, while increasing proteins and especially fats. The main purpose of this imbalance in the proportions of macronutrients in the diet is to force the body to use fats as a source of energy.

In the presence of carbohydrates, in fact, all cells use their energy to carry out their activities. But if these are reduced to a sufficiently low level they begin to use fats, all except nerve cells that do not have the ability to do so. A process called ketosis is then initiated, because it leads to the formation of molecules called ketone bodies, this time usable by the brain. Typically ketosis is achieved after a couple of days with a daily carbohydrate intake of about 20-50 grams, but these amounts can vary on an individual basis.

BREAKFAST

Cream Cheese Blueberry Muffins

Preparation Time: 10 minutes

Cooking Time: 12 minutes

Servings: 6

Ingredients:

- Nonstick cooking spray

- 1 cup almond flour

- 2 teaspoons ground cinnamon

- 3 to 4 tablespoons erythritol

- ¾ tablespoon baking powder

- 2 large eggs

- 2 tablespoons cream cheese

- 2 tablespoons heavy whipping cream

- 4 tablespoons butter, melted and cooled

- 2 teaspoons vanilla extract

- 2 tablespoons blueberries (fresh or frozen)

Directions:

1. Preheat the oven to 400°F. Spray a muffin tin using cooking spray or line it with muffin liners.

2.   In a small bowl, put and mix the almond flour, cinnamon, erythritol, and baking powder.

3.   In a medium bowl, place then mix the eggs, cream cheese, heavy cream, butter, and vanilla with a hand mixer.

4.   Put the flour mixture into the egg mixture and beat with the hand mixer until thoroughly mixed.

5.   Put the mixture into the prepared muffin cups.

6.   Drop the berries on top of the batter in the muffin cups.

7.   Bake for at least 12 minutes, or until golden brown on top, and serve.

Nutrition: Calories: 160 Total Fat: 15g Protein: 4g Total Carbs: 10g Fiber: 2g Net Carbs: 8g

Macadamia Nut Square

Preparation Time: 10 minutes 1 hour chilling

Cooking Time: 0 minutes

Servings: 4

Ingredients:

- ¼ cup macadamia nuts

- ¼ cup nut butter

- 1 teaspoon erythritol

- 2 tablespoons butter, melted

- 2 tablespoons shredded coconut or cacao nibs

(optional)

Directions:

1. In a food processor, pulse the macadamia nuts until they are a little smaller than rice size.

2. In a bowl, combine the macadamia nuts, nut butter, erythritol, and butter and mix well. Add the shredded coconut or cacao nibs (if using) and stir well.

3. Line a loaf pan using parchment paper then pour the mixture into the pan.

4.   Refrigerate for 1 hour, remove, and cut into squares.

Keep in an sealed container, refrigerated or in the freezer.

Nutrition: Calories: 208 Total Fat: 21g Protein: 3g Total Carbs: 3g Fiber: 1g Net Carbs: 2g

Mozzarella Bagels

Preparation time: 30 minutes

Cooking time: 15 minutes

Servings: 6

Ingredients:

- 1 egg

- 1½ cups almond flour

- 1½ cup mozzarella, shredded

- 2 oz cream cheese, cut into pieces

- 1 tsp baking powder

- 1 tbsp oat fiber

Directions:

1.   Put the mozzarella and cream cheese for 1 minute in a microwave. Stir and microwave for 30 seconds more.

2.   In a food processor combine egg with microwaved cheese.

3.   Add dry ingredients and process well. Scrape the dough out, wrap in plastic wrap, and place in the freezer for 20 minutes.

4. Preheat oven to 400°F and line a baking sheet with parchment paper.

5. Divide the dough into 6 portions.

6. Make each piece into a sausage shape and seal the ends together forming a ring.

7. Place on the parchment paper and bake for 12–15 minutes.

Nutrition: Calories: 245 Fat: 17g Carb: 5.6 g Protein: 7.2g

KETO BREAD

Banana Bread

Preparation Time: 2 hours

Cooking Time: 30 minutes

Serves: 12

Ingredients:

- 2 cups almond flour
- 1/4 cup coconut flour
- 1/2 cup walnuts, chopped
- 2 tsp baking powder
- 2 tsp cinnamon
- 1/4 tsp Himalayan salt
- 6 tbsp. coconut oil, melted
- 1/2 cup erythritol
- 4 eggs
- 1/4 cup almond milk, unsweetened
- 2 tsp banana extract
- 1/2 tsp xanthan gum

Directions:

1.   Place all the wet ingredients into the pan of the bread machine.

2.   Add all dry ingredients next.

3.   Set bread machine to quick bread setting.

4.   When the bread is done, remove bread machine pan from the bread machine.

5.   Let cool slightly before transferring to a cooling rack.

6.   You can store your bread for up to 5 days.

Nutrition: Calories: 224 Carbohydrates: 5 g Protein: 8g Fat: 20g

Cheddar Biscuits

Preparation Time: 10 minutes

Cooking Time: 25 minutes

Servings: 12

Ingredients:

- 4 eggs

- 1/4 cup unsalted butter, melted

- 1 1/4 cups, coconut milk

- 1/4 tsp. salt

- 1/4 tsp. baking soda

- 1/4 tsp. garlic powder

- 1/2 cup finely shredded sharp cheddar cheese

- 1 Tbsp. fresh herb

- 2/3 cup coconut flour

Directions:

1.   Preheat the oven to 350F. Grease a baking sheet.

2.   Mix together the butter, eggs, milk, salt, baking soda, garlic powder, cheese, and herbs until well blended.

3.	Add the coconut flour to the batter and mix until well blended. Let the batter sit then mix again.

4.	Spoon about 2 tbsp. batter for each biscuit onto the greased baking sheet.

5.	Bake for 25 minutes.

6.	Serve warm.

Nutrition: Calories: 125 Fat: 7g Carb: 1g Protein: 5g

Purple Yam Pancakes

Preparation Time: 5 minutes

Cooking Time: 10 minutes

Serves: 4

Ingredients:

- 1/2 cup Coconut Flour

- 4 Eggs

- 1 cup Coconut Milk

- 1 tsp. Guar Gum

- 1/2 tsp. Baking Powder

- 1 tbsp. Coconut Oil

- 1/4 cup Purple Yam Puree

Directions:

1. Mix all ingredients in a blender.

2. Preheat a skillet and coat with non-stick spray.

3. Ladle in the batter and cook for 1-2 minutes per side.

Nutrition: Calories: 347 Fat: 31 g. Protein: 11 g. Carbs: 3 g.

Sweet Coffee Bread

Preparation Time: 2 hours

Cooking Time: 25 minutes

Servings: 10

Ingredients:

- 2 cups of almond fine flour

- Salt, half a teaspoon

- Cinnamon, three-quarters of a teaspoon

- Eggs, four

- Swerve Keto sweetener half a cup

- 1/2 cup of unsalted melted butter

- 1/4 cup of protein powder that is not flavored

- 4 tsp. of coconut flour

- 2/3 cup of almond milk that is not sweetened

- 2 tsp. espresso

- Extract from vanilla, half a teaspoon

- Active dry yeast, two teaspoons

- Baking powder, two teaspoons

Directions:

1.   Mix together the almond flour, coconut flour, sweetener Swerve, cinnamon, salt, baking powder, espresso, and unflavored protein powder in a container.

2.   Mix the unsweetened almond milk, eggs, extract of vanilla, and unsalted melted butter in another container.

3.   As per the instructions on the manual of your machine, pour the ingredients in the bread pan, taking care to follow how to mix in the yeast.

4.   Place the bread pan in the machine, and select the sweet bread setting, together with the crust type, if available, then press start once you have closed the lid of the machine.

5.   When the bread is ready, extract it from the pan and place it on a wire mesh surface to cool before cutting it.

Nutrition: Calories: 177.7 Fat: 3.8g Carb: 3.1g Protein: 4.6g

Apple Butter Bread

Preparation Time: 2 hours

Cooking Time: 25 minutes

Servings: 10

Ingredients:

- Melted butter, half a cup unsalted

- Swerve sweetener, one cup

- An egg

- Unsweetened apple butter, one cup

- 1 tsp. of cinnamon powder

- Almond flour, two cups

- Baking soda, two teaspoons

- Nutmeg ground, one teaspoon

- Extract of vanilla, one teaspoon

- 1/2 cup of unsweetened almond milk

- 2 tsp. of active dry yeast

Directions:

1.   Mix the almond flour, Swerve, cinnamon, nutmeg powder, and baking soda in a container.

2.   Get another container and combine the unsweetened apple butter, unsalted melted butter, vanilla essence, and almond milk that are unsweetened.

3.   As per the instructions on the manual of your machine, pour the ingredients in the bread pan, taking care to follow how to mix in the yeast.

4.   Place the bread pan in the machine and select the sweet bread setting, together with the crust type, if available, then press start once you have closed the lid of the machine.

5.   When the bread is ready, using oven mitts, remove the bread pan from the machine. Use a stainless spatula to extract the bread from the pan and turn the pan upside down on a metallic rack where the bread will cool off before slicing it.

Nutrition: Calories: 217 Fat: 13g Carb: 4.2g Protein: 4g

Buttery Bagels

Preparation Time: 10 minutes

Cooking Time: 23 minutes

Servings: 6

Ingredients

- 1/2 tsp. baking soda

- 1 3/4 Tbsp. butter, unsalted and melted

- 3 eggs, separated

- 1/4 tsp. cream of tartar

- 2 Tbsp. coconut flour, sifted

- 1 3/4 Tbsp. cream cheese, full-fat and softened

- 2 tsp. Swerve sweetener, granulated

- 1/4 tsp. salt

- Coconut oil cooking spray

Direction:

1. Preheat the oven to 300F. Coat a 6-cavity donut pan with coconut oil spray.

2. Divide the eggs between whites and yolks.

3. Blend the cream of tartar with the egg whites and pulse with a hand mixer for 5 minutes.

4. Combine the egg yolks with salt, baking soda, Swerve, coconut flour, melted butter, and cream cheese.

5. Gently blend the whipped eggs into the mix and blend well.

6. Fill the pan with the batter.

7. Bake in the oven for 23 minutes.

8. Cool and serve.

Nutrition: Calories: 83 Fat: 3g Carb: 1.2g Protein: 6g

Turmeric Bread

Preparation time: 5 minutes

Cooking time: 3 hours

Servings: 14

Ingredients:

- 1 teaspoon dried yeast

- 4 cups strong white flour

- 1 teaspoon turmeric powder

- 2 teaspoon beetroot powder

- 2 tablespoon olive oil

- 1.5 teaspoon salt

- 1 teaspoon chili flakes

- 1 3/8 water

Directions:

1. Merge all the ingredients and place it to the oven.

2. Close the lid,

3. When the bread machine has processed baking, detach the bread and put it on a cooling rack.

Nutrition: Carbs: 2.4g Fat: 3g Protein: 2g Calories: 129

Sugar-free cream cheese frosting bread

Preparation Time: 5 minutes

Cooking Time: 10 minutes

Servings: 6

Ingredients:

- 4oz cream cheese

- 2 tbsp. butter, cubed, softened

- 1/2 cup erythritol, powder or granulated

- 1 tsp. vanilla extract

- 1 tbsp. heavy cream

Directions:

1.   Merge the cream cheese, butter, vanilla, and Erythritol. Mix using a hand mixer.

2.   Attach in heavy cream 1 tablespoon at a time until you reach a smooth consistency.

Nutrition: Calories: 12 Carbohydrates: 5 g Protein: 2g Fat: 11g

American cheese beer bread

Preparation time: 5 minutes

Cooking time: 60 Minutes

Servings: 8

Ingredients

- 1 1/2 cups of fine almond flour

- 3 tsp. Of unsalted melted butter

- Salt, one teaspoon

- An egg

- Swerve sweetener, two teaspoons

- Keto low-carb beer, one cup

- 3/4 tsp. Of baking powder

- 1/2 cup of cheddar cheese, shredded

- 1/2 tsp. Of active dry yeast

Directions:

1. Prepare a mixing container, where you will combine the almond flour, swerve sweetener, salt, shredded cheddar cheese, and baking powder.

2.   Prepare another mixing container, where you will combine the unsalted melted butter, egg, and low-carb Keto beer.

3.   As per the instructions on the manual of your machine, pour the Ingredients in the bread pan, taking care to follow how to mix in the yeast.

4.   Place the bread pan in the machine, and select the basic bread setting, together with the bread size and crust type, if available, then press start once you have closed the lid of the machine.

5.   When the bread is ready, using oven mitts, remove the bread pan from the machine. Use a stainless spatula to extract the bread from the pan and turn the pan upside down on a metallic rack where the bread will cool off before slicing it.

Nutrition: Calories: 80 Fat: 1.5g Carb: 13g Protein: 3g

Keto Almond Sweet Bread

Preparation Time: 10 minutes

Cooking Time: 50 minutes

Servings: 14

Ingredients:

• 2 1/4 cup almond flour

• 2 eggs

• 2 tbsp. ground flaxseed

• 1/4 tsp. ground star anise

• 1/4 tsp. ginger powder

• 1 tsp. baking powder

• 1/2 tsp. xanthan gum

• 1/2 cup heavy cream

• 1/2 cup sugar substitute

• 1/2 cup butter

Directions:

1.   Melt the butter in a pan. Add heavy cream and sugar substitute. Stir until mixed well. Remove from the heat and cool.

2.   Place the rest of the dry ingredients in a bowl and whisk. Pour in the cooled cream and butter mix. Add 2 eggs and mix.

3.   Line bread in with parchment paper and pour the bread dough.

4.   Bake at 350F for 45 to 50 minutes.

5.   Remove, cool, and serve.

Nutrition: Calories: 206 Fat: 19.8g Carb: 2.3g Protein: 5.2g

Italian blue cheese bread

Preparation time: 3 hours

Cooking Time: 30 minutes

Servings: 8

Ingredients:

- 1 teaspoon dry yeast

- 2 1/2 cups almond flour

- 1 1/2 teaspoon salt

- 1 tablespoon sugar

- 1 tablespoon olive oil

- 1/2 cup blue cheese

- 1 cup water

Directions

1. Mix all the Ingredients. Start baking.

Nutrition: Carbohydrates 5 g Fats 4.6 g Protein 6 g Calories 194

KETO PASTA

Vermicelli

Preparation time: 2 minutes

Cooking time: 5 minutes

Serves: 2

Ingredients:

- 1 oz. cream cheese

- 2 eggs

- A pinch of salt and pepper

- 1/2 tsp. vital wheat gluten

Directions:

1. Mix cream cheese, eggs, vital wheat gluten, salt, and pepper in a blender until smooth.

2. Preheat the oven.

3. Line baking tray with parchment paper.

4. Bake for 5 minutes.

5. Detach from the oven and let it rest for 10 minutes.

6. Using a pizza wheel, cut very thin strips along the pasta sheet to resemble vermicelli noodles.

7. Let the noodles dry for 30 minutes.

8. Simmer with the sauce for a minute before serving.

Nutrition: Calories 236 Carbs 1.2 g Fiber 3 g Fat 9.6 g Protein

7.5 g

Kelp noodle salad.

Preparation time: 10 minutes

Cooking time: 0 minutes

Serves: 4

Salad Ingredients;

* 3 green onions (sliced)

* 1 (11oz/340g) pack kelp noodles

* 1 cucumber (julienned)

* 1/4 cup carrots (grated)

* 1/2 cup cashews (crushed)

* 0.5 oz. cilantro (minced)

* Dressing ingredients;

* 2.3oz almond butter

* 1 garlic clove (minced)

* 1 tablespoon tamari/ coconut aminos

* 1 tablespoon swerve

* 2 tablespoons lime juice

* 1 teaspoon chili oil/ chili infused extra-virgin olive oil

* 1 teaspoon ginger root (grated)

* 1 teaspoon sesame oil

- Red pepper flakes (pinch)

- Sea salt (pinch).

Directions:

1. In a bowl mix the salad ingredients.

2. In a jar, mix the dressing ingredients.

3. Pour the dressing into the initial bowl.

4. Toss to mix and serve.

Nutrition: Calories 240 Carbs 4.6 g Fiber 1 g Fat 11 g Protein 7

g

Rosemary lasagna noodles

Preparation time: 3 minutes

Cooking time: 40 minutes

Serves: 4

Ingredients:

- 2 eggs

- 4 oz. cream cheese

- 1/4 cup parmesan, shredded

- 1 1/4 cup mozzarella, shredded

- 1/8 tsp. rosemary

- pinch of marjoram

- pinch of thyme

- 1/2 tsp. basil

- 1/2 tsp. oregano

- 1/4 tsp. garlic powder

- 1/4 tsp. onion powder

- 1/4 tsp. salt

Directions:

1. Preheat the oven.

2. Mix the cream cheese and eggs in a bowl until smooth.

3.   Add in the remaining ingredients.

4.   Pour the mixture on a baking tray lined with parchment paper.

5.   Bake for 25 minutes.

6.   Cut the lasagna noodles while the pasta sheet is still warm.

7.   Prepare the filling (Meaty Keto Lasagna Filling).

8.   Layer the noodles and the filling.

9.   Bake for another 20 minutes.

10.   Serve while hot.

Nutrition: Calories 199 Carbs 1.9 g Fiber 0.5 g Fat 11 g Protein 12.7 g

Chicken Noodle Soup Recipe

Preparation time: 5 minutes

Cooking Time: 30 minutes

Serving Size: 10

Ingredients:

- 1 tablespoon sea salt or to taste
- 1 garlic clove (pressed)
- 4 chicken thighs (skins removed)
- 3 tablespoon fresh dill
- 1 teaspoon salt-free seasoning
- 4 cups chicken broth
- 2 carrots (sliced)
- 1/2 lb. rotini pasta
- 10 cups water
- 2 medium celery sticks (finely chopped)
- 2 tablespoon olive oil
- 1 medium onion (finely chopped)

Directions:

1. Mix ten cups of water with four cups of chicken broth and one tablespoon of sea salt in a big soup pot.

2. Bring to a simmer, include chicken thighs and cook partly covered for twenty minutes while the vegetables are cooked, skimming off any bubble that floats on the surface.

3. Put two tablespoons of olive oil and sauté the onions and celery in a large skillet once soften, then switch to the bowl.

4. In the stockpot, 1/2 lb. of pasta and diced carrots and proceed to cook at a low simmer for fifteen minutes or until the pasta is tender.

5. Erase the chicken thighs from the container when cooking the pasta and use either tools or your fingers to slice the chicken, removing any bone and fat that can come off quickly.

6. Place the shredded chicken back in the pot.

7. Season with 1 teaspoon your preferred seasoning and if appropriate, additional salt to adjust.

8. Add one clove of garlic in the pan. Finally, insert three tablespoons of dill and extract it from the heat.

Nutrition: Calories: 213 Total Fat: 2g Carbs: 3g Protein: 9g

Egg whites pasta

Preparation time: 4 minutes

Cooking time: 10 minutes

Serves: 2

Ingredients:

- 2 oz. cream cheese

- 1/2 cup egg whites

- 1 large egg

- 1 1/3 tbsps. whole psyllium husk

- 1/2 tsp. glucomannan powder

- 1/4 tsp. granulated garlic

- 1/4 tsp. dry parsley

- 1/8 tsp. salt

- coconut oil spray

Directions:

1. Dissolve the cream cheese.

2. Stir in the garlic, salt, glucomannan powder, parsley, psyllium husk, and 1 whole egg.

3. Slowly add half of the egg whites until the mixture become a paste.

4. Mix well until everything is smooth.

5. Once smooth, add the rest of the egg whites and stir well.

6. Spray the foil with coconut oil.

7. Preheat oven to 350F.

8. Pour the mixture on the tray and bake for 10 minutes.

9. Remove from oven and cool until you can touch the foil.

10. Remove the foil and roll the pasta sheet.

11. With a sharp knife, cut the rolled-up sheet into 3/4-inch-wide slices.

Nutrition: Calories 366 Carbs 3 g Fiber 3 g Fat 12 g Protein 12 g

Shirataki noodles (with coconut Basil chicken).

Preparation time: 10 minutes

Cooking time: 15 minutes

Serves: 4

Ingredients;

- 1 lb. raw chicken breast, thinly cut

- 8ounces cucumber

- 10 basil leaves, large

- 1 can coconut milk, full-fat

- 1 tablespoon coconut oil

- Miracle noodles, 2 packages

- Sour sauce;

- 2 tablespoons fish sauce

- 2 tablespoons sweetener

- 1/4 cup lime juice

- 1/2 teaspoon toasted sesame oil

- Sesame seeds

- Toasted coconut, shredded

- Red pepper flakes

- Mint

- Basil

- Cilantro

Directions:

1.   Cut the chicken into thin strips. Add all the chicken strips, sautéing for about 7 minutes. Ensure the pieces are entirely cooked before removing.

2.   Ensure you've juiced up a 1/4 cup of lime juice. Add the fish sauce and your sweetener to the cup and stir to mix well. Take out 3 tablespoons of the sauce and add into your blender with a pinch of salt. Add 1/2 teaspoon toasted sesame oil to the blender too.

3.   Pee your cucumber and spiralize it with a spiralizer. (You can dice it instead if you lack one)

4.   Allow the chicken juice residing on the pan to turn brown and solidify. Add basil leaves and pour in coconut milk while scraping the brown bits. Thereafter, bring it to boil over high heat for 5 minutes. When done, pour it into the blender blending till smooth. (Vent the lid since the liquid is hot)

5.　　Rinse and drain the noodles. Using a bowl (microwave-safe), heat up the noodles to warm.

6.　　Add the remaining sweet and sour sauce over the cucumber noodles and toss.

7.　　Add the sauce and chicken back into the pan. (heat over medium heat till hot)

8.　　Divide the kelp noodles among 4 bowls.

9.　　Top the noodles with basil chicken.

10.　　Garnish the cucumber salad as you wish.

11.　　Enjoy the meal!

Nutrition: Calories 285 Carbs 5 g Fiber 5 g Fat 22 g Protein 18 g

Spinach pasta

Preparation time: 2 minutes

Cooking time: 3 minutes

Serves: 5

Ingredients:

- 3 oz. spinach

- 2 eggs

- 1/2 tsp. salt

- 1 1/2 tsp. olive oil

- 2 cups almond flour

- 1/2 cup coconut flour, for kneading

Directions:

1. Cook the spinach until it turns bright green.

2. Prepare an ice bath for the spinach by combining ice and water in a large bowl.

3. Remove the spinach from the skillet and submerge it in the ice water.

4. Once the spinach is lukewarm, drain and squeeze the extra water with a cloth.

5. Combine the spinach, eggs, salt, and olive oil in a bowl.

6. Mix until everything is smooth.

7. Slowly add the almond flour to make the dough.

8. Once the dough is formed, let it sit for 25 minutes.

9. Dust a flat workplace with a generous amount of coconut flour and knead the dough with it until the dough is no longer sticky. Add as needed.

10. Cut the dough into 4 pieces.

11. Roll each piece with a rolling pin.

12. Using a pizza wheel, cut 3-4 inch blocks out of the dough.

13. Cut the blocks in a zigzag motion to create medium sized triangles.

14. Once all of them are cut, dust the triangles with some coconut flour.

15. Take a piece of the triangle shaped pasta, wet your fingers and stick two of the ends together.

16. Repeat with all of the triangle pieces.

17. Lower the pasta gently in a pot of boiling water and cook for 3 minutes.

18. Remove each piece and transfer to a plate.

Nutrition: Calories 165 Carbs 5 g Fiber 6 g Fat 17 g Protein 13.6 g

Empanada Green Pepper Noodles

Preparation time: 10 minutes

Cooking time: 15 minutes

Serves: 4

Ingredients:

- 1 tablespoon extra-virgin olive oil

- 1 medium yellow onion, diced

- 2 garlic cloves, minced

- 1 pound ground beef

- 1 cup sliced green olives

- 2 green peppers, spiralized

- 2 hard-boiled eggs, diced

- Salt

- Freshly ground black pepper

Directions:

1. In a large skillet over medium heat, heat the olive oil and sauté the onion and garlic. After about 5 minutes, add the ground beef and stir everything together for about 3 minutes more.

2.   Add the sliced olives and green pepper noodles. Sauté for another 3 to 4 minutes, or until the noodles start to become fork-tender, add the diced eggs and season with salt and pepper. Remove from the heat and serve immediately.

Nutrition: Calories 336 Fat 17g, Protein 38g, Sodium 692mg, Total Carbs 3g, Fiber 3g

Daikon radish pasta

Preparation time: 2 minutes

Cooking time: 8 minutes

Serves: 2

Ingredients:

- 2 Daikon radishes

- 1/2 cup bagel seasoning

- 4 cloves of garlic

- 5 tbsps. olive oil

Directions:

1. Wash and peel the radishes with a vegetable peeler.

2. Spiralize the radishes using the smallest noodle attachment.

3. Let the spiralized radish sit in saltwater for 2-3 minutes.

4. Finely chop the garlic.

5. Using a medium sized pan, heat the olive oil.

6. Add the chopped garlic and stir.

7. Drain the water from the radish and add to the pan.

8.   While mixing the garlic oil with the radish, slowly add the seasoning.

9.   Cook for 7-8 minutes and serve.

Nutrition: Calories 242 Carbs 3 g Fiber 2 g Fat 13 g Protein 1 g

Cheese head lasagna sheets

Preparation time: 3 minutes

Cooking time: 15 minutes

Servings: 8

Ingredients:

- 1 egg

- 2 tbsps. cream cheese

- 3/4 cup almond flour

- 1 3/4 cups shredded mozzarella cheese

- 1/4 tsp. salt

- 1/2 tsp. Italian seasoning

Directions:

1.   In a microwave safe bowl, mix the shredded cheese and almond flour.

2.   Add the cream cheese on top of the mix.

3.   Put the mix in the microwave for 30 seconds.

4.   Mix in the Italian seasoning, salt, and egg.

5.   Shape into a sphere with your hands.

6.	Put the ball in in the middle of the two pieces of parchment paper.

7.	Roll the dough out into a sheet using a rolling pin.

8.	Remove the parchment paper on top.

9.	Cut into 4 wide 6-inch-long pieces.

10.	Prepare the lasagna sauce and filling.

11.	Preheat the oven to 400F.

12.	Cook for 12-15 minutes.

Nutrition: Calories: 275 Total Fat: 7.6g Carbs: 1.6g Protein: 6.3g

Classic Minestrone Soup

Preparation time: 5 minutes

Cooking Time: 1 hour 5 minutes

Serving Size: 6 bowls

Ingredients:

- 2 teaspoons lemon juice

- Fresh (grated) Parmesan cheese

- 4 tablespoons virgin olive oil (divided)

- 1 can beans

- 2 cups (chopped) collard greens

- 1 onion (chopped)

- (Freshly ground) black pepper

- 1 cup (whole grain) elbow or shell pasta

- 2 medium carrots (chopped)

- 2 ribs celery, (chopped)

- 2 bay leaves

- Pinch of red pepper flakes

- 1/3 cup tomato paste

- 2 cups (chopped) seasonal vegetables

- 2 cups of water

- 1 teaspoon fine sea salt

- 4 cloves garlic (minced)

- 1/2 teaspoon (dried) oregano

- 1 large can (diced) tomatoes

- 4 cups vegetable broth

- 1/2 teaspoon (dried) thyme

Directions:

1. Heat a skillet with oil.

2. Insert the sliced onions, cabbage, celery, tomato sauce and a touch of salt until the oil glitters.

3. Cook until the veggies are darkened, and the onions become translucent.

4. Seasonal tomatoes, ginger, oregano and chives can be added.

5. Cook until aromatic, for about two minutes, while whisking frequently.

6. Pour the sliced tomatoes, their liquids, broth, and water into the mixture.

7.   Add lime, bay leaves and flakes of red pepper. With salt and black pepper, season generously.

8.   Increase the heat to medium-high and put the mixture to a boil, then cover the pan with the lid partly, allowing a space of around one inch for steam to escape.

9.   To sustain a gentle simmer, reduce the heat as needed.

10.   Heat and remove the cap for fifteen minutes, then insert the spaghetti, beans and greens.

11.   Continue to boil for twenty minutes, exposed, or until the pasta is prepared al dente and the vegetables are soft.

12.   Erase the jar, then extract the bay leaves from the steam.

13.   Add the lemon juice and the remaining tablespoon of essential oil and mix well.

14.   Flavor it with more pepper and salt. Spice the soup bowls with parmesan cheese.

Nutrition: Calories: 111 Total Fat: 2g Carbs: 0g Protein: 9g

KETO CHAFFLE

Garlic And Parsley Chaffles

Preparation time: 2 minutes

Cooking Time: 5 Minutes

Servings:1

Ingredients:

- 1 large egg

- 1/4 cup cheese mozzarella

- 1 tsp. coconut flour

- 1/4 tsp. baking powder

- 1/2 tsp. garlic powder

- 1 tbsp. minutesced parsley

- For Serving

- 1 Poach egg

- 4 oz. smoked salmon

Directions:

1. Switch on yourDash minutesiwaffle maker and let it preheat.

2. Grease waffle maker with cooking spray.

3. Mix together egg, mozzarella, coconut flour, baking powder, and garlic powder, parsley to a mixing bowl until combined well.

4. Pour batter in circle chaffle maker.

5. Close the lid.

6. Cook for about 2-3 minutesutes or until the chaffles are cooked.

7. Serve with smoked salmon and poached egg.

8. Enjoy!

Nutrition: Protein: 45 Fat: 51 Carbohydrates: 4

Scrambled Eggs On A Spring Onion Chaffle

Preparation time: 5 minutes

Cooking Time:7–9 Minutes

Servings:4

Ingredients:

- Batter

- 4 eggs

- 2 cups grated mozzarella cheese

- 2 spring onions, finely chopped

- Salt and pepper to taste

- 1/2 teaspoon dried garlic powder

- 2 tablespoons almond flour

- 2 tablespoons coconut flour

- Other

- 2 tablespoons butter for brushing the waffle maker

- 6-8 eggs

- Salt and pepper

- 1 teaspoon Italian spice mix

- 1 tablespoon olive oil

- 1 tablespoon freshly chopped parsley

Directions:

1. Preheat the waffle maker.

2. Crack the eggs into a bowl and add the grated cheese.

3. Mix until just combined, then add the chopped spring onions and season with salt and pepper and dried garlic powder.

4. Stir in the almond flour and mix until everything is combined.

5. Brush the heated waffle maker with butter and add a few tablespoons of the batter.

6. Close the lid and cook for about 7–8 minutes depending on your waffle maker.

7. While the chaffles are cooking, prepare the scrambled eggs by whisking the eggs in a bowl until frothy, about 2 minutes. Season with salt and black pepper to taste and add the Italian spice mix. Whisk to blend in the spices.

8. Warm the oil in a non-stick pan over medium heat.

9. Pour the eggs in the pan and cook until eggs are set to your liking.

10.	Serve each chaffle and top with some scrambled eggs.

Top with freshly chopped parsley.

Nutrition: Calories 194, Fat 14.7 g, Carbs 5 g, Sugar 0.6 g,

Protein 1 g, Sodium 191 mg

Simple Savory Chaffle

Preparation time: 5 minutes

Cooking Time: 7–9 Minutes

Servings:4

Ingredients:

- Batter

- 4 eggs

- 1 cup grated mozzarella cheese

- 1 cup grated provolone cheese

- 1/2 cup almond flour

- 2 tablespoons coconut flour

- 21/2 teaspoons baking powder

- Salt and pepper to taste

- Other

- 2 tablespoons butter to brush the waffle maker

Directions:

1. Preheat the waffle maker.

2. Add the grated mozzarella and provolone cheese to a bowl and mix.

3.   Add the almond and coconut flour and baking powder and season with salt and pepper.

4.   Mix with a wire whisk and crack in the eggs.

5.   Stir everything together until batter forms.

6.   Brush the heated waffle maker with butter and add a few tablespoons of the batter.

7.   Close the lid and cook for about 8 minutes depending on your waffle maker.

8.   Serve and enjoy.

Nutrition: Calories 352, Fat 27.2 g, Carbs 4.3 g, Sugar 0.5 g, Protein 15 g, Sodium 442 mg

Chili Chaffle

Preparation time: 3 minutes

Cooking Time:7–9 Minutes

Servings:4

Ingredients:

- Batter
- 4 eggs
- 1/2 cup grated parmesan cheese
- 11/2 cups grated yellow cheddar cheese
- 1 hot red chili pepper
- Salt and pepper to taste
- 1/2 teaspoon dried garlic powder
- 1 teaspoon dried basil
- 2 tablespoons almond flour
- Other
- 2 tablespoons olive oil for brushing the waffle maker

Directions:

1. Preheat the waffle maker.
2. Crack the eggs into a bowl and add the grated parmesan and cheddar cheese.

3.   Mix until just combined and add the chopped chili pepper. Season with salt and pepper, dried garlic powder and dried basil. Stir in the almond flour.

4.   Mix until everything is combined.

5.   Brush the heated waffle maker with olive oil and add a few tablespoons of the batter.

6.   Close the lid and cook for about 7–8 minutes depending on your waffle maker.

Nutrition: Calories 36 Fat 30.4 g, Carbs 3.1 g, Sugar 0.7 g, Protein 21.5 g, Sodium 469 mg

Delicious Raspberriestaco Chaffles

Preparation time: 5 minutes

Cooking Time: 15 Minutes

Servings:1

Ingredients:

- 1 egg white
- 1/4 cup jack cheese, shredded
- 1/4 cup cheddar cheese, shredded
- 1 tsp coconut flour
- 1/4 tsp baking powder
- 1/2 tsp stevia
- For Topping
- 4 oz. raspberries
- 2 tbsps. coconut flour
- 2 oz. unsweetened raspberry sauce

Directions:

1. Switch on yourround Waffle Maker and grease it with cooking spray once it is hot.

2. Mix together all chaffle ingredients in a bowl and combine with a fork.

3.   Pour chaffle batter in a preheated maker and close the lid.

4.   Roll the taco chaffle around using a kitchen roller, set it aside and allow it to set for a few minutesutes.

5.   Once the taco chaffle is set, remove from the roller.

6.   Dip raspberries in sauce and arrange on taco chaffle.

7.   Drizzle coconut flour on top.

8.   Enjoy raspberries taco chaffle with keto coffee.

Nutrition: Protein: 28% 77 Fat,: 6 187 Carbohydrates: 3% 8 kcal

Coconut Chaffles

Preparation time: 2 minutes

Cooking Time: 5 Minutes

Servings: 2

Ingredients:

- 1 egg
- 1 oz. cream cheese,
- 1 oz. cheddar cheese
- 2 tbsps. coconut flour
- 1 tsp. stevia
- 1 tbsp. coconut oil, melted
- 1/2 tsp. coconut extract
- 2 eggs, soft boil for serving

Directions:

1. Heat you minutesi Dash waffle maker and grease with cooking spray.

2. Mix together all chaffles ingredients in a bowl.

3. Pour chaffle batter in a preheated waffle maker.

4. Close the lid.

5.   Cook chaffles for about 2-3 minutesutes until golden brown.

6.   Serve with boil egg and enjoy!

Nutrition: Protein: 21 Fat: 117 Carbohydrates: 3

MAIN, SIDE & VEGETABLE

Mediterranean Pork

Preparation time: 10 minutes

Cooking time: 35 minutes

Servings: 2

Ingredients:

•   2 pork chops, bone-in

•   Salt and pepper, to taste

•   1/2 teaspoon dried rosemary

•   garlic clove, peeled and minced

•   Directions:

•   Season pork chops with salt and pepper. Place in a roasting pan. Add rosemary, garlic in the pan.

•   Preheat your oven to 425 degrees F. Bake for 10 minutes. Lower heat to 350 degrees F. Roast for 25 minutes more. Slice pork and divide on plates.

•   Drizzle pan juice all over. Serve and enjoy!

Nutrition: Calories: 165 Fat: 2g Carbohydrates: 2g Protein: 26g Fiber: 1g Net Carbohydrates: 1g

Sunny Side Up Eggs on Creamed Spinach

Preparation time: 5 minutes

Cooking time: 10 minutes

Servings: 2

Ingredients:

- 4 oz of spinach leaves

- tbsp mustard paste

- 4 tbsp whipping cream

- eggs

- Seasoning:

- ¼ tsp salt

- ¼ tsp ground black pepper

- ½ tsp dried thyme

- tbsp avocado oil

Directions:

1.   Take a medium skillet pan, place it over high heat, pour in water to cover its bottom, then add spinach, toss until mixed and cook for 2 minutes until spinach wilts.

2. Then drain the spinach by passing it through a sieve placed on a bowl and set it aside.

3. Take a medium saucepan, place it over medium heat, add spinach, mustard, thyme, and cream, stir until mixed and cook for 2 minutes.

4. Then sprinkle black pepper over spinach, stir until mixed and remove the pan from heat.

5. Take a medium skillet pan, place it over medium-high heat, add oil and when hot, crack eggs in it and fry for 3 to 4 minutes until eggs have cooked to the desired level.

6. Divide spinach mixture evenly between two plates, top with a fried egg and then serve.

Nutrition: 280 Calories; 23.3 g Fats; 10.2 g Protein; 2.7 g Net Carb; 2.8 g Fiber;

Special Veggie Side Dish

Preparation time: 10 minutes

Cooking time: 12 minutes

Servings: 4

Ingredients:

- 2 cups cauliflower rice
- cup mixed carrots and green beans
- cups water
- ½ teaspoon green chili, minced
- ½ teaspoon ginger, grated
- garlic cloves, minced
- 2 tablespoons ghee
- cinnamon stick
- tablespoon cumin seeds
- bay leaves
- whole cloves
- black peppercorns
- whole cardamoms
- 1 tablespoon stevia

- A pinch of sea salt

Directions:

1.   Put water in your instant pot, add cauliflower rice, mixed veggies, green chili, grated ginger, garlic cloves, cinnamon stick, whole cloves and ghee and stir..

2.   Also add cumin seeds, bay leaves, cardamoms, black peppercorns, salt and stevia, stir again, cover and cook on High for 12 minutes.

3.   Discard cinnamon stick, bay leaves, cloves and cardamom, divide among plates and serve as a side dish.

4.   Enjoy!

Nutrition: Calories 152, fat 2, fiber 1, carbs 4, protein 6

Mushroom Pork Chops

Preparation time: 10 minutes

Cooking time: 40 minutes

Servings: 2

Ingredients:

- 8 ounces mushrooms, sliced

- teaspoon garlic

- onion, peeled and chopped

- cup keto-friendly mayonnaise

- pork chops, boneless

- 1 teaspoon ground nutmeg

- 1 tablespoon balsamic vinegar

- ½ cup of coconut oil

Directions:

1. Take a pan and place it over medium heat. Add oil and let it heat up. Add mushrooms, onions, and stir. Cook for 4 minutes.

2. Add pork chops, season with nutmeg, garlic powder, and brown both sides. Transfer the pan in the oven and bake

for 30 minutes at 350 degrees F. Transfer pork chops to plates and keeps   it warm.

3.   Take a pan and place it over medium heat. Add vinegar, mayonnaise over the mushroom mixture, and stir for a few minutes.

4.   Drizzle sauce over pork chops

5.   Enjoy!

Nutrition: Calories: 600 Fat: 10g Carbohydrates: 8g Protein: 30g Fiber: 2g Net Carbohydrates: 5g

Garlic 'n Sour Cream Zucchini Bake

Preparation Time: 10 minutes

Cooking Time: 35 minutes

Servings: 3

Ingredients:

- ½ cups zucchini slices

- 5 tablespoons olive oil

- tablespoon minced garlic

- 1/4 cup grated Parmesan cheese

- (8 ounces) package cream cheese, softened

- Salt and pepper to taste

Directions:

1. Lightly grease a baking sheet using cooking spray.

2. Place zucchini in a bowl and put in olive oil and garlic.

3. Place zucchini slices in a single layer in dish.

4. Bake for 35 minutes at 390oF until crispy.

5. In a bowl, whisk well, remaining ingredients.

6. Serve with zucchini

Nutrition: Calories: 385 Fat: 32.4g Carbs: 9.5g Protein: 11.9g

Creamy Kale Baked Eggs

Preparation time: 10 minutes

Cooking time: 20 minutes

Servings: 2

Ingredients:

- bunch of kale, chopped
- 1-ounce grape tomatoes, halved
- tbsp whipping cream
- tbsp sour cream
- 2 eggs
- Seasoning:
- ½ tsp salt
- ½ tsp ground black pepper
- ½ tsp Italian seasoning
- ½ tbsp butter, unsalted

Directions:

1. Turn on the oven, then set it to 400 degrees F and let it preheat.

2. Meanwhile, take a medium skillet pan, place butter in it, add butter and when it melts, add kale and cook for 2 minutes until wilted

3. Add Italian seasoning, 1/3 tsp each of salt and black pepper, cream and sour cream, then stir until mixed and cook for2 minutes until cheese has melted and the kale has thickened slightly.

4. Take two ramekins, divide creamed kale evenly between them, then top with cherry tomatoes and carefully crack an egg into each ramekin.

5. Sprinkle remaining salt and black pepper on eggs and then bake for 15 minutes until eggs have cooked completely.

6. Serve.

Nutrition: 301.5 Calories; 25.5 g Fats; 9.8 g Protein; 4.3 g Net Carb; 4 g Fiber;

Delicious Creamy Crab Meat

Preparation Time: 5 minutes

Cooking Time: 10 minutes

Servings: 3

Ingredients:

- lb Crab meat

- ½ cup Cream cheese

- tbsp Mayonnaise

- Salt and Pepper, to taste

- tbsp Lemon juice

- cup Cheddar cheese, shredded

Directions:

1.	Mix mayo, cream cheese, salt and pepper, and lemon juice in a bowl. Add in crab meat and make small balls. Place the balls inside the pot. Seal the lid and press Manual.

2.	Cook for 10 minutes on High pressure. When done, allow the pressure to release naturally for 10 minutes. Sprinkle the cheese over and serve!

Nutrition: Calories 443, Protein 41g, Net Carbs 2.5g, Fat 30.4g

Great Broccoli Dish

Preparation time: 10 minutes

Cooking time: 12 minutes

Servings: 6

Ingredients:

- 31 oz broccoli florets

- cup water

- 5 lemon slices

- A pinch of salt and black pepper

Directions:

1. Put the water in your instant pot, add the steamer basket, add broccoli florets and lemon slices, season with a pinch of salt and pepper, cover and cook on High for 12 minutes.

2. Divide among plates and serve as a side dish.

3. Enjoy!

Nutrition: Calories 152, fat 2, fiber 1, carbs 2, protein 3

Radish with Fried Eggs

Preparation time: 5 minutes

Cooking time: 10 minutes

Servings: 2

Ingredients:

* ½ bunch of radish, diced

* ½ tsp garlic powder

* tbsp butter

* tbsp avocado oil

* eggs

* Seasoning:

* 1/3 tsp salt

* ¼ tsp ground black pepper

Directions:

1.   Take a medium skillet pan, place it over medium heat, add butter and when it melts, add radish, sprinkle with garlic powder and ¼ tsp salt and cook for 5 minutes until tender.

2.   Distribute radish between two plates, then return pan over medium heat, add oil and when hot, crack eggs in it and fry for 2 to 3 minutes until cooked to desired level.

3.   Add eggs to the radish and then serve.

Nutrition: 187 Calories; 17 g Fats; 7 g Protein; 0.4 g Net Carb; 0.5 g Fiber;

SOUP AND STEWS

Tomato Bisque Soup

Preparation time: 10 minutes

Cooking time: 40 minutes

Servings: 6

Ingredients:

- 3 cups canned whole, peeled tomatoes

- 4 cups chicken broth

- cup heavy cream

- cloves garlic, chopped

- tablespoons butter

- teaspoon freshly chopped thyme

- Salt & black pepper, to taste

Directions:

1. Add the butter to the bottom of a stockpot.

2. Add in all the remaining ingredients minus the heavy cream. Bring to a boil, and then simmer for 40 minutes.

3. Warm the heavy cream, and then stir into the soup.

Nutrition: Calories: 144 Carbs: 4g Fiber: 1g Net Carbs: 3g Fat: 12g Protein: 4g

Broccoli Curry Soup

Preparation Time: 10 minutes

Cooking Time: 30 minutes

Servings: 4

Ingredients:

- Salt & Black pepper (as needed)

- Onion, chopped

- tbsp. Curry

- tbsp. Coconut oil

- liter Vegetable stock

- 1 cup Coconut cream

- 75 g Cheese substitute - your choice, grated

- 1 lb. Broccoli

Directions:

1. Pour coconut oil into a frying pan on the stovetop using the med-high heat setting.

2. Mix in the onion. Simmer for approximately six minutes.

3.   Lower the temperature to medium. Then, add in the broth until it begins to simmer. Mix in the broccoli as well as any seasonings before adding curry. Simmer for 20 minutes.

4.   Pour into a blender before mixing in the cheese substitute.

5.   well.

Nutrition: Calories: 375 Total, Fat Content: 20 g Net Carbs: 5 g Protein: 17 g

Vegetarian Fish Sauce

Preparation Time: 5 minutes

Cooking Time: 20 minutes

Servings: 16

Ingredients:

- 1/4 cup dried shiitake mushrooms

- 1-2 tbsp. tamari (for a depth of flavor)

- 3 tbsp. coconut aminos

- ¼ cup water

- tsp sea salt

Directions:

1. To a small saucepan, add water, coconut aminos, dried shiitake mushrooms, and sea salt. Bring to a boil, then cover, reduce heat, and simmer for 15-20 minutes.

2. Remove from heat and let cool slightly. Pour liquid through a fine-mesh strainer into a bowl, pressing on the mushroom mixture with a spoon to squeeze out any remaining liquid.

3.   To the bowl, add tamari. Taste and adjust as needed, adding more sea salt for saltiness.

4.   Store in a sealed container in the refrigerator for up to 1 month and shake well before use. Or pour into an ice cube tray, freeze, and store in a freezer-safe container for up to 2 months.

Nutrition: Calories: 39.1 Fat: 2g Carbs: 5g Protein: 0.3g

Broccoli Cheddar & Bacon Soup

Preparation time: 10 minutes

Cooking time: 10 minutes

Servings: 6

Ingredients:

- 2 cups chicken broth

- cup broccoli florets finely chopped

- cup heavy cream

- cup shredded cheddar cheese

- ½ white onion, chopped

- cloves garlic, chopped

- slices cooked bacon, crumbled for serving

- ½ teaspoon salt

- ¼ teaspoon black pepper

Directions:

1.   Add all the ingredients minus the heavy cream, cheddar cheese and bacon to a stockpot over medium heat.

2.   Bring to a simmer and cook for 5 minutes.

3.   Warm the cream, and then add the warm cream and cheddar cheese. Whisk until smooth.

4.   Serve with crumbled bacon.

Nutrition: Calories: 220 Carbs: 4g Fiber: 1g Net Carbs: 3g Fat: 18g Protein: 11g

DESSERT

Keto Buttercream

Preparation Time: 12 minutes

Cooking Time: 15 minutes

Servings: 4

Ingredients:

- Unsalted butter 8 oz.

- Vanilla extract 2 tsp.

- Ground cinnamon 11/2 tsp.

- Erythritol 1 tsp.

Directions:

1. In a small saucepan, brown 1/4 of the butter before it becomes amber in color, but without burning.

2. Pour browned butter into a beaker and stir little by little with a hand mixer until it is moist in the remainder of the food.

3. Toward the end, add vanilla, cinnamon, and sweetener.

Nutrition: Calories 136 Total Fat 10.7 g Total Carbs 1.2 g Sugar 1.4 g Fiber 0.2 g Protein 0.9

Keto Chocolate and Hazelnut Spread

Preparation Time: 12 minutes

Cooking Time: 10 minutes

Servings: 6

Ingredients:

- Hazelnuts 5 oz.

- Coconut oil 1/4 cup

- Unsalted butter 1 oz.

- Cocoa powder 2 tbsp.

- Vanilla extract 1 tsp.

- Erythritol 1 tsp.

Directions:

1.   In a dry, hot frying pan, roast the hazelnuts until they develop a good golden color. Pay careful attention-the nuts can quickly burn. Let them cool a bit.

2.   Place the nuts and roll them in a clean kitchen towel so that any of the shells fall off.

3.   Put the nuts in a blender or food processor with the remaining ingredients. Mix in the desired consistency. The more you blend, the smoother the distribution.

Nutrition: Calories 195 Total Fat 14.3 g Total Carbs 4.5 g Sugar 0.5 g Fiber 0.3 g Protein 3.2 g

Keto Caramel Sauce

Preparation Time: 3 minutes

Cooking Time: 1 hour

Servings: 4

Ingredients:

- Raw macadamia nuts or cashews 1/2 cup

- Coconut cream melted 1/2 cup

- Mito Sweet granulated erythritol and monk fruit sweetener, or liquid stevia to taste 1 tbsp

- Vanilla extract 3 tsp

- Grass-fed ghee melted 2 tbsp

- Pinch of salt

- Grain-Free Granola

- Creamy Coconut and Avocado Smoothie

- Dark Chocolate Trail Mix Bites

Directions:

1. Preheat the oven to about 320 degrees.

2. Put nuts on the baking tray, then toast them for 20 minutes in the oven, or until golden & crunchy.

3. Allow the roasted nuts to cool slowly, then add them to a mixer and combine until smooth to most.

4. Add rest of the ingredients, then blend until smooth. Be cautious not to over-blend because coconut cream will separate from it.

5. If you would not use your keto caramel on the same day, place it in the refrigerator in a glass pan. Apply the material to a saucepan at medium heat and gently microwave to reheat to render it more pourable.

6. Serve it with ice cream, or some gourmets treat

Nutrition: Calories 323 Total Fat 12 g Total Carbs 1 g Sugar 5 g Fiber 11 g Protein 25 g

Lemon Curd - Keto, Low Carb & Sugar-Free

Preparation Time: 3 minutes

Cooking Time: 13 minutes

Servings: 10

Ingredients:

*   1/2 cup fresh lemon juice

*   2 tablespoons Lemon zest

*   3/4 cup swerve confectioners (or erythritol)

*   1/4-pound grass-fed unsalted butter (at room temperature)

*   2 Whole eggs

*   3 Egg yolks

*   1/4 teaspoon salt

Directions:

1.   Add butter in a saucepan and stir in the swerve. Stir the eggs and the flour, lemon juice & zest for lemons. Switch the heat to medium-low, and simmer for 6-8 minutes until it thickens sufficiently to cover a spoon's back surface.

2.   The secret to smooth and fluffy coming out of this curd is to stir the whole time.

3.   Remove from heat and cover this with plastic wrap to ensure that it properly touches the curd. Chill out the refrigerator and relax.

Nutrition: Calories 376 Total Fat 11 g Total Carbs 2.9 g Sugar 5 g Fiber 13 g Protein 21 g

Easy Lemon Coconut Custard Pie with Coconut Milk

Preparation Time: 10 minutes

Cooking Time: 55 minutes

Servings: 8

Ingredients:

- Large eggs can use 3 for stiffer custard 3

- Coconut Milk canned 1 cup

- Low carb sugar 3/4 cup

- Coconut flour 1/4 cup

- Unsalted butter melted and cooled 2 tbsp.

- Vanilla extract 1 tsp.

- Baking powder 3/4 tsp.

- Lemon zest 1 tsp.

- Lemon Extract 1/2 tsp.

- Unsweetened Shredded Coconut 4 ounces

Directions:

1. Spray a cooking spray on a 9-inch pie dish and preheat oven to 350 degrees.

2. Mix the ingredients, sweetener, coconut milk, coconut flour, sugar, baking powder, citrus zest, garlic, and lemon extract in a big dish. Stir until mixed.

3. Fold in untreated hemp. Pour mixture into a serving platter.

4. Bake for 40-45 minutes until it is crispy on the sides and a medium golden brown on top.

5. Remove from oven and let it cool before trying to cut as well as serve.

6. Keep the remaining in the fridge for up to three days.

Nutrition: Calories 23 Total Fat 12 g Total Carbs 3 g Sugar 5 g Fiber 12 g Protein 21 g

Simple Low-Carb Chocolate Tart (Sugar-Free)

Preparation Time: 10 minutes

Cooking Time: 25 minutes

Servings: 8

Ingredients:

- Almond flour 1 1/4 cup

- Unsweetened shredded coconut 3/4 cup

- Medium egg 1

- Coconut cream 3/4 cup

- Coconut oil melted 1/4 cup

- Drops stevia or more

- Cacao powder unsweetened 2 tbsp and 1 tsp

- Vanilla essence 1 tsp

- Pinch of salt

- A small handful of chopped hazelnuts to garnish

Directions:

1. Preheat oven about 180 centigrade.

2.	Mix almond flour, eggs, and shredded coconut in the food processor or stick blender until it shapes into a doughy ball.

3.	Press dough into a loaf tin that is covered with baking paper. On the sides, it should be about 2 fingers wide. To make it look good, press the corners with your fingertips if you wish.

4.	Bake the base tart for about 20 minutes, until its lightly browned. Take it out from the hot oven and allow cool.

5.	Now turn ganache into chocolate. Heat the coconut oil and then whisk in the cream of coconut, vanilla essence, cacao powder, pinch of salt, and powdered erythritol or stevia. If required, sample the sweetener and change it.

6.	Pour over the cool tart base & put in the refrigerator until completely set (about 1 1/2 hours).

7.	Until serving, on medium heat, dry roast a few sliced hazelnuts in the pan until golden.

Nutrition: Calories 32 Total Fat 7.2 g Total Carbs 1 g Sugar 3 g Fiber 0.7 g Protein 14 g